He hadn't really been going to kiss her, had he?

That wasn't what those moments had been about, was it? Those moments when he'd found himself leaning toward her without realizing why?

It couldn't be, he told himself, but he was shaken. He hadn't wanted, or even been aware of, a woman in a sexual way for longer than he could remember.

"Fine state of affairs," he said to the dog who had been his main listener for five years. "Don't want to sleep in case the dream comes back, but if I stay awake, I can't stop thinking about...things I shouldn't be thinking about."

Even the dream was better than these ridiculous thoughts about things that no longer applied to him, about a woman he had no business thinking of.

Dear Reader,

Spring always seems like a good time to start something new, so this month it's Marilyn Pappano's wonderful new Western miniseries, HEARTBREAK CANYON. *Cattleman's Promise* is a terrific introduction to the men of Heartbreak, Oklahoma—not to mention the women who change their lives. So settle in for the story of this rugged loner and the single mom who teaches him the joys of family life.

Unfortunately, all good things must end someday, and this month we bid farewell to Justine Davis's TRINITY STREET WEST. But what a finale! Clay Yeager has been an unseen presence in all the books in this miniseries, and at last here he is in the flesh, hero of his own story in *Clay Yeager's Redemption*. And, as befits the conclusion to such a fabulous group of novels, you'll get one last look at the lives and loves of all your favorite characters before the book is through. And in more miniseries news, Doreen Roberts continues RODEO MEN with *A Forever Kind of Cowboy*, a runaway bride story you'll fall in love with. *The Tough Guy and the Toddler* is the newest from Diane Pershing, and it's our MEN IN BLUE title, with a great cop hero. Christine Scott makes the move to Intimate Moments with *Her Second Chance Family*, an emotional and memorable FAMILIES ARE FOREVER title. Finally, welcome new writer Claire King, whose *Knight in a White Stetson* is both our WAY OUT WEST title and a fun and unforgettable debut.

As always, we hope you enjoy all our books—and that you'll come back next month, when Silhouette Intimate Moments brings you six more examples of the most exciting romance reading around.

Yours,

Leslie J. Wainger
Executive Senior Editor

Please address questions and book requests to:
Silhouette Reader Service
U.S.: 3010 Walden Ave., P.O. Box 1325, Buffalo, NY 14269
Canadian: P.O. Box 609, Fort Erie, Ont. L2A 5X3

JUSTINE DAVIS

CLAY YEAGER'S REDEMPTION

Published by Silhouette Books

America's Publisher of Contemporary Romance

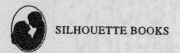

SILHOUETTE BOOKS

ISBN 0-373-07926-5

CLAY YEAGER'S REDEMPTION

This edition published by arrangement with Harlequin Books S.A.

® and TM are trademarks of Harlequin Books S.A., used under license. Trademarks indicated with ® are registered in the United States Patent and Trademark Office, the Canadian Trade Marks Office and in other countries.

Look us up on-line at: http://www.romance.net

Printed in U.S.A.

Chapter 1

If she hadn't seen the flash of black and white disappearing into the woods, he might have gotten away clean.

"Hey, dog!"

Casey's shout of surprised annoyance had barely faded away when the heavy screen door slammed with a crash that heightened her frustration; if the thing wasn't sagging and the hinges so shot, she could have brought in all the groceries at once, instead of having to leave one bag on the steps outside while she wrestled with it. The bag, she thought ruefully as she raced after the fleeing thief, that had held the paper-wrapped roast that had proved too tempting for some visiting canine.

The dog was quick, even weighted down as he was, and was through the broken section of fence that separated the yard from the grove of walnut trees in seconds. Casey was soon deep into the trees, following the raiding animal more by sound than sight.

"Give it up," she panted to herself as she slowed to duck under a low branch. "It's dog food now."

Then she caught another flash of black and white, heard a joyous bark and realized the animal had stopped. She quickly broke into a run again. Then, as she came through the trees into a small clearing, just as quickly stopped dead.

The pickup truck parked beneath the trees was green, nearly the same shade as the leaves, and the small camper shell was wooden—exquisitely made and carved, she noted—which explained why she hadn't seen it until she was nearly on top of it. This small grove was well off the main road, so she had no idea what the truck was doing there. Unless its driver was trying to hide it, she thought warily.

She could hear the dog, who was giving short, sharp little barks that sounded somehow quite proud. The animal was on the other side of the truck, out of her line of sight, and all Casey could think at the moment was that if he was barking, he wasn't eating; maybe there was a chance for the roast yet, what with all the excess wrapping Amos Tutweiler inevitably put on his meats.

She nearly laughed aloud at the thought of serving a prime rib that had been dragged through the woods by a dog to the refined ladies of the River Bend Historical Society. Then she heard the voice, and all laughter died in her throat.

It was deep, rich, husky, and sent a shiver up her spine. A completely different kind of shiver from the one the persistent voice on the phone caused. How, she wondered, could the human species come up with two masculine voices that had such different effects? She took another step, listening.

"What've you got?"

Another bark—Casey could almost see the plumed tail wagging. To a dog, she supposed, a successful hunt was a successful hunt, no matter the method or the prey. She heard the rustle of paper, then, as she approached the front of the truck, a low groan.

"Mutt, where did you get that?" More barks, then, suddenly, a warning growl. Both dog and man turned as she rounded the front fender.

He was tall, was her first thought. Tall and lean. No, he was beyond lean, and the looseness of his clothes—worn jeans and a faded red T-shirt—indicated that he hadn't always been that way. His hair was a dark, shaggy mass, long enough to drag along his shoulders when he turned his head, but his face was clean shaven, with long, angular planes. His eyes were...

They were dead. It was the only word she could come up with to describe them. Not the color, which was a striking combination of shades she supposed would be called hazel, but the lackluster flatness of them, the hollow lack of any life or emotion, except, perhaps, a mild chagrin at her sudden appearance.

She'd first thought him to be about thirty, but after seeing those eyes, she figured her guess might be several years low.

She fought the involuntary fear that tried to grip her at the sight of him. She had long ago acknowledged the inevitability of the feeling, but she refused to let it rule her. Besides, his voice truly was nothing like the voice that haunted her nights. And it wasn't strangers she had to watch out for. She'd learned that the hard way.

She watched him silently. He looked at the worse-for-wear package the dog had laid at his feet, then back at her. His mouth twisted as he looked back down at the furry hunter.

"Mud, you've really done it this time." The dog yipped happily.

She'd thought he'd said mutt before. The question popped out before she could stop it. "Your dog's name is Mud?"

He turned his head toward her again, and she knew she'd

been wrong about his eyes. They looked perfectly normal now, if a bit weary.

"Well," he said wryly, in that voice that still shivered up her spine, "if it wasn't before, it would be now, wouldn't it? I suppose you're the owner of this piece of meat he...liberated?"

"That piece of meat—" Casey said sternly, trying to ignore the lolling-tongued grin of the dog, an expression emphasized by the parti-coloring of his face, one dark eye surrounded by black, one blue eye surrounded by white— "is a prime rib roast I was supposed to serve Sunday afternoon."

Any trace of amusement vanished from his lean face. He let out a long breath. "What does prime rib go for these days?" he asked, a resignation she didn't understand in his tone.

"That piece was worth about seventy dollars, until your friend there got hold of it." She looked at the dog again. He was, she realized, nearly as lean as his master; she could practically count his ribs.

The man shifted his gaze back to the half-unwrapped piece of meat, which was obviously beyond saving now. "I'm sorry," he said lowly. "He's never done anything like this before. Even on short rations."

"He learns fast, then. I only set the bag down for a moment because my screen door is broken, and I can only hold it and one bag at a time."

"I'm sorry," the man repeated, running a hand through the tangle of his almost black hair. Casey saw the flex of ropy muscles in his arm and again got the impression that he hadn't always been so thin, that once this had been a well-muscled, much more solid man. Had he been ill? she wondered. Was he still?

The dog moved restlessly, creeping forward with a low growl as if to warn this visitor, apparently oblivious of the fact that she was the owner of what he fancied for his dinner. Border collie, she thought suddenly. Like Corky had been. Only Corky had had better manners; Aunt Fay had seen to that.

"Mud, stop." The dog dropped into a motionless crouch.

"Maybe," Casey said as she eyed the nearly gaunt animal, "if you fed him more, he wouldn't be stealing from people."

The man stiffened. When he spoke, his voice was taut and formal, and he looked past her rather than at her. So much for lack of emotion, Casey thought. She'd clearly struck a nerve.

"I can't pay you for the meat. Not in cash. But I can work. Fix that door you mentioned, and the hole in your fence, and anything else that's broken."

"That would take a lot of fixing." The sour words were out before Casey fully realized what he'd said. He knew about the hole in the fence? Had he been watching her? Fear, sudden and sharp, welled up inside her. She fought it down, supplanted it with the realization that if he was that broke, it was doubtful he'd been shelling out change to make midnight phone calls or had a cell phone to make them on.

"I've got nothing but time," he said.

His words were so bitter, his voice so utterly exhausted sounding that for a moment Casey's fear subsided. She was surely being paranoid, she thought. There was no way Jon could find her here. And she would have recognized his voice, wouldn't she? Even that hoarse whisper couldn't disguise it completely, could it? The phone calls were a fluke, just some sicko who had hit her number by accident.

Still, that didn't mean she wanted a total stranger around, especially one who looked as if he'd been on the road for months. Years maybe, she amended, glancing into the bed of the truck. It was full of belongings, yet neat; the clever hand that had built the camper shell was in evidence here, as well. Even in the fading evening light she could see the shelves that lined the perimeter around a raised sleeping area, which gave more storage underneath. Everything was tidy, in its place. She imagined it had to be; order would be a necessity for anyone to live in such a small space. Which was, she realized, what he was doing.

For the first time she looked around more carefully. A small folding canvas chair sat in the shade of the largest tree; a book lay open beside it. There were books, lots of them, in the truck, as well, she realized, along with a small light clipped up over the sleeping area for reading at night. The thought comforted her somehow. A dish that held water for the dog sat next to the truck's front wheel, and a pair of apparently just washed jeans lay over a line strung from the back of the chair to a low branch of the tree.

"Camping out?" she asked, stating the obvious.

He looked at her sharply, then shifted his gaze downward, seeming to stare at the toes of his worn brown leather hiking boots.

"I haven't bothered anybody."

"But you are on private property."

His head came up then. "There were no signs. Or any fence, except yours. That's why I stopped here."

"We don't need signs here. Everybody in River Bend knows whose land it is."

He drew himself up with an effort that made Casey weary just to watch it. "I'll be over in the morning to fix the door and whatever else you think necessary to pay for the meat," he said in clipped, emotionless tones. His jaw tightened slightly. "I don't suppose you could hold off turning me in to the property owner until tomorrow?"

The rising evening breeze lifted a strand of red gold hair and pressed it against her cheek. She brushed it away. "Too late," she said.

His eyes, which had naturally followed the movement of her hand—or the errant strand of hair, she wasn't sure which—snapped back to her face. Understanding dawned on his strong, hollow-cheeked features.

"Oh. You."

A sharp, quick bark from the collie drew their attention downward. The dog had been busy; he'd again snatched up his prize, and nearly half of the roast had disappeared. The torn wrapping flapped around the rest. From the looks of him, Casey thought, he could have devoured it all and still been hungry.

"You've gone that far, dog," she said wryly, "you might as well finish it."

The dog ignored her, his varicolored eyes fastened on his master.

"Why doesn't he just eat it?" Casey asked.

"Because," the man said a little gruffly, "the rest of it's for me." He knelt suddenly beside the dog, putting a broad, strong hand atop the animal's head. "Go ahead, boy," he said softly. "Just don't go getting the idea you can go raiding every time you get a little too hungry."

The collie whined, confused. He lifted the remaining meat gently in his jaws, as if offering it. Casey felt an odd, painful tightening in her throat at the simple gesture of love from an animal most would call dumb.

"All right, Muddy." The man's voice was low and husky, as if his throat were as tight as hers. "We'll share, like always. Thanks."

He took the meat, gave the dog a long, gentle stroke from head to tail and stood up. The collie yipped happily, his plumed tail waving, all once more right in his world. With a wary look at Casey, he trotted over to the bowl of water and lapped noisily.

Casey had to swallow against the lump in her throat. She'd tried so hard to control her emotions for so long now, tried to keep them on a level plane, neither up nor down, and now all her efforts had been shattered by a skinny dog no higher than her knee. Choking back tears, she turned swiftly, barely stopping herself from breaking into a run.

"Mrs. Scott?"

She froze. Her breath caught, and fear flooded her again. She glanced back over her shoulder, half-expecting him to be coming after her. But he hadn't moved, merely stood there, the Border collie now back at his heels. Just the sight of the loyal animal eased her terror, although her common sense told her she was foolish to believe in the instincts of a dog, and a not-too-friendly one at that.

"How did...?" She couldn't get the words out, but he guessed her meaning.

"The mailbox," he said, quickly, as if he'd seen her fear and wanted to ease it.

Dear God, Casey thought. That simple. She'd never even thought of it, never realized that her beloved aunt's name on the battered old tin box out by the road was an advertisement for her own presence.

"Do you want me to leave?" He was studying her intently, and Casey knew what he was seeing. A guarded, jumpy woman, with flame-colored hair that should have been evidence of an equally fiery spirit but wasn't, and a pair of wide blue eyes that were wary more often than not.

And she also knew, with a certainty whose source she couldn't be sure of, that if she told him to leave, he would go. He wouldn't ignore her request; she wouldn't be reduced to pleading, all the while knowing he was bigger, stronger, and could...

With an instinct born of long practice, she bit her lip, using the pain to stop the storm of thoughts that threatened to overwhelm her. God, she hadn't been like this in so long; she'd thought she'd beaten it, that she'd truly left it behind her....

"It's nearly dark," she said, a little breathlessly.

"Yes." He waited silently for a moment, then repeated his words. "Do you want me to leave now?"

He'd been here for days, and she'd never seen him, Casey thought, trying to calm herself. If he'd meant her any harm, surely it would have happened by now. He'd had ample opportunity. Even if she hadn't been convinced by his voice, she was sure now that this stranger had nothing to do with the almost nightly calls.

"I...no. Not tonight. It's late."

"Thank you," he said simply.

Casey said no more, just turned and hurried back through the trees and the broken fence. And as she locked up that night, going through the routine of carefully checking all the doors and windows, even those that had never been unlocked since she'd moved in, she wondered if she would sleep at all, knowing that there was a stranger, a male stranger, camped out less than a hundred yards away. But as she'd so often reminded herself, it hadn't been a stranger who had given her these nightmares.

Oddly, her last thoughts as she drifted toward sleep late that night were of a dog's tongue-lolling grin and the tightness of a man's voice as he solemnly thanked his four-footed friend for his gift.

Casey thought she'd dreamed the sound, but when it came again she knew it was what had awakened her. And close behind that realization came the instinctive fear. Someone was trying to break in. Her heart began to race.

The decision to move the phone out of the bedroom—in the hope that the almost nightly calls wouldn't wake her from her badly needed sleep—had seemed so easily made then. Now, as she sat quivering in her big brass bed in the early morning light, that lifeline to help sitting uselessly on the desk in the living room, she felt like a fool. It didn't make sense, anyway, since she felt guilty not answering when it could be a neighbor needing help. She should have moved it back as soon as she realized it woke her up from the living room, anyway. Never mind that it would take a sheriff's deputy twenty minutes to get all the way out here; at least help would be coming.

Then the noise came again, and her heart leaped, as if trying to hammer its way out of her chest.

She couldn't just sit here. She had to at least try to get to the phone. The one in the kitchen—maybe he wouldn't see her go in there. Biting her lip, trying to suppress her shivers, she ordered her recalcitrant body to move. It was a moment before it obeyed, and she had to steady herself with a hand on the solid brass bedpost before she trusted her shaky legs to support her.

Easy, she thought. She took the first step. It's only fifteen feet from the bedroom to the kitchen, she told herself. She could be there, make the call and be locked safely in the bathroom before he saw her. On the strength of that thought, she made it to the doorway of the kitchen, her eyes fastened on the cheery red telephone on the wall beside the window.

The window. She froze, staring out through the sheer curtains—the frilly, lacy things her aunt had had a penchant for—at what had immediately caught her eye. There in the yard, parked next to the small, ramshackle barn, was a battered green truck. A truck she had seen once before.

Tugging at the long, soft T-shirt she slept in, she tiptoed across the cool linoleum floor of the kitchen until she could lean around and peer at her front door. She gave a muffled little gasp as the sharp, pounding noise came again. Then she saw the heavy screen door move. Not swinging on its broken hinges, but actually moving away from the front door. Carried, she saw then, in broad, masculine hands. She heard the distinctive sound of a dog's toenails clicking on the wooden porch.

Mud. And his owner. He'd really shown up. She let out a long, relieved sigh. And then sucked her breath quickly back in again, berating herself once more for her instinctive relaxation the moment she'd heard the dog.

She turned away, hurrying back to her room to quickly dress in jeans and a soft, loose blue sweater. Then she went back to the front door and quietly pulled it open.

Standing at the foot of the steps, he had his back to the door, a screwdriver in one hand as he worked on the broken upper hinge. His hair was tied neatly back with a leather thong this morning, and he wore a faded, red plaid flannel shirt against the chill. It was stretched taut over his broad shoulders as he worked on the door.

Mud made a small, slightly less threatening noise—a greeting this time, rather than a warning? Casey wondered—and the man's head swiveled around to look at the dog. Mud started up the steps, and in sudden realization the man glanced up at the door just as Casey stepped outside.

He seemed startled. "I…you're home."

"So it seems," she said, her voice a bit dry after the scare he'd given her. Mud sat down before her, studying her with an intensity she found amusing—and a touch unnerving.

"I'm sorry," the man said quickly, lowering the screwdriver. "I didn't see a car, so I thought you'd gone."

"It's in the barn."

"Oh." He hesitated, then added, "I'm sorry if I woke you."

Only then did Casey realize she hadn't stopped to brush the sleep-tangled mass of her hair; color tinged her cheeks as she lifted a hand to try to smooth it down. "Don't be sorry about that," she said, embarrassment making her voice tight. "Be sorry that you scared me to death. I thought someone was breaking in."

He seemed puzzled. "I told you I'd be here to fix this." He gestured at the door.

"I know. But I didn't think you really would."

He drew back a little, and she saw that stiffness again. She saw a return of that flat deadness in his eyes before they became merely shuttered once more. "I said I would be. I owe you seventy dollars, remember?"

Casey knelt beside the Border collie, holding her hand out to the wary animal. "I'd say it's your plundering friend here who owes me."

The black-and-white dog pondered her overture for a moment that seemed to go on and on. Then Mud reached out his white-striped nose to nuzzle her hand. When his master didn't speak, Casey looked up to find the man studying her with an intensity that put the dog's to shame. And made her definitely uneasy. Only the touch of surprise in his expression kept her from getting up and running back inside. With a hasty pat for the black-and-white head, she straightened up just as he spoke.

"We both owe you. Who do you think ate the rest of that roast?"

Her eyes widened. "You ate it?"

He shrugged. "About a third of it was still wrapped. After I cut off the chewed end for Mud, it seemed a shame to waste it."

"So that's why I smelled smoke last night?"

"I'm sorry if it bothered you, but I didn't have any other way to cook it. I was careful with the fire."

"It's all right," Casey said. "We had a very wet spring, so there's not much fire danger right now despite the heat. I'm just glad the meat didn't go to waste."

"It didn't, believe me." His mouth twisted wryly. "I haven't even seen prime rib in longer than I can remember."

Casey glanced at the truck. "You've been...traveling a long time, then?"

"Yes."

It was flat, emotionless, yet unmistakably a warning against any more questions. A warning that reminded Casey that she should be listening to the warnings sent out by what was left of her common sense. She backed up a step, stopping within reach of the door.

"I have a great respect for privacy," Casey began slowly, "but—"

"I understand," he interrupted in a quiet voice that somehow assured her he did. "You don't know me, don't know that I wouldn't ever hurt..."

His voice trailed off, and for an instant Casey saw pain flash across his lean face, a pain so great it made her wince inwardly. But then it was gone, so swiftly that she couldn't even be sure she'd seen it.

"I'll fix this door," he said after a moment, his voice brisk, as if in an effort to deny the break in his words.

"If you can, I'd appreciate it." She glanced over at his truck. "You built that, the camper?" He nodded. "Then I guess the door should be a piece of cake. That's nice work."

"Thank you. After the door, I'll do the fence. And it looks like these steps could use some work. And that porch railing, and the screen that's coming loose."

"You only owe me seventy dollars," Casey said wryly. "If I had the local carpenter out to do all that, he'd charge me seven hundred."

"His dog didn't steal from you."

Casey studied him for a moment. "You're taking this very seriously, aren't you? Most people would just say that's what I get for leaving it outside where Mud—" the dog, who had gone back to his inspection of her front porch, turned at the sound of his name "—could get to it. And then they'd sue me if the dog got sick after eating it."

Again that look, that pain flashed across his face, only this time she was watching his eyes, those heavily lashed hazel eyes that should be so beautiful yet seemed so dead, and was sure of it.

"I learned a long time ago to take responsibility for my

own actions. Or inaction.'' His voice was flat, again denying the pain she'd seen.

And you learned the hard way, didn't you? Casey wasn't sure where the thought had come from, but she was somehow certain it was true. Eyes like that didn't come from sliding easily through life.

Casey jumped at the shrill of the phone. She pressed a hand to her chest as if that could slow the sudden racing of her heart, closing her eyes as she told herself she was being silly. He never called in the daylight, anyway, she reminded herself. Her mouth quirked wryly; that gravelly, threatening voice would lose much of its effect in the sunlight, she supposed.

When she opened her eyes again, the stranger was watching her, his dark brows slightly furrowed. When another ring came, his gaze flicked to the phone, then back to her face.

''Excuse me,'' she said hastily, realizing her reaction must seem strange to him. She hurried over to the desk and grabbed the receiver. And breathed a silent prayer of thanks that the voice on the other end wasn't the one that haunted her.

Chapter 2

One of the fates—certainly one with a better sense of humor than the one that had led Mud to her shopping bag—was with her.

"Casey, honey, I know it's late notice, and it's awful of us, but you know, the girls and I were talking about tomorrow while we were playing cards at Mable's last night—she's such a poor loser, I just can't believe it—but anyway, we got to thinking that prime rib might be a teeny bit rich for an afternoon tea, don't you agree?"

Casey found herself drawing in a long, deep breath; when she realized her need for air was in response to Phyllis Harrington's amazing ability to get all those words out without taking a single breath, she smothered a laugh. And managed not to point out just how long she had spent trying to convince the ladies of just that.

"Why, I do believe you're quite right, Mrs. Harrington," she said, aware that she could still hear the sound of movement out on the porch.

"You're not angry? I know you already bought the prime

rib, because Amos told me you were in yesterday, but the girls and I decided a nice, light chicken dish would be so much better. I don't know what we were thinking of, prime rib at midday, but then Pamela remembered that lovely chicken casserole you did for little Karen's wedding, and we thought, well, we'll just call and see if there's anything else she can do with that roast, because we'd hate to see it go to waste—''

''It won't, Mrs. Harrington. Believe me, it won't.'' She heard a loud pounding and nearly smiled.

''What is that noise, dear?''

''I, er, I'm getting my screen door fixed,'' Casey said, then hastily changed the subject; the last thing she needed was Phyllis Harrington, in whose dictionary the word *secret* was listed right before *semaphore,* getting wind of the fact that she had a total stranger—and one of those ''awful homeless transients,'' to boot—working on her house. ''The chicken will be fine, but I'll need to get started. I'll be there tomorrow morning right at eleven.''

''We'll have everything set up at the hall for you, dear. And you will stay, won't you? We don't get to see you nearly enough since you came home. You shouldn't keep to yourself so much, it's not—''

''I'll be sure and see everyone tomorrow,'' Casey promised, cutting off another spate of breathless advice; everyone in River Bend seemed to have some for her, but only Phyllis Harrington could deliver so much in so little time.

A knock on the door gave her the excuse she needed. ''I have to go now, Mrs. Harrington. The...repairman needs something.''

When she got to the door, he was staring off into the distance, toward the fields that stretched beyond her dilapidated fence. The dog sat at his feet, plumed tail still, his attention fixed on his master as if he sensed...something.

You're going to totally anthropomorphize that dog before long, she told herself sternly.

She opened her mouth to speak, then realized she had no idea what to call the man. And she felt a little shiver of misgiving that she'd never even thought to ask his name before allowing him to start working. Of course, she'd been distracted by the phone call, and she somehow doubted that he would have stopped even had she told him to, but still, it was no excuse. If something awful happened, if he did anything, she should at least have a name to give the police.

She smothered an inward sigh, longing for a time when that wouldn't have occurred to her.

"Did you need something?" she said.

Although he'd obviously been lost in thought, he didn't even jump when she spoke. Exceptionally steady nerves? she wondered. Or simply a lack of them?

He turned around, his lean face expressionless. His eyes were the same, flat and unreadable. But his voice was normal enough as he asked, "Do you have any wood screws, for the door hinges? And galvanized nails, for the fence?"

She gave him a wry smile. "I have no idea. There are nails and screws in the toolroom, but beyond that, I couldn't tell you."

She waited for some comment about the foolishness of living on a farm with her minimal knowledge of such things, but it didn't come.

"And the toolroom is...?" was all he said.

"That small door, there," she said, gesturing toward the barn. "It's not locked."

He nodded and began to turn away. She stopped him, saying something she knew she should have made clear earlier.

"You know, you really don't have to do this. I was just upset before."

"Rightfully so," he muttered, glancing at the dog, who had leaped to his feet at the man's first move.

"He thought he was...hunting. I don't generally hold it

against animals when they act instinctively.'' She smiled. ''Besides, it turns out I don't need the roast, anyway.''

He lifted a brow at her, then, rather quickly she thought, made an accurate guess. ''The phone call?''

''Yes. The ladies of the River Bend Historical Society decided they would rather have chicken for their monthly brunch.''

An odd expression crossed his face, as if he couldn't understand such a choice. Or, she thought suddenly, as if it had been a long time since he'd been faced with that kind of choice. She glanced down at the dog, who didn't seem to be lacking in energy for all his thinness, and wondered if there had been times that the dog ate when the master didn't. Somehow it wouldn't surprise her.

''You...cook for them, these ladies?''

''It's what I do. I'm a caterer.''

She said it proudly. When she'd first come back, she'd gotten business from some of the small town's population out of respect for Aunt Fay. The rest was probably because they felt sorry for her, having to scramble back here from the big city, or possibly out of simple curiosity about her. Or maybe it was just the novelty of having a caterer in town.

But she'd always known that the initial rush would only carry her so long, that sooner or later she would have to stand or fall on the quality of her work. And now, three years later, she knew she had carved a place for herself. She was the caterer of choice in the county for weddings, anniversaries and parties. And when she had landed the historical society brunches, she'd known she was on her way. In a couple of months they were holding a big fund-raiser; if that went well, her name would be made.

He gave her an intent look, as if he'd heard the emphasis in her tone. But he only nodded and turned to head down the steps.

''Wait,'' Casey said suddenly, remembering. He stopped

and looked back over his shoulder at her. "I...don't even know your name."

"Clay," he said.

Her brow furrowed. "Just Clay?"

After a moment he shrugged. "Yeager, if you need another name."

What an odd way to put it, she thought. But he'd answered her easily enough. Not that that meant anything.

It wasn't until he had disappeared into the toolroom that she realized he'd ignored her declaration that he didn't have to pay her back for the meat.

She wasn't going to push it again. If he was so set on doing this work, she would let him. Lord knew the place needed it; she had little time and less knowledge when it came to household repairs. In the city she'd always paid to have things fixed.

And in the city she'd learned that some things could never be fixed.

She turned on her heel and strode back into the kitchen, determinedly shoving the unwelcome thoughts out of her mind.

By the time she had the chicken casseroles prepared to be baked in the morning—a large one for the ladies and a smaller one that she herself would dine on for a couple of days—along with the trimmings and extra touches that helped spread her reputation for remembering all the little details, she was flushed from the kitchen heat. The early afternoon sun beat down on this side of the house this time of year, and it seemed it was turning out to be another hot, humid August here on the Iowa flatland. Even the inevitable thunderstorms passing through didn't help much; they only lasted long enough to make the ground—and the people—steam.

The hammering, she realized, had stopped. It had been going on almost steadily since she'd directed Clay Yeager to the toolroom; apparently he'd found what he needed there. She'd seen little of him since, but his presence had been undeniable, with the constant noise of work being done. She'd glanced out a couple of times after he'd finished with the screen door—which now swung neatly and stayed put when asked—but he'd been out of sight, apparently working on the fence on the far side of the barn.

She'd found the noise soothing rather than annoying, which she supposed was odd. She hadn't realized how alone she sometimes felt out here until now.

That's not true, she told herself. You like it that way. It's one of the reasons you came here.

When the silence continued, she wondered if Clay had quit for the day. Even if it was only one o'clock, he'd done more than enough to pay back the seventy dollars. She was sure the local man would have charged her that just for the door. And wouldn't have done as nice a job, either. He had a habit of—

A sharp string of barks from Mud interrupted her musings. The dog sounded almost anxious, and she didn't think she was assigning him human characteristics this time. She had the thought that having a dog around might not be a bad idea. Mud might not be guard-dog big, but she had a feeling he would be tenacious and brave in defending anyone he considered his. If nothing else, he could bark a warning.

Or a signal, she thought as she washed up—she was a hands-on cook in the literal sense—and went to see what was happening. She should offer the man something cool to drink, she supposed; it was awfully hot already. There was lemonade in the fridge. Maybe he would like—

Her thoughts came to an abrupt halt as she rounded the corner of the barn and saw what Mud had been barking at.

Clay was down. He was almost flat on his side against the wall of the barn, propped up only by one elbow. He was shaking his head sharply. As if he'd gotten dizzy. It wasn't unheard-of, in this kind of heat and humidity, for people to pass out, but not usually people as young and apparently healthy as Clay Yeager.

She ran to him, kneeling beside him as he shook his head sharply again. He looked pale, and his skin was clammy and cold, even in the heat. Mud danced beside her; apparently even she was welcome if she could help.

"Are you all right?"

He raised one arm, motioning as if to brush her away, but instead, when his hand landed on her wrist, he held on. He went still then, as if her steadiness had been all he'd needed.

"Have you been drinking water?" she asked, thinking first of the usual reason for such reactions to excessive heat.

He started to nod, apparently thought better of it and muttered, "Yes," under his breath.

She frowned; something else must be wrong, then. "Are you sick?"

This time he shook his head slowly, as if trying out the motion. It must not have made him feel any worse, because he made an effort to push himself upright. He braced his back against the wall and let his head loll back, eyes closed.

Mud whined, sounding as worried as any human she'd ever heard. She glanced at the dog, and he subsided. Then she heard another sound, low and gurgling. It took her a moment to recognize it as a growling stomach. She turned back to Clay quickly.

"Have you had any lunch?"

His mouth twitched slightly, and he said nothing. Suspicion spiked in her.

"Have you eaten anything today?"

"I thought I'd better not chance it," he muttered. "That prime rib was a little...rich."

"It made you sick?" she guessed. His mouth twisted wryly, but again he didn't answer. "Well, no wonder you're passing out," she said, "if you lost that and haven't eaten since. And doing all this work on an empty stomach, in this heat," she added, noticing that he'd indeed made repairs on a good fifty feet of her rickety fence.

"I'll be fine."

His voice was low, and she thought she saw a slight tremor go through him. "You will be," she said, "as soon as you get some food in you. Can you get up? I've got plenty of things I can fix in a hurry."

One eye flickered open. "I already owe you—"

"You've more than paid it back," she said, cutting him off. "Can you stand?"

Both eyes closed again, and for a moment he was silent. Then, slowly, he got to his feet. His left hand never left the side of the barn, betraying his lack of faith in his own strength.

"Are you sure you're not ill? Maybe it wasn't just the prime rib."

"I'm fine."

His voice was a little tight, but steady enough. She had a sudden feeling that he'd been going without food a lot longer than just today. *Short rations,* he'd said. And if he shared everything with Mud...

"Wash up and come in," she ordered, not caring that it sounded peremptory. "I'll find something for Mud, too." She turned on her heel and walked toward the house before he could argue with her.

And she lectured herself on her too soft heart all the way. He was a complete stranger, but she was treating him like a friend. She should know better. Had she learned nothing?

Yes, she thought rather fiercely. *I did learn. I learned professed friendship is no safeguard.*

If he cared about that kind of thing anymore, he would be embarrassed, Clay thought. But he didn't. He was long past the point when embarrassment had any place on his priority list.

His mouth quirked. He wasn't sure he *had* a priority list anymore.

But if he did, he thought as he tested his balance by letting go of the barn wall, food just might be on it. And since he'd abandoned pride about as long ago as embarrassment, he would take her handout—and he would admit it wasn't just for the dog's sake.

He did as instructed, welcoming the cool water from the outside tap; he wasn't used to this Midwest humidity. He knew the relief the water offered wouldn't last, that he would soon feel clammy and hot again, but it was worth it for the minute or two of respite.

"You can help me clear out some leftovers," she said as he came in; she was already heating something up in a rather sizable microwave. "That is," she added, "if you don't mind eating them."

"Mrs. Scott, judging by the smell in here, your leftovers are better than anything I've eaten in months."

His stomach rumbled suddenly, as if to underline his words. He felt a sudden queasiness and wondered if perhaps he had pushed too far, when just the thought of food made him wobbly.

"Call me Casey," she said as she pulled a large dish out of the microwave and forked some of the contents onto a plate. "Mrs. Scott was my aunt."

He wondered briefly if she was purposely not making clear if the "Mrs." appellation applied, then laughed at himself; old habits truly died hard, if after all this time questions like that occurred to him so instinctively.

But his inward laughter died quickly; there was nothing funny about it. He hated that the instinct was so ingrained in him, hated that even after he'd tried so hard to exorcise the man he'd once been, it still persisted.

The aroma that hit his nose as she set a plate down in front of him set off another rumble in his midsection. "You have to be the best caterer in town," he said, eyeing the plate full of what appeared to be pork chops, a scoop of pasta salad and a slice of bread he would swear was home baked.

"I am," she agreed with a smile. "But in a place the size of River Bend, that's not saying much. I'm also the *only* caterer in town."

She had a lovely smile, he thought. Sweet, in contrast to the fiery color of her hair. Which was the real her? he wondered. Or was she some combination? Some paradox that would keep the man in her life on his toes? Not that he'd seen any sign of a man around.

He shook his head, wondering where all that speculation had come from. It must be the smell of this food making him crazy. Only the manners his mother had so long ago pounded into him kept him from pouncing on the food while she set a plate down for Mud, who sniffed it eagerly, then looked up at Clay.

"Go ahead, boy," he said. And with a little whine the dog dug in.

"Don't wait on me," Casey said as she began to fill her own plate.

"I'll wait."

She gave him a stern look over her shoulder. "I'm not the one who nearly passed out. Eat."

He tried to go slowly, but still he ate much more quickly than she did. And much more. Her plate wasn't nearly as full as his. But once he'd tasted the pork chops with their surprising and delicious citrus tang, the pasta salad with a unique touch of both sweet and tart in the dressing, and the bread that proved to indeed be home baked—with not a bread machine in sight—he couldn't stop. And while anything edible would have done the job, he had to admit that this kind of food was a treat he'd almost forgotten existed in the world.

She kindly waited until he slowed down before speaking. "You're a long way from California."

His head came up sharply; he knew he hadn't said a word about where he was from. But then, he recalled, she'd seen the truck, so she'd probably seen the license plate. His father kept renewing the registration, so although he didn't have the current tabs, a simple computer check showed it was current. He'd thought of reregistering it somewhere else, but you needed an address for that, and he was never in one place long enough. Too bad. He could have picked a state where the registration fees were a bit less astronomical.

"A very long way," he agreed, leaving it at that.

"Usually it's people from Iowa heading to California on vacation, not the other way around."

He made a sound that he hoped she would take as answer.

"Unless you have family in the area?"

He managed, thanks to long practice, to keep his expression even. "No." *Not here. Not anywhere. Not who'd be willing to claim him anymore.*

"I suppose not, or you'd be staying with them," she said. "I've always wanted to go there. Where in California are you from?"

"South. Marina Heights."

Her brow furrowed. "I haven't heard of that. Is it near L.A. or San Diego?"

He set down the glass of milk she'd poured him. "You're on a farm in Iowa, drink the milk," she'd teased when he'd lifted a brow at it, and when he had, he'd found it surprisingly good. But now he just looked at her, speaking carefully.

"I'm not on the run from the law, I'm not a serial killer or a thief, nor do I mean you any harm. Beyond that, with all respect, my life is not your business."

She took it well, he thought. She didn't flinch, didn't look shocked or even hurt at his brusqueness. Odd, he would have expected at least one of those reactions.

"Point taken," she said coolly. And then, to his surprise, she went on. "I have a...proposition for you, Mr. Yeager."

"Clay, please," he said, wishing he'd given her another name, any name; his own had too much baggage. "What proposition?" he asked warily.

"As you can see, this place needs work. There are dozens of jobs like the ones you've done today. I don't have the time or the knowledge to do them. You seem to have both."

He stared at her. She couldn't mean what it seemed like she was suggesting. Could she?

"I can offer you meals, and a modest wage. However you want to work it out, whatever work you think it's worth. Oh, and Mud, too." She glanced at the dog, who was sitting patiently at Clay's feet, his gaze on her as she spoke. "Although I'm not sure leftover people food is the best for him. I'll pick up something more appropriate in town—you can just tell me what to get."

"You want...me to work for you?"

Her brows lowered slightly. "Isn't that what I said?"

He took a deep breath, then let it out slowly. Laying his silverware across his now nearly empty plate, he leaned forward and asked, "Are you crazy?"

She blinked. "What?"

"Are you crazy?" he repeated, more emphatically this time. "You ask a total stranger to come to work for you, here, out on this place, where you're completely alone?"

"You told me that the law's not after you, you're not a serial killer or a thief, and that you don't mean me any harm."

"And just like that, you believe me? Wouldn't I say the same thing if I were one or all of those things?"

"Probably," she agreed, annoyingly calm about it.

"How close is your nearest neighbor? Half a mile? And the nearest cop is...what, half-an-hour, twenty minutes' response time at best?"

For some reason he couldn't fathom, she smiled then. It was a sad, painful smile touched with bitterness, and he both wanted and didn't want to know what had made her capable of a look like that.

"Yes, to all of it. And believe me, I know you're a stranger. And I know how isolated I am out here. I also know that sometimes it's the ones who call themselves your friends that you have to watch out for."

She rose quietly, gracefully, gathered her dishes and Mud's plate, took them to the sink and left him wondering who and what had taught this quiet, innocent-seeming woman such a harsh lesson.

And the sudden spurt of anger at whoever it was startled him. It had been a very long time since he'd felt anything like that. And he wasn't sure he liked the fact that it had happened here, now, and with her.

The answer was clear and simple. He would tell her no, thank her for the food, apologize again for Mud's hunting expedition, and then, having done all he could to even the accounts, he would be on his way. He'd hoped to stay in the area awhile longer—both he and the truck were weary—but...

The truck.

It needed work. A lot of it. It had been new when he'd left California, but that had been five years and more than one hundred thousand miles ago, and now it needed new hoses and belts, probably an alternator, not to mention a valve job, and it was due for tires and more. It could break down at any moment, and he didn't have the money to fix it. Not that he couldn't go on without it—none of his meager possessions, except maybe a few books, meant much to him—but Mud needed shelter, since dogs weren't welcome in many places, and he spent a lot of time in the truck while Clay worked at some short job that would get them back on the road again.

She'd said a "modest" wage, but if she provided meals,

he could save it all and maybe get some of that badly needed work done. At least he would have a start, enough to get him to somewhere where he could get a better-paying job. Not to mention that he could get some rest and regular food; that episode out by the barn had scared him more than he cared to admit.

He heard the slap of the dishwasher closing. Casey straightened up and turned around. She leaned against the front of the dishwasher and looked at him.

"Well?" she asked.

He took a deep breath, hoping he wasn't making a big mistake. And knowing somehow that he was. "You're still crazy to hire somebody you don't even know," he said. "But if the offer is still open...I'll take it."

"That you're a stranger," she said, her voice sounding as that smile had looked, sad, tinged with bitterness, "is the only reason I offered. You're hired."

I'm also an idiot, Clay thought. But Lord knows I'm an expert at it. One of the very best at being deaf, dumb and blind, too.

Mud yipped, as if sensing his thoughts. And when he looked down at the little collie, the animal cocked his head to one side quizzically, as if to ask what he was doing.

I wish I knew, buddy. I wish I knew.

Chapter 3

Maybe she *was* crazy, Casey thought as she stood at the kitchen sink, looking out into the growing dusk. He'd worked hard all day, but she still knew only his name, and he'd been oddly hesitant about that. And when it came to anything else, he'd clammed up completely.

She wasn't even sure what had driven her to impulsively make the offer, but now that it was done, she wasn't sorry. Yes, he'd refused to speak of himself, where he'd come from or what he was doing so far from home, but she sensed it was a reticence stemming from pain, not secretiveness or some more nefarious reason. And even if he'd refused to tell her who and what he was, he'd been telling the truth when he'd told her what he wasn't. She was as sure of that as she could be of anything anymore. His response had been instant and incredulous; he truly thought she was crazy for trusting him, which, in a perverse way, convinced her that she could.

Besides, she'd resolved long ago that she could not go

through life second-guessing everyone she met just because she'd once been so horribly wrong.

She wasn't, however, foolish enough to invite him to take up residence in one of the spare rooms in the house. It had occurred to her, but she'd discarded the idea immediately. She was nowhere near ready for such a thing as a man living under her roof. It had been tension-inducing enough just to have him around last night.

And he'd been grateful enough when she'd told him that he could move his truck into the yard and stay there at night if he wanted to. That she'd carefully checked the locks on every door and window—not that she didn't do that regularly, anyway—before she'd offered was something she didn't tell him. In this quiet, bucolic area her actions would be viewed as paranoid, if not plain suspicious. Of course, she'd lived in the big city for five years, which got her forgiven for a lot of what the locals would consider odd behavior.

They're right. I never should have left, she thought, as she had so many times before. *I should have stayed here in River Bend.*

She sighed as she finally rinsed the casserole dish she'd been washing, wondering vaguely how long she'd been rubbing at it with the scrub pad. The luncheon had gone well. The food had been a hit, and only three of the ladies had insisted on telling her exactly what she should be doing with her life, getting married and having babies being first on all their lists.

The remonstrations for leaving River Bend in the first place had finally faded away. Had she been born here, rather than having come to live with Aunt Fay after her parents had been killed when she was ten, she supposed it would have taken even longer for them to die out. As it was, it had been nearly a year before they'd finally given up telling her that she never should have gone to Chicago.

She knew that nothing could have stopped her from

heading for the big city back then. She'd been eager to leave small-town life behind her, had been young, full of energy, enthusiasm and optimism.

And, she added to herself wryly, naiveté. She'd had lots of that. Five years later she'd come running back, ruing the day she'd ever left.

She hadn't intended to stay here on the farm forever, had only intended to heal, to get over it and go on with her life, but the quiet peace here had been too alluring, too much a balm to her wounded soul to leave easily. And by the time she didn't need it quite so badly, she had a life here. It wasn't the frantic, high-powered pace she'd once thrived on, but it was a life.

That it had recently become a life behind locked doors and windows at night, a life of jumping at every noise, of panic at every phone call, didn't erase the peace she'd found here.

She knew she'd done all she could about the calls. She'd reported them to the sheriff's department when they'd begun a week ago, although she hadn't told them her entire story. She didn't want to drag it all out again unless she had to, and she had no proof it was Jon. As far as she knew, it couldn't be, and she didn't want to make the call that would disprove that. She would much rather believe it was some adolescent-minded male who got his jollies this way.

They'd promised to send an extra patrol her way periodically, but she knew she was too far out for them to come by very often. And that there was little they could do about anonymous calls. The best suggestion they'd had was to change her number, but she couldn't see that that would do much good unless she kept it unlisted, and she could hardly do that and run a business.

And in spread-out farmland like this, you couldn't just not answer your phone. She'd realized that when she'd moved the bedroom phone out to the living room and it had awakened her, anyway. With help far away, the neighbors out here had to be able to count on one another in case of fire or other emergency. Just last year she'd had to go get Cathy Stokes and take her to the hospital to have her baby, when her husband had been snowed in in Minneapolis.

So she'd let it go and yesterday she'd put the phone back in her bedroom, hoping the calls would stop when whoever it was got bored.

Unless it *was* Jon.

She suppressed a shiver. It couldn't be. It didn't *sound* like Jon; there was a raspy tone to the voice that didn't fit, even in that disguised whisper. He didn't know where she was. He couldn't just get to a phone in the middle of the night, could he? And it had been years. He couldn't still be—

The sound of the old pump handle outside drew her attention. She used it only often enough to keep it working, but Clay was washing up after his day of work. Through the kitchen window she saw him shiver—the well was deep enough that the water was cool, even at this time of year, especially on a day as warm as this one—but he kept on.

For a moment she was again aware of how broad his shoulders were, but his T-shirt was wet and clinging to him, and almost immediately she focused on what she could see of his too visible ribs even through the fabric; he was indeed far too thin. The memory of him sagging against the barn wall came back to her, and she realized he most likely had passed out from a combination of heat and hunger. The idea gave her an odd little chill, and she quickly began to expand her plan for meals of hearty, weight-producing food.

Midwest food, she thought with a smile. Including beef, potatoes, gravy and fresh-from-the-fields corn. She got her share of the sweet vegetable from the Wilsons, who leased her acreage for corn and soybeans. The money helped pay the farm's bills, and not being a farmer herself, she was content with the arrangement.

Clay was right on time; she'd told him dinner was at five. It was earlier than she normally ate, but he'd started early, and he had to be hungry.

He looks like he's been hungry for a long time, she thought, feeling that little internal tug anew. And she wondered yet again who he was, how he'd arrived at this pass, apparently homeless, living out of his truck, without even enough food to eat. He seemed more than willing and able to work, and from all she read, the job market wasn't nearly as bad as it once had been. Could it be by choice? Or had he lied, and was there some hidden reason why he couldn't settle in one place and work at least until he was healthily strong again?

She made herself quash her wonderings as she served up the meal she'd just finished, a savory hash of potatoes, chicken, tomatoes and peppers that was one of her specialties.

"Is there something I can do?" he asked politely as he came in.

"Nothing except eat," she said; she'd set the table while the hash had been simmering to doneness.

"That," he said as she set a full plate in front of him, "I can do."

He seemed so serious, so shadowed that she was a little startled by the quip. There was no trace of a smile, only a slight quirk of his mouth at one corner.

"You've earned it," she said. "I can't believe all you've accomplished today. Hello, Mud. Have fun chasing the squirrels today?"

The dog gave a little yip, then sat as she prepared and put a plate down for him. He politely waited until her hand was clear before he attacked the food. She felt Clay's gaze on her and hastened to assure him, "No peppers for the furry one, just chicken and potatoes. I'll get to the store soon for actual dog food."

For an instant he looked surprised when she sat down with him, but the expression vanished before she could be sure. He took a couple of bites before answering her.

"If he'll even eat it, after meals like this," Clay said. "You must have customers lined up for miles."

"I'm fairly well established now," she said. "And it's going to pick up as soon as they start bringing in the corn. Everybody works, and a lot of the wives are happy not to have to cook every night for a crew of voracious workers. Took a while to get them used to the idea, but I keep pretty busy now."

"I thought most of it was done by machines."

"Spoken like a city boy," she said with a grin that she hoped took any sting out of the words. "A lot of it is mechanized, but somebody still runs the machines and sorts the crop—unless you're talking about factory farms."

"That's quite a frown," he said.

She shrugged. "It's not a pleasant topic around here these days. Family farms are going under. They just can't compete with the big operations."

She didn't want to get off onto that, and he'd looked a bit wary when she'd said "city boy," so she quickly changed the subject.

"I know that well water's chilly, so if you'd like, you're welcome to use the shower off the mudroom. It's small, but it works, and the water's as hot as you want."

He looked at her assessingly, and she wondered if he was about to tell her she was crazy again. She wasn't sure she could argue with him on that. But after a moment he said merely, "Thank you. A real shower would be... welcome."

"I'll put out some towels."

Again he looked at her silently for a long moment before he spoke. "You're being awfully...kind."

She shook her head. "You're working awfully hard."

She glanced down as Mud took up an attentive position at her feet. He hadn't waited for Clay's okay to eat, she realized suddenly. And now he sat there licking his lips as if to express his pleasure in the meal.

Or thirst, she thought suddenly, realizing she'd forgotten to put down water for him. She rose and did so, and the little collie gave her a look she could only describe as approving. She smiled at him.

"Give me time, my furry friend. I'll figure out all the signals."

When she sat back down, Clay was looking from her to the dog and back, one dark brow raised. "He doesn't usually take like that to people," he said. "He's pretty standoffish. But then, they don't usually read him that well."

Casey suspected that the dog was a lot like his owner, too hurt to be anything but aloof. Not that he'd been physically injured, there was no sign of that, and certainly no sign of abuse, but there was a sadness in the quiet dignity of the dog that matched that of his owner. Unlike Corky, who had been a bit madcap and had had moments of puppyhood up until the day she died.

"My aunt had a Border collie when I was little," Casey explained. "Corky was smart as a whip and stubborn as a Missouri mule, Aunt Fay used to say. But that dog and I got along fine."

"It's the nature of the breed," Clay agreed. "They take time, but they're worth the trouble."

"I was the only child she knew. I think to her I was just another creature to guard, herd and generally watch out for."

His fork clattered to his plate. She thought there was an odd sharpness to his motion as he looked downward, as if he had jerked his gaze away from her rather than simply followed the fall of the fork.

"Sorry," he muttered. And she didn't think she was

wrong in her guess that he'd purposely changed the subject. "I'll finish the gate tomorrow, then get started on the roof before you get any more rain damage."

"This is Iowa in August," she said wryly. "It could stay dry, rain or hail at any given moment."

"Depends on your interpretation of dry," he said, his wry undertone almost matching hers. He was recovered now from whatever had bothered him.

"It is a bit humid," she agreed.

"A bit? This is a sauna."

A clue? she thought. He was used to drier air. Even in August? That would narrow down where he could be from. Desert area, perhaps? Mountains? Coast?

"We remember days like this fondly in January, when we're under a couple of feet or more of snow."

"I think I'd like that better."

Think? He didn't know? Did that mean he wasn't used to snow, either? Eliminated mountains, then, she guessed.

Then she laughed at herself. *Who do you think you are, Sherlock Holmes?*

And she had the grace to realize that she wouldn't care for him to return the favor and pry into her life, and vowed to let it be.

And vowed, as well, that she would not lie awake as she had last night, waiting for any noise, any sign that she'd made the horrible mistake of inviting a predator into her small, safe world.

"You think you're safe, don't you? You're wrong."

Casey's hand clenched the receiver as she sat there in the darkness. The sheriff's deputy had told her to just hang up on the caller if she wouldn't change her number, but she couldn't help straining to listen, to hear any clue in the low, harsh, whispering voice that would tell her if it was Jon. But it was impossible. Jon hadn't had any accent or verbal quirks that might betray him. He'd sounded...

average. And looked average. Perfectly normal. No one would ever have guessed what he was capable of. No one ever had, until he'd done it. Most especially her.

But there was no hint that it was Jon making the calls, nothing truly personal that would tell her that it was anything more than just bad luck that this psycho had fastened on her. That it was so much more out of place here in the quiet Iowa countryside only made it more frightening; you almost expected this in the city, but not here.

"I know where you are. I'm coming after you."

That was normal, too, they'd told her. She'd stared at the deputy, incredulous that he could use the word *normal* in such a context. He'd had the grace to be embarrassed and explain that what he'd meant was that it was typical of such a caller to say he knew where she was and threaten her with his personal appearance. They almost never followed through. If they had the guts to do that, they wouldn't be making relatively safe phone calls, she'd been assured.

It was that *almost* that had stuck in her mind, of course.

"You'll never get away, Casey."

She shivered, despite the relative warmth of the night air. She knew he had her name the same way he'd no doubt gotten her number, and not for the first time she wished she'd thought of something besides Casey's Catering as a business name.

But she was through trying to figure out this voice. She hung up with a determination to continue to do so from now on. If she hadn't been able to tell if it was Jon from the half-dozen calls so far, she wasn't likely to be able to in the next half dozen. And she didn't think it was, not really. He'd sworn she would pay, and she doubted he would be able to resist letting her know he was making good on that oath. Jon had never been one for delayed gratification, as she'd learned to her great regret.

So if it wasn't Jon, maybe if she took away some of the

guy's fun, he would give up. She would hang up immediately from now on. Oddly, that small decision to take back some control brought her comfort. Foolish, perhaps, but she would take it and be grateful.

Odder still was the sense that she was somehow safer from this twisted man, whoever he was, because Clay Yeager was here, asleep in his truck just a dozen yards away.

"Now, *that's* foolish," she muttered to herself as she pounded her pillow back into the right shape.

But she couldn't deny the feeling. However, she did manage to resist the urge to go look out the window just to see his truck sitting in the yard.

The predator wasn't inside her world, she assured herself. He was out there somewhere, hiding behind the anonymity of phone calls. And he, she thought with sudden fierceness, could just go to hell. She was not going to let this coward ruin—or run—her life. She would consider him no more important than a persistent mosquito.

And that burst of determination enabled her to go back to sleep much sooner than she normally did after a call.

"You've really taken to her, haven't you?" Clay asked as Mud's ears pricked up when Casey pulled into the drive. "I'd say it was the great food, but you let her get close before she ever fed you. Well, except for the prime rib."

He rarely thought anymore about the fact that he talked to the dog as if he were human. They'd been alone on the road together so long that it seemed natural. Not to mention that he still felt a qualm now and then at how close he'd come to having the clever animal put down. Now he couldn't imagine how cold and lonely this journey would have been without him.

That he deserved for it to be as cold and lonely as it could be was something he tried not to think about.

The dog trotted toward her as she got out of her car,

plumed tail up and wagging. Clay concentrated on replenishing his supply of roofing nails, filling the pocket on the utility belt.

"Hi, Mud!"

She sounded cheerful, bright, carefree, and Clay felt a tightness in his chest he hadn't experienced in a long time. The collie barked a greeting that seemed to echo her tone.

"You may not be so glad to see me when you find out I have boring old dog food in this bag here," she teased the animal.

Mud didn't seem to hold it against her, instead just followed her into the house. The screen door closed nice and slow behind them, just like it was supposed to.

If it had closed that way before, he wouldn't even be here now, Clay thought. And where would he be? Out on some country road, either broken-down or starving, no doubt. But instead he was here, the proverbial city boy, as she had called him, on a farm, eating regularly and resting a truck that was on the verge of major problems and that he couldn't afford to put gas in, anyway.

So why was he so uneasy? He'd stayed in one place on occasion, sometimes even for weeks. And this would only be...well, the list of things to be done could take a month, even more, but he wasn't about to stay that long. He'd already prioritized them, would do the most crucial first, the roof and repairing that rain gutter, and fixing that leak in the kitchen, and a couple of other damage-producing things. After that, he could break away anytime and not feel guilty about it.

That feeling guilty even occurred to him was not something he liked. And there was no reason for it, really. Casey was self-sufficient enough; she'd been the one to clear the rain gutters of debris, had done a credible job on weatherproofing the windows, she'd even repaired the ladder he was using until it was secure and safe. She would have gotten to the most important stuff eventually.

He walked back toward the ladder leaning against the eaves of the house. He settled the hammer in its loop on the carpenter's belt—it was a little light for roofing; he would have preferred a roofing hatchet, but with some extra muscle and time it worked—and put his foot on the first rung.

He heard the sound of the door opening again and barely squelched the urge to dash up the ladder to the roof; what the hell was wrong with him? Why was he feeling this crazy urge to dodge her?

She would just come up after you if she wanted to, he told himself, and stayed put.

"How's it going?" she asked, in the same chipper tone she'd used with Mud.

"I found another bad patch. It's going to take a bit longer."

Her mouth quirked at one corner. "I'm not surprised. I doubt it's been looked at much since my uncle died. Will we need more shingles?"

"Maybe. It'll be close."

She nodded. "Let me know. I'll get them. Oh, and I got the lumber you wanted for that brace."

"Good. That should hold the truss that's starting to split."

She gave him a quizzical look. "How do you know all this? Are you a professional carpenter?"

"No."

She waited, looking at him. It was an approach he knew well; most people felt compelled to fill a silence like this. It prompted more than one person to come out with something they normally wouldn't have said; he'd used the tactic many times himself. But recognizing it didn't make being on the receiving end any more comfortable. Finally he gave in to the subtle pressure.

"My father's a contractor." He couldn't see what harm it could do to tell her that. And the smile she gave him made it seem worth it.

"Ah. So you grew up around this kind of thing."

"Yes."

"Does he do houses, or commercial?"

"Both."

"Did you work with him?"

"Sometimes."

She let out a small, exasperated sound and glanced down at Mud. "And how are you today, Mud? Find any more squirrels to herd?"

The dog barked, paused, then barked twice more in quick succession.

"My, but you're quite the conversationalist! Are you sure you belong to him? Or maybe you just have better manners."

To his own amazement, Clay felt himself flush. "I'm sorry. I don't mean to be rude. I guess I'm just not much for…"

He trailed off, not sure whether what he'd been about to say wouldn't be more rude than his single-word answers. But she guessed what he'd been about to say and finished the sentence for him.

"Small talk?" She grimaced slightly. "I'm sorry. I was being rude, too. You're trying to work." She gestured around her. "And you're doing amazing things. Getting to all the things I haven't had time for, or wouldn't know how to do, anyway."

"Looks like you've done all right," he said, tacitly accepting her apology as she'd accepted his, and making an effort at being at least civil, if not talkative.

"Not like this," she insisted. "The screen, the fence, the roof… It's hard to keep things up, being alone on the place and trying to run a business, as well."

He let out an exasperated sound that echoed her own. "You really shouldn't advertise that you're alone out here."

"I wasn't advertising. You're the only one here, and you already know."

He couldn't argue with that logic, so he didn't even try. "The place isn't in such bad shape, except for the roof, and that'll be fixed soon."

"It's good to see it looking like it did when Aunt Fay was alive. She loved this place."

"It shows. Did she actually farm it?"

Casey nodded. "She took over after my uncle passed away. Up until the day she died, she had crops ready to go in and harvesting lined up."

She looked out over the yard to the distant fields bursting with the cash crop Iowa was renowned for, the corn that was, Clay thought rather inanely, truly as high as an elephant's eye.

"She used to tell me old farmers' tales, like how the Seneca Indians said you shouldn't plant corn until it was warm enough to sit on the ground naked and be comfortable."

Clay let out a short bark of a chuckle at that piece of lore. "Now, that's a visual," he said.

"Indeed," Casey agreed, smiling back. "It was very hard work for little return, though. I'm glad I don't need to count on it to survive."

"The catering business is less of a gamble, I'd guess."

"Not just that," she said. "My folks had lots of life insurance, and Aunt Fay set up a trust fund for me after they were killed. Since I lived with her, I never had to touch it, and it's quite sizable now."

He stared at her. She was still looking out over the fields. Her expression was tinged with a long-ago sadness, but that wasn't enough to stop him from grabbing her by the shoulders and turning her to face him.

"You really are crazy! What the hell are you doing, telling me you have a rich trust fund?"

He saw her focus snap back from wherever her mind had gone as she looked out over the farmland. "What?"

"You are either stupid, certifiable or naive beyond belief. I know you're far from stupid, so it has to be one of the other two."

Something came over her then, a chill that was almost tangible. He felt it in the sudden stiffness of her shoulders, saw it in the wintry look that frosted her bright blue eyes. And then he heard it in her voice, as cool now as it had been bright and cheerful before.

"Any naiveté I ever had disappeared long ago, *Mr.* Yeager. If you want that trust fund badly enough to try to swindle me out of it, then you're welcome to it. There are a lot more important things to lose in life."

She turned on her heel and went into the house, closing the door quietly but firmly behind her.

He stood there for a moment, wishing fiercely that he hadn't seen what he just had. Wishing he hadn't seen that look that spoke of knowledge gained in ugly ways.

Wishing he didn't have a better idea than most what it took to put that kind of look in a person's eyes.

Chapter 4

"More hardware, Casey? You building a new house out there or what?"

Casey kept her face even with an effort as Joe, the cashier at the Exchange, River Bend's combination hardware, feed and lumber store, rang up her purchases. She knew she would have to keep her voice light, casual, or she would draw attention like a harvested field drew crows.

"No, just trying to keep the old one from caving in," she joked, hoping he would leave it at that.

"Oh, come now, not much likelihood of that." The rather querulous female voice came from just behind her. "Ray, he built solid."

Casey took a bracing breath before turning to face Phyllis Harrington. If there was a reason she was hesitant to let anyone know about Clay being at her place, it was this woman. It wasn't just that she was of the mind-set that unmarried males and females should be chaperoned at all times, and that there was only one kind of relationship possible between men and woman, but she was also the biggest gossip in River Bend. For as long as Casey could remember, Aunt Fay had joked there were three ways to communicate, telephone, telegraph and tele-Phyllis. The woman was notorious for both her inability to keep her mouth shut and her ability to keep it running once she'd opened it.

It wasn't that she was ashamed or embarrassed to have Clay there, Casey told herself, but she knew the way the minds ran among Phyllis and the Ladies. They would have a simple business arrangement worked up into a romantic relationship before she had time to blink. And no matter how much she explained that it wasn't that way at all, their minds would be set, and she would be the hot topic in town. It would rumble on for days, until she dreaded coming into town at all.

And she did *not* want that. She'd already been through it when she'd first come home, when she hadn't quite had herself under control yet and she'd been caught a couple of times crying or reacting oddly. Phyllis and her cronies had been sure she'd run away from a broken romance, and she'd been more than willing to let them think that. She only wished it had been true.

But she didn't want to go through it all again.

"Hello, Mrs. Harrington," she said, as cheerfully as she could manage, forgoing the familiarity of using the older woman's first name, a formality Casey knew she expected. "Yes, if it wasn't for my uncle, the place would have tumbled over by now."

"You should have stayed home and taken care of it," Phyllis said, waggling her finger at Casey.

She'd learned long ago not to argue with Phyllis Harrington. "You're right," she said, taking the wind out of the woman's sails, and knowing Phyllis had no idea just how right she was. "But I'm trying to catch up now."

There was little more the woman could say, so she switched tack. "Who's doing your work?"

She should be glad, Casey supposed, that Clay had

shown no inclination to go into town. The sight of any stranger drew attention, and if he was spotted more than once, the pack would be on the hunt, after every detail of who he was, where he was from and what his connection with River Bend was. Or, more important, *who* his connection was.

She answered carefully, not wanting to lie outright. "I'm a big girl, Mrs. Harrington. I can fix things. I can even pound nails."

"But someone was hammering while you were on the phone with me the other day."

So much for not lying, Casey muttered to herself. No one could ever accuse Phyllis Harrington of being forgetful, even when it might be more comfortable for others if she was. And Casey knew that if she didn't salve the woman's curiosity somehow, it was entirely likely she would climb in that huge boat of a car of hers and risk the lives and limbs of everybody in town to come out to the farm and find out just what was going on. If they ever named tornadoes as they did hurricanes, her vote for the first one would be Phyllis.

"Oh," Casey said in what she hoped was a breezy voice, "that was just the screen-door guy, working on my door."

Phyllis frowned. "Screen-door guy? There's no one in town who—"

"He came out from Ames," she said quickly, figuring the college town had to have someone who could pass for a "screen-door guy."

"Humph. Out-of-towners. You should have used someone from River Bend."

Casey managed not to laugh at the self-contradiction, knowing it would mortally offend the woman.

"Next time I will," she assured her, knowing that Clay had fixed the screen door so well that she probably wouldn't need it worked on for at least another ten years. Even Phyllis would have forgotten by then.

She would probably have forgotten all this herself by then.

In ten years, she thought as she carried her bag out to her car, Clay Yeager would be just a distant memory. He would be that aloof, reticent man she'd never gotten to know, but who had saved her so much time and, if she was honest, money; she knew what his kind of help cost, and she thought she was getting off easy with meals and fifty dollars a day. Especially for the kind of days he put in, generally working twelve hours or better.

Which reminded her that after she stopped at Jean Harvey's bookstore to see if she could order that vegetable cookbook she wanted, she needed to stop at the bank; Clay had asked if she could pay him in cash. She'd felt a small qualm at his request, wondering again if he was hiding somehow, afraid of leaving any kind of paper trail.

But then she'd laughed at her overactive imagination. He probably didn't have a checking account, since he never stayed in one place long enough. Cash was easier. And she didn't mind; it was a small enough favor to ask. Plus, it would only be for a while; they hadn't talked about how long he would stay, and that fact alone hinted to her it wouldn't be long.

Something, she told herself, that you'd be well advised to keep in mind.

She was getting used to him being around, even after only a week. He was never intrusive; sometimes she went for hours never seeing him, only hearing the sounds of his work, but it was oddly comforting. Which surprised her, since the solitude and the associated safety had been the primary attractions the farm held for her, besides the fond memories.

And she enjoyed the meals they shared, although he insisted on eating his lunch while working and was hardly what you could call a talkative dinner companion. It wasn't totally that he was secretive, reluctant to talk about himself, although there seemed enough of that; it was also that he seemed truly out of practice in conversation.

A guy who doesn't want to talk about himself, and you're complaining? she thought wryly.

But it was best that she not get too comfortable with having him around. Not that "comfortable" was the right word to use about Clay Yeager. He would leave, and soon, she suspected. There was just something...restless about him. Something unsettled. Something edgy.

She looked at the money the teller handed her for a moment before she tucked it away in her purse. She wondered how much cash it would take to send him on his way again.

And she wondered why the idea left her feeling the tiniest bit bereft.

The week had passed for Clay with an odd combination of speed and slowness. He was up and working early every morning, and he forced himself to concentrate on the job at hand to keep his mind from straying to other, less welcome, things. So the days had passed, for the most part, fairly quickly.

It was the nights in between and the evenings that seemed painfully endless. It was the meals, at a table shared with a woman who had a mane of red-gold hair supermodels would kill for and a curvaceous figure those skinny models would consider excessive, but that he found essentially female. It was the evenings when she came out and sat on the screen porch at the rear of the house, in the rocker he guessed had been her aunt's, and he felt torn between a desire to spend those quiet minutes with her and the urge to put as much distance between them as he could.

And even hours spent reading by the light in his camper, the cure for most of his restless nights, didn't succeed in putting her out of his mind. And not solely because he'd been borrowing from her own library, with her cheerful blessing.

He swung the hammer more energetically than necessary and made himself focus on what he was doing. He'd decided to fix the old wrought-iron weather vane that lay useless atop the house, and had started as soon as he'd finished the roof. It was a great old piece. He couldn't guess how old, but old enough. The iron had been bent and shaped into the traditional four-directional wind vane, but the flat, hammered-iron ornament was not the usual horse or chicken or other stock animal, but a dog. A dog who looked for all the world like Mud.

He supposed it had to be fashioned after Casey's aunt's dog, the Border collie she had told him about. Or perhaps her aunt had simply found the vane and bought it because of the resemblance. But he'd figured he could fire up the old potbellied stove in the toolroom of the barn and make enough of a makeshift forge out of it to straighten the bent spire, and he could fashion a new base for it. Although it would end up a bit shorter, he could at least get it back up and functional, if not make it like new. He hoped she would be happy about it.

But then, she might think this frivolous when there were so many other things to be done. No, he thought as soon as the idea had formed, that didn't sound like Casey. She'd loved her aunt, and this had been important to her, therefore it would be important to Casey. He was sure of it.

"Yeah, like you're an expert," he muttered under his breath.

Truth be known, he had no idea how to deal with Casey Scott. On the surface, she seemed so open and, as he'd accused her, so naive. Or maybe it was just that this mostly rural area where people didn't even lock their doors was so utterly strange to him that it all seemed too innocent to be believed.

If you'd asked him years ago, he would have said there wasn't a place left on the planet where mankind and innocence could coexist. The former arrived and the latter left. That was just the way things were.

Or so he'd thought. Yet there was a peace here, a serenity, that seemed almost unreal to him. But he had to admit, unreal or not, it seemed to seep into the bones until you quit thinking about threats from your fellow man and worried more about threats from Mother Nature. Too much rain or not enough. Snow too early. Hail. Tornadoes. These were the things you worried about in River Bend.

It was a trite phrase, but even he could feel it, that connection to the land. It didn't seem to matter that he'd grown up in suburbia and the closest he'd gotten to nature was the occasional camping trip. He'd known the streets, had been able to sense a shift of mood in a crowd in a split second, but this... this was different.

As Casey was different.

As the thought formed in his mind, he nearly hammered his finger instead of the vane. What the hell was he thinking? If Casey Scott was different, it was because she was too darn trusting. She even trusted him, a stranger.

And if there was anything that struck fear into Clay Yeager's heart, it was the thought of being trusted. Especially by a woman.

He slammed the hammer down one more time on the heat-softened iron, figured it was as straight as it was going to get, and plunged it into the bucket of water he'd set up for that purpose. He watched the steam rise, trying not to think of anything else. Trying not to think about Casey and the politeness they'd retreated into since he'd railed at her for telling him about her trust fund.

I was right, he insisted inwardly. *She had no business rattling on to me about such things. No business trusting me like that.*

But she *could* trust him, at least that far. He wasn't going to steal from her. He knew she could trust him with everything she'd told him—her aloneness, her money—so was she foolish if she somehow knew that? Or was she just a good judge of people?

He pulled the vane out of the bucket and watched it drip, cool now. He hadn't thought of it that way before—that perhaps she wasn't so naive if she knew she could trust him. Maybe if he'd been someone else, she wouldn't have.

And there was no way he could hang the word *naive* on that look he'd seen in her eyes. There had been nothing of innocence and everything of world-weariness in that look. There was something else in Casey Scott, some dark, hidden thing that shadowed blue eyes that should be as bright as the Iowa sky on a summer day. He knew it, knew it because he'd become all too sensitive to the undercurrents people hid behind their daily masks.

He knew it because he hadn't been, once. And it had cost him his world.

Light. Pure, bright California sunlight. Nothing bad could ever happen in a place with such light. The feeling was incomparable. For once things had gone the way they were supposed to. The sun was out, and all was right with the world.

He was home early for a change, so maybe even Linda would be happy. He would take her out to dinner, both her and Jenny. They hadn't seen much of him lately, and he had to try to make it up to them. And he would. He'd even made arrangements to take some time off. They would be like they used to be, laughing, having fun, something there had been too little of in recent years. Jenny would love the stuffed elephant he'd bought her to add to her huge collection. She would solemnly name it and drag it around for weeks until it was suitably broken in.

He was feeling so good he started to whistle as he pulled into the drive and hit the button for the garage-door opener. The door began to lift.

Instead of the semitidy garage, the door opened on a

yawning maw of darkness and horror. It seemed to suck away every trace of sunlight, every bit of warmth. It had been daylight, but now the tunnel of light created by the headlights of his truck, lights he hadn't even known were on, was the only illumination. It seemed oddly red. But it still showed all too well what awaited him in that gaping, dark cavern.

He sat, staring, barely aware that he'd hit the brakes, barely aware that he heard the puppy in there somewhere, whimpering, but fully aware that his world had just shattered. Permanently.

"No," he whispered, clenching his hands on the steering wheel.

He'd been to countless scenes as bad as this or worse. His instinct and training had never failed him. But now he couldn't function, couldn't move, couldn't even think. He heard an odd scrambling, an almost metallic sound, but it didn't really register.

"No. God, no…"

He heard his own voice as if from a distance. It was a hollow, horrible thing. A chill swept him, making him shiver. He heard Mud whimpering again. The cold increased. He was shuddering now. Small bursts of sound escaped him, helplessly. Mud whimpered. Something icy touched his neck, then his cheek. Mud yipped, worried.

He came awake abruptly. For an instant he had no idea where he was, didn't know if the pale light he saw was morning or evening. Mud nudged him, gently, almost tenderly. The full-grown Mud, not the whimpering pup of the dream.

The dream.

It was only the dream, back again. He let out a sound that he was sure sounded about like Mud's whimpering. Maybe even more despairing than the worried dog had sounded.

God, it had been so long he'd dared to think, to hope, he was free of it. And he had been, for a long time; the dream hadn't come in nearly two years.

But it hadn't lost any of its vividness in that time, or any of its power. And, most especially, it had lost none of its horror. Or its ability to terrify him. He'd almost forgotten how harrowing the dream was, how it drained him, shook him to the soul.

But Mud had not forgotten. Nor had he forgotten what to do.

"Thanks, buddy," he said softly, reaching out to scratch one silky black ear. "Again," he added on a long, compressed, weary breath.

"Are you all right?"

He sat up sharply, nearly rapping his head on the shelf over his pillow. He stared toward the back of the truck, where the windowed top half of the shell was propped open. And where Casey was standing in the morning light, looking at him.

"What are you doing here?" he snapped.

"I was already awake," she said, brow furrowing at the sharpness of his tone. "Mud and I were on the porch when all of a sudden he took off running for the truck and scrambled in the back here. Then I heard him whimpering, and I thought he might be hurt."

"Oh."

He said it flatly, his anger at being caught this way draining away. It would be beyond churlish to be angry at her for that, no matter how hideously he was embarrassed that she'd glimpsed his torment. No matter that all he wanted to do at this moment was run.

It was bad enough that she'd guessed he'd been practically starving and had probably come up with this temporary handyman job for the sole reason of feeding him, but now she'd witnessed the misery he tried so hard to hide. And he succeeded, most of the time. Just his luck she'd caught him when his guard was down, the one time he couldn't suppress the thoughts, the memories, when he was asleep.

Now the questions would start. And he couldn't face that. Almost desperately, he tried to shake off the remnants of the dream and think, to calculate; she'd paid him yesterday for this week, so he had plenty to get rolling again. The truck repairs would have to wait; he would just have to hope the thing would hold together and keep running a little longer.

"Dreams can be so very ugly, can't they?" she said softly, in a rhetorical tone that told him she wasn't expecting an answer. And then she said, in a completely normal voice, "Breakfast will be ready in about twenty minutes. Coffee's ready now."

She turned and walked away.

That was it? Clay thought. No questions? No prying? She just said that and then walked away? She was acting as if nightmares that left you shaking and sweating and drained were a normal part of life.

And then he remembered her eyes, that look that had clouded them. And thought that maybe, to her, they were.

Chapter 5

In the end, he didn't run.

"It'd be dumb, Mud," he said after she called them in for dinner a couple of days after the dream had returned. "I mean, what better place for a couple of starving nomads to stay than with the best caterer in the state?"

Mud yipped in assent. The collie had more than taken to Casey; he'd included her in his rounds, checking on her whenever he took off in response to some internal signal Clay had never been able to figure out. Casey had been amused but understanding. Border collies were working dogs, she said; they needed jobs to do. She'd taken to leaving the screen unlatched and the sliding barn door open enough for the dog to get through, saying she wasn't at all averse to a diligent watchdog around.

This had never happened before; no matter how long they'd stayed in any one place, the dog had remained aloof, disdainful of whoever they encountered. But Mud's acceptance of Casey had even survived the switch to regular dog food—although he suspected Casey slipped the dog some treats when he checked in while she was cooking. His first clue had been when he'd seen Mud nose open the screen door and go inside, the second when he inevitably emerged licking his chops.

Now Clay headed for the shower first, clean clothes in hand. Casey had offered to do his laundry in with hers, but he'd declined. It was silly, he supposed, but there was something…intimate about that, and it made him uncomfortable. So he did his own, which was no great project; he had about enough clothes for a couple of weeks and that was it.

He finished quickly, stepped out of the small shower and grabbed a towel. He raised it to his hair, rubbing it dry, wondering again if he should spend the money for a haircut. He'd had a short, precision cut for years, and it had taken a while to get used to the strands brushing his shoulders. But the long hair seemed appropriate, and one more thing that set him apart from the man he'd been back then.

When he caught a glimpse of himself in the mirror, he stopped, the towel now damp in his hands. Gone was the gaunt, hollow look. His ribs were still prominent, but the concave stomach didn't look like it was meeting his backbone anymore. Amazing what ten days of good, regular food could do.

And desserts, he added silently. He grinned as he went back to drying his hair. Casey turned out some mean pies, and he'd learned just how good they could be.

She was setting the table when he got to the kitchen. He hadn't wanted to put his dirty work boots back on, so he was barefoot and made no noise as he paused in the doorway. She was humming something slow and melancholy, murmuring a phrase or two of the lyrics now and then, something about too many memories for one heart to hold. Her hair was neatly held at her nape with some kind of stretchy cloth band, as she wore it most days. But he could still remember the first morning he'd come here, when it had been loose and sleep-tousled, not tamed as it was now, but wild, as if expressing some emotion she normally didn't allow herself.

He watched as she laid out silverware with a loving touch; it had been her aunt's, she'd told him, and her great-aunt's before her, and she cherished it for that reason alone, despite the ornate pattern that wasn't really to her taste.

As she put down the last fork, moved by an urge he didn't understand and probably never would have given in to had he stopped to think, Clay crossed the room swiftly and took her elbow.

She gave a little start.

"Oh! I didn't hear you!"

"Sorry. Come on, I want to show you something."

Her red-gold brows furrowed. "Now what did you find that needs repairing?"

"No, this is something that's already fixed. I finished it today."

She brightened a little as they went outside. "Is that what you were doing back on the roof this afternoon?"

"Yes." He'd been up there when she'd returned from a job, and she'd been curious, since he'd finished the roof the day before, but he'd managed to keep what he was doing hidden. He wasn't sure why he'd felt the need to do that, but now he was glad he had.

"The roof looks wonderful, by the way. Nice and weather-tight."

"It shouldn't leak," he said, leading her out into the yard. He turned her around. He didn't bother to tell her where to look. She was already tilting her head back, and she would see it soon enough. Besides, he wanted to watch her reaction when she saw it. Merely curiosity, he told himself. Nothing wrong with that, even if he hadn't felt so much as a spark of it in years.

"I'll be grateful for that when the next rain hits. If it had gotten any worse, there could have been—oh!"

She stopped abruptly. He saw her eyes widen, her lips part, and then a slow, delighted smile crossed her face. And it was worth every burned finger and even the singed hair he'd ended up with on the project to see it.

She turned to him then, her eyes alight. "You fixed it! You fixed Corky!"

In the face of her joy, he couldn't help smiling back at her. It was such a simple thing, but it clearly meant to her all he'd suspected and more.

"Aunt Fay adored that vane, and I was so upset when it broke. It seemed like an omen or something, just another reminder that she was gone. But there it is, good as new!"

She laughed joyously, and to his shock, he found himself chuckling along with her. It was a foreign, unfamiliar sound and felt even stranger than it sounded.

"Not quite as good as new," he said, shying away from his own unexpected reaction. "It's a bit shorter, and I had to change the base a little."

"It doesn't matter, really, it doesn't. It looks wonderful." Suddenly, unexpectedly, she threw her arms around him in a fierce hug. "Thank you, Clay. This means so much to me."

She might as well have fired a flash-bang grenade at him. He couldn't move, couldn't think, couldn't react. Except for routine, unavoidable touches and the occasional hand-shake on a job, he'd had little physical contact with another human being for five years. He avoided it, withdrew from it, even the backslapping camaraderie of men seeming pain-ful, where it had once been part of his life.

And now here he was, with a lovely, delicious woman wrapping her arms around him, embracing him as if he'd just handed her the moon instead of doing a little metal-work. Holding him in a way he hadn't been held in a very long time, even before...

He shivered inwardly and didn't know if it was from the memory or the feel of a warm, soft female body pressed against his. Not that she meant it that way, of course; she was simply delighted to see what he'd done. But that didn't change the chaos she was causing. And he couldn't even stop her. Couldn't pull away, couldn't push her arms away.

Couldn't? Or didn't want to?

Before he could begin to deal with that shocking thought, she had released him. Perhaps she'd sensed his unease, because she was looking at him oddly, as if she thought she'd done something wrong.

He spoke hastily, wanting the awkward moment to pass. "My dad used to have an ironworker he hired for some projects. I hung out with him, because I liked watching him work on wrought-iron pieces. I remembered just enough to get this done. If it had been any newer, I probably wouldn't have had a clue."

"Bless your father, then," she said, accepting his rush of words as if there were nothing unusual about them. "And thank you again. I never expected you to do that."

He shrugged, feeling a bit easier. "I thought it might be important to you."

"It is," she said, her tone heartfelt. "Very."

She gave it one more loving look before they went back inside to eat. And he was very satisfied with his decision and the results.

"So tell me," he said, after he'd taken the edge off his hunger from the day's work, "why did somebody who can cook like this not start a catering business until three years ago?"

Casey lifted a brow at him, and only then did he realize he had initiated a personal conversation for the first time. But after a moment she answered easily enough.

"I thought I wanted to live in the big city."

"Why?"

She shrugged, picking at the last slice of potato on her plate. "Why does any twenty-five-year-old want to leave a small town? I was bored, I wanted excitement and I thought a place like Chicago would have everything I wanted.''

Her tone answered the question he hadn't yet asked; whatever she'd found in the city, it hadn't been what she wanted. And, having more than a few of his own, he recognized a "hands off" sign when he saw one. He finished the delicious scalloped potatoes before speaking in a neutral tone.

"So you came back home."

She nodded, apparently willing to go on, since he hadn't pressed for answers she wouldn't give. "Three years ago."

There was something, some faint undertone in her voice, much more subtle than the warning had been, but also much tenser. As if the memory of her homecoming were less than pleasant.

He said nothing, just watched her as he took a sip of the milk he'd grown to look forward to, as long as it was ice-cold, which she made certain it was, to finish off the meal. She seemed to realize he'd heard something she hadn't meant him to and hastened to go on as if it were nothing.

"Aunt Fay left me a small inheritance in addition to the farm, and I put that together with what I got for leasing out the fields that first year and remodeled the kitchen for my purposes."

Not touching the trust fund, he noted. Wise woman.

He glanced around; he'd seen the first time he was in here that this was a serious kitchen. A huge silver commercial range with two ovens, and two more ovens on the next wall—with doors that opened conveniently on side hinges, he'd noticed, wondering why everybody didn't make them that way. Two dishwashers and a huge island topped half with a cutting board and half with a slab of granite, which she'd told him was for pastry and breads.

"And then you were in business?"

"Then I took out ads in the paper and the phone book, and posted some flyers. I got sympathy and curiosity jobs at first, but I'm good, and pretty soon I was getting taken seriously.''

"And rightfully so," he said with heartfelt sincerity. Then, even though his gut warned him not to let this get too personal, not to let this easy companionship continue, he asked, "You and your aunt were very close, weren't you?"

Her mouth curved into a soft smile that was sad and loving at the same time. "Yes. She was wonderful. She took me in without hesitation when my parents were killed in a car accident."

He drew back slightly. Somehow he'd gotten the idea that she was only here because her aunt had left her the place, not because she'd actually grown up here.

"I'm sorry," he said tentatively. "I didn't know."

"It's all right. It's not...fresh anymore. And Aunt Fay made up for a lot. I was only ten, so it was pretty traumatic for me."

"So you really did grow up here."

She nodded. "And it was wonderful. I'd lived in St. Louis with my folks, but I spent every summer here. I adored it, the space, the animals...of course, what little girl wouldn't adore having her very own pony to ride?"

He went very still. As clearly as if it were real, he heard the small voice begging, *Please, I really, really want a pony! Oh, please?*

He clenched his jaw, managing to suppress the shudder. "Of course," he said tightly. "What little girl wouldn't?"

He was amazed he'd been able to speak at all, but thought he'd done all right. Until she looked at him with such concern.

"Clay? Are you all right?"

"Fine. Excuse me."

He got up and carried his plate and glass to the sink, rinsed them carefully, then put them in the dishwasher, moving with methodic precision.

"Clay…"

"Thank you for dinner."

"What's wrong?"

"Nothing. I'm going to go for a walk."

"There's apple pie for dessert," she said, still not sounding convinced.

"Later." Then, trying a little harder, he added, "Thank you."

He nearly ran down the steps. And kept running, toward the woods where he'd parked his truck what seemed like aeons ago. Where he'd first met Casey, thanks to Mud's hunting expedition. He slowed a little as the trees got thicker. This was not a neatly planted grove, like the walnuts on the other side of the yard; this was a thick stand of mixed trees, most of which he didn't recognize. He only knew California trees, the Joshuas of the desert and the evergreens of the mountains, the scrub oak, the willow and the ubiquitous eucalyptus, the Australian import some wished had never arrived.

He slowed his pace to a walk. Felt the uneven ground beneath his feet and realized that doing this in his bare feet wasn't the smartest move he'd ever made.

He was back under control, he assured himself. She'd just caught him off guard. He hadn't been prepared, hadn't been ready, and the unintentional blow had hit him harder than it should have.

It was his own fault, he told himself. He'd let himself slip into something far too comfortable, too tempting. Long, easy, revealing chats over a good meal, savoring a smile, delighting in her joy…and her laughter. Something he'd never, ever expected to be part of his life again.

And beneath it all, flowing like a bright, dangerous river, the growing awareness that Casey was a beautiful, charming and very alluring woman.

* * *

Had she really thought, not very long ago, that her life was not running at the frantic pace she'd grown used to in the city?

Casey wiped a strand of unruly hair out of her face with her arm, careful not to burn her nose with the cake pan she'd just removed from the oven. This was the last of the baking; now all she had to do was finish with the hors d'oeuvres, and by that time the cake would be cool enough to put together into that chocolate-and-fruit conglomeration called Black Forest. Not what she would have chosen with the rest of the menu, but she only suggested; the customer chose.

She glanced at the clock on the oven. She had plenty of time; the Newmans' party wasn't until seven. The mushrooms were ready to be stuffed, the pâté nicely molded, and the caviar she'd had to order from New York was ready to be put on ice. Mrs. Newman, who was here under duress, the city born and bred wife of a factory farm executive assigned to the area for a year, was quite a different customer from most of the local women. And Casey wasn't sure she didn't prefer the less pretentious tastes she had once thought, in youthful arrogance, provincial.

With a smile at the marvel of growing up, Casey ran through her schedule in her head. She would deliver the hors d'oeuvres twenty minutes before the first guest was expected, giving the mushrooms the final broiling in Mrs. Newman's huge, but rarely used, oven—she'd rented the house because it was the only place that looked civilized out here amid the rustics, as she put it. Then it would be back home to check on the pork tenderloin she was roasting and to finish the cake. Then she would pack it all up, heading over again an hour before Mrs. Newman required that dinner be served. While the meat was cooling for slicing, she would fix the green beans with sour cream sauce, then put the roast under the broiler for a few minutes to give it a nice, browned crust. If she was lucky, it would all come out just right. And if she wasn't, well, she would adapt. She'd gotten quite good at that.

She started on the mushrooms, filling each nicely matched cap with the crab-and-cheese mixture she'd prepared earlier. It was a steady, repetitive chore, and her mind began to wander to the other things that had joined with her work schedule to turn her life into something quite opposite the quiet, peaceful life she'd envisioned when she'd first conceived the idea of opening her own small business here.

First and foremost was the enigma, the puzzle, the annoyance and fascination by turns of Clay Yeager. Some level of interest and curiosity was only to be expected, she guessed. He was the first person, and certainly the first man, she'd been around this much in a long time. But it wasn't simply that. There was something about him that she suspected would have drawn her attention no matter what the circumstances. Something dark and mysterious, yet not frightening. Something that kept her from taking offense when he snapped at her, because somehow she was sure it wasn't her he was angry at, any more than a wounded animal who bit was angry at the person trying to help.

It wasn't the first time the analogy of a wounded animal had come to her. There were many times when he would withdraw, when a sudden shadow in his eyes, a sudden tightness in his body or tension in his face, would make her think of some wild creature, hurt, trapped, helpless. Which was odd, because in all other respects, she couldn't imagine anyone less helpless than Clay Yeager. Everything he did, he did with assurance and an economy of motion that spoke quietly of strength and power. She'd watched him work more than once with a rapt fascination, then blushed when she'd realized she was more fascinated with him than with the work he was doing.

And more than once he'd caught her watching him, but he'd never commented, had always assumed she was merely checking on his work. Which was, she'd thought, all she should have been doing. It wasn't as if she were interested in him as anything other than her hired helper. She wasn't interested in any man in that way. She wasn't sure she ever would be.

Which made her think of the other factor that was making her life chaos. But this time, when she thought of her midnight phone caller, it was with a small sense of pride; she'd hung up on him the last two times and managed to go right back to sleep. He'd barely gotten a couple of words out when she'd quietly—she didn't want to give him the satisfaction of doing it angrily—replaced the receiver. Hopefully he would move on to other prey soon.

Not, she thought wryly, that she would wish him on anyone else.

She wiped at her forehead again; with all this cooking and baking, she'd heated up the kitchen pretty well, enough that the small air conditioner in the living room wasn't able to keep up. She'd been elbow-deep in cake batter when she'd decided that the first bit of spare cash she had was going for a separate cooling unit for the kitchen.

She wondered how Clay was doing outside. It was hot there, too, and he'd been chopping up the firewood left over from last year's fairly mild winter and cutting the unusable scrap lumber that had been scattered around in various places for kindling. The rhythmic sound of the ax and the saw—the power saw hadn't worked, but he'd insisted it wasn't necessary when she'd offered to get it fixed or replaced—had been the counterpoint to her work in the kitchen, and she'd found it oddly soothing. But it was hot work under any conditions, and especially today.

Quickly she finished the mushrooms, packed them in a covered plastic dish and set them in the refrigerator. Then she pulled out the pitcher of lemonade she'd made yesterday, filled a large glass with ice and the tangy liquid and headed outside.

She followed the sound of the ax around the barn to the woodpile. And stopped dead in her tracks.

He was crouched down, gathering some smaller pieces of wood. He'd pulled off his shirt in the heat, and in the first few seconds all she could do was stare at the play of powerful muscles in his back and shoulders, and the sheen of sweat on his skin. He might be too thin for his build, but what was there was solid. And nicely constructed.

Her eye tracked to the waistband of his jeans and the gap between the worn fabric and his spine. It was there that he'd lost the most weight, she guessed—and she wondered just how low on his hips those jeans would slip when he stood up. Her face heated fiercely, the kitchen now seeming cool by comparison.

And then another kind of shock overtook her. Her eyes narrowed, focused, and a chill went through her at the realization that what she was seeing was real, not some trick of the light or Hollywood makeup job. Clay Yeager carried scars. Lots of them.

Low on his left side was a round, thickly ridged mark that even to her untutored eye looked like a bullet wound. Across his back were a couple of thin white marks, and across his right shoulder was a patch of skin that looked twisted and shiny, like a burn.

She didn't think she'd made a sound, but his head came up, and he turned toward her. Without thinking, she looked for further signs of damage, finding them before she even realized what she was doing. A series of small circles, some larger than others, some faintly reddish, some white and thick-looking. An oddly tidy *X* of faint white lines like the ones on his back. And a thicker line, marked with the tiny dots of stitches, marched at a curving angle up his right arm from just above the elbow nearly to his shoulder.

He moved then, and she became suddenly aware of how intently she'd been staring. Flushing, she lifted her gaze to see him reaching for his shirt. Only as he twisted and reached for the T-shirt he'd tossed over the top of the woodpile did she realize she had the answer to her earlier question; the unbelted jeans hung low on his narrow hips, inviting her eyes to trace the trail of dark hair that arrowed down from his navel and enticing her mind to wonder at what was hidden.

"Sorry," he said as he picked up the shirt.

Sorry? He was apologizing to her? She was the one standing here gaping at him like some kind of voyeur, speculating on the intimate parts of his body, reacting like a schoolgirl to the parts she could see. She couldn't believe it. She, of all people, to fall prey to imaginings like that, to have her fingers curling with a desire to touch....

"I didn't mean to shock you," he said, and began to pull the gray T-shirt over his head. "I don't usually take my shirt off around strangers."

The scars. He was talking about the scars. Maybe he hadn't even noticed that she'd been eyeing him like a prize bull.

She should be relieved, but somehow she didn't like the idea that he thought she'd been gawking at his scars much better. "I'm the one who's sorry," she said quickly, feeling unbearably awkward. "I didn't mean to be rude, staring like that."

He tugged the shirt down, which couldn't have been easy over sweaty skin. "It's all right," he said dismissively. "I'm used to it."

She knew he didn't mean being stared at by females wondering what he would look like naked—which she still couldn't quite believe she'd done—so she decided to cut her losses and let him think it was indeed the scars that had so transfixed her. It wasn't really a lie; that had been part of it.

She handed him the glass of lemonade, only realizing when she went to let go of it how tightly her hand had been gripping it. He took it and drained about half of it in a single gulp.

"My God, Clay, what happened to you?" It burst from her before she could stop it.

"Things."

"Was that a...bullet wound?"

He gave her a narrow look over the rim of the glass. "Changing your mind about me?"

"No," she said quickly. "I just...wondered. And those burns are so regular, and that X looks like a cut, almost like it was...drawn."

"It was," he said flatly.

Casey couldn't help her gasp.

"Look, I apologized that you had to see them, but I'm not about to give you a cheap thrill by telling you how I got them all."

His voice was cold, harsh, and while it stung, Casey supposed she had some of it coming. He had a right to his privacy, and she could see why his battered body would be something he didn't care to display or explain. But she didn't care for his assessment of her, and this time, she couldn't let it pass.

"Judging by those marks, whatever the thrills were, they were anything but cheap," she said levelly. "I'm sorry you think I'd get some kind of charge out of whatever happened to you. I get no thrill out of pain and suffering. That's not who or what I am."

Then she turned and left him there, before her wayward tongue ran amok and she blurted out more than she wanted to about pain and suffering.

Chapter 6

The dream had come again last night, so he was more tired than usual tonight. He'd forgotten how harrowing it was, how drained it left him. And he'd put in an even longer day than usual today. He'd been working inside on a bit of ceiling that had been damaged by the leak in the roof, and he had lost track of the time until Casey had arrived home from a job long after dark and been startled, even upset, that he was still working. She'd fed him on leftovers that were incredible, as usual, and with his stomach full, he'd been almost falling on his face.

He was so exhausted now that his rather wild thoughts that the dream was a sign almost seemed reasonable.

For the first time in five years, he hadn't been thinking about what he'd lost. He'd been fascinated by who was here now, hadn't thought about moving on for days. And the moment he'd realized that, guilt had swamped him, guilt for allowing himself even a moment's peace and relief. And he couldn't help thinking the dream had come back to remind him of that.

"You'd better turn in," she said as she gathered up their plates, jerking him out of the daze he'd drifted into. There was a lingering touch of excess politeness in her tone that had been there ever since their encounter by the woodpile.

He couldn't blame her, not after what he'd said to her. He hadn't meant to snap at her, or accuse her of getting some twisted charge out of the signs of battle he carried. As she'd said, she wasn't the type, and he knew that. But she'd stared so long that he'd started to wonder, even when he knew what she was feeling was much more likely to be simple pity. And he'd had enough of that to last him the rest of his miserable life.

The phone rang.

Casey let out a little gasp and dropped the plates.

Sleepiness retreated instantly; that wasn't a typical re-action to a ringing phone. And she was staring at the phone as if it were coiled and rattling. He got hastily to his feet and covered the three feet between them in one long stride.

He grasped her shoulders. "Casey?"

Her head snapped around toward him, and for a moment he saw pure fear in her eyes. Then the ring came again, and she looked away; he saw her take a deep breath. "I was just…startled."

For a moment she stood there, silent, seemingly waiting for…something. His fingers tightened involuntarily, as if he sensed she was going to pull away and he didn't want her to. And he wasn't sure his unruly hands weren't right. He leaned toward her uncertainly, until he could feel the warmth of her body. Then he stopped, unsure of what he was doing or what was going on.

After a moment, instead of reaching for the still-ringing phone, she bent to pick up the shattered plates, breaking his grip. Something wasn't adding up here, he thought, and it didn't take his old instincts for him to know it.

"Aren't you going to answer it?"

Silently she straightened, set the broken pieces on the

counter and reached for the receiver. She said hello, listened for no more than a second and hung up.

"Wrong number," she said briefly, without looking at him.

"Casey...," he began.

"At least they don't have to be washed," she said.

The words were joking, but her tone didn't match. She tossed the pieces into the trash, put the one glass that had survived into the dishwasher and slammed the door shut. She picked up a dish towel and wiped off the counter.

"You'd better get some sleep," she said. "You were about to fall asleep in your dinner."

And you jumped out of your skin at a phone call, he thought. But she'd so clearly closed the subject that he had little choice but to let it go.

It was tough, he thought as he and Mud headed outside to the truck. You couldn't very well push someone else to answer questions when you avoided them yourself.

But what really bothered him was the fact that he *wanted* to push, that he wanted answers, that he wanted to know about her, especially what had her so frightened. He supposed it was natural to be wary of a late-night phone call, especially for a woman living alone, but she had been more than wary; she'd been downright scared.

And almost secretive.

He stopped in his tracks and glanced back at the house. The front was already dark, the single light in the house glowing from her bedroom in the back.

Secretive.

He turned away and made himself keep going. She had a right to keep things from him; he was, after all, just the hired help, and nearly a stranger at that. She had a right to privacy, just as he had. And if he expected her to observe his right, he would have to observe hers.

It would be better that way, anyway, he thought, continuing his internal lecture as he sat on the tailgate of the truck and pulled off his boots and socks. The last thing he needed was to become any more involved than he already had. And he sure as hell didn't need to do anything as stupid as...kiss her.

He froze in the act of tossing his socks on the small pile of laundry he was going to have to attend to tomorrow.

Kiss her?

He hadn't really been going to kiss her, had he? That hadn't been what those moments had been about, had it? Those moments when he'd found himself leaning toward her without realizing why?

It couldn't be, he told himself, but he was shaken. He hadn't wanted, or even been aware of, a woman in a sexual way for longer than he could remember. At first, the trauma of five years ago had made the idea repellent. As time passed, the active aversion faded but left in its place something he could only describe as indifference. He'd assumed his ability to feel desire had been destroyed. It had been an odd feeling, realizing he was for all intents and purposes impotent, and then realizing that he didn't really care. It was distant, remote, something that would have bothered the man he'd been but meant little to who he was now, a hollow shell in the guise of a human being. He had simply accepted it as part of the punishment he felt he deserved.

And it had been so long that he hadn't even recognized the sensation when it had happened.

Mud made a low sound, as if he sensed his master's sudden distress. He jumped up on the tailgate and nuzzled Clay's hand with his nose.

"I'm losing it, buddy," Clay muttered. He scooted inside the truck bed, pulled up the tailgate after them, leaving the windowed section open so Mud could get in and out if he needed to.

He lay back on the bed, a thick foam pad cut to fit the space between the side cabinets and over the raised storage in the truck bed. Mud went to his niche beside Clay, circling until things were arranged to his liking and then settling in. Clay reached down and scratched the dog's ears in that sweet spot that made the little collie get as close as a dog ever did to purring.

"Fine state of affairs," he said to the dog who had been his main listener for five years. "Don't want to sleep in case the dream comes back, but if I stay awake, I can't stop thinking about…things I shouldn't be thinking about."

Mud whined his understanding of the mood, if not the words.

"Don't know why I'm telling you," Clay said dryly. "You're ready to adopt her. If you haven't already."

Clay sighed. Maybe Mud was tired of the road; maybe that was why he had taken to Casey so quickly. He liked the place. Lots of open space to roam, squirrels to chase and regular meals.

Maybe *he* was tired of the road, to even be thinking like this.

He shied away from the thought. It didn't matter if he was tired of it. It wasn't as though he had any other choice. He hadn't just burned his bridges, he'd blown them up midspan, and he couldn't go back, even if he wanted to. But he didn't want to. There was nothing for him there, nothing but constant reminders of the one huge failure of his life, the one that made all the successes seem minor and pointless. The one final, deadly mistake he'd made that had destroyed everything. He was just as dead as his once happy life, but his body kept going. He'd thought of ending the pain permanently, but he didn't deserve that kind of peace. Maybe someday he would.

Maybe someday he would take the .38 he'd carefully packed away in a hidden compartment of the truck and eat it, as he'd wanted to all those years ago. He kept it hard to get at; he didn't want it to be too easy, too tempting. Didn't want to be able to end the torment at any moment when it got to be too much.

He didn't think about it that often anymore. Maybe that was a sign he should move it, make it easier. The whole point had been to never forget, to endure the punishment, pay the price no one else would exact from him. Maybe it was a sign he'd healed too much, maybe…

"I'm just full of maybes and signs tonight, aren't I?" he said under his breath to Mud.

With a sigh he rolled onto his side and closed his eyes. Even the dream was better than this endless string of maybes and wonderings and ridiculous thoughts about things that no longer applied to him, about a woman he had no business thinking of.

But the maybes chased him into sleep, and only the dream had the power to vanquish them.

The night was dotted with fireflies, and knowing it would be one of the last shows of the season, Casey took her iced tea out on the back screen porch and sat on the built-in bench to watch. The darting, faintly green lights never failed to amaze and entertain her. They were as much a part of her childhood as the chickens, cows and other livestock, as much a part of the passing seasons as the fields of corn starting as tiny sprouts and ending up taller than she was.

"Fireflies?"

She looked up to see Clay, fresh out of the shower, his hair damp and combed back. "Yes. They're putting on quite a show tonight."

"I've heard about them, but I've never seen them."

Another clue, Casey thought, although she wasn't sure why she persisted in wondering about him, where he was from, where he'd been.

"Then sit down and watch," she said. "You're lucky to see this many. They've fallen victim to the spraying for other bugs, I'm afraid."

After a moment's hesitation he joined her on the bench.

The only other place to sit was Aunt Fay's rocker, and she noted his reluctance to sit there. She appreciated his sensitivity even as she was coping with the thought that she wouldn't really have minded.

As he watched the aerial dance, she watched him. He'd been very careful never to let her catch him without his shirt again, and she didn't know whether to be grateful or disappointed.

Some tiny part of her mind was telling her that she should be grateful for even a spark of interest in a man; she'd wondered if that part of her would be crippled forever. Every one of the ladies of the historical society seemed to have a son, nephew or grandson they just knew would be perfect for her, but not one of those she'd met had evoked the slightest bit of reaction beyond casual friendship. Not one of them had made her want more.

Not one of them had set her mind to fantasizing and her hormones to humming.

A sharp yap from Mud snapped her out of her reverie. She looked for the dog, but before she found him, Clay laughed.

She stared at him. He had actually laughed. He'd been here nearly two weeks, and she'd never heard him laugh. Chuckle, maybe, for about two seconds, but never laugh. And she found she loved the sound of it.

"You catch one of those, Mud, what are you going to do with it?" he called out.

She looked again for the dog, and found him out in the yard, trying desperately to catch one of the flitting little powerhouses. Looking like one of the dogs she'd seen on TV chasing Frisbees, the collie leaped up, often doubling back on himself in midair, landing flyless and barking his frustration at them. Then he tried again, determinedly.

She understood why Clay had laughed; in fact, she couldn't stifle her own amusement at the dog's antics.

"Get one, Mud!" she called out. He looked over his

shoulder at her with a tongue-lolling grin. Successful or not, it was clear the dog was enjoying himself. And he seemed content to go on trying endlessly.

It was a few moments later that Clay spoke softly, almost absently. "I haven't seen him act like this since he was a puppy."

"How old is he?"

Still in that abstracted tone, he answered, "Five years and three months."

Rather exact, she thought, for a dog. But he seemed to be all Clay had in the world, so maybe it was to be expected. She leaned forward on the bench and rested her elbows on her knees.

"Has he grown up on the road?"

"Pretty much. He was—" He stopped suddenly, as if he'd just realized what he'd been about to say.

She let it pass. "So you've been on the move for a long time. Do you like it?"

"That's not an issue."

She carefully kept her tone even. "And not something you discuss, right?"

"No."

He didn't sound angry or curt, as he had in the past when she'd inadvertently trespassed. In fact, he hadn't sounded like that ever since he'd rather awkwardly apologized for his comments when she'd caught him shirtless that day.

"Fair enough," she said. "We'll just watch the circus act."

He smiled then, and her breath caught. How could such a simple thing as a smile be so incredible? Was it simply the rarity of it? Or was it the amazing difference between the smile and his usual somber expression?

They watched Mud play. The dog was taking a new tack now, trying to chivy the uncooperative bugs into a corner. After a moment Casey said, "My aunt used to say that the instinct in Border collies is so strong that if they can't find anything else to herd, they'll herd running water.''

Clay laughed. Again. Even lighter, more genuine, this time. And it was, Casey thought, a lovely sound. "Or, in his case, fireflies," he said. "How do they do it, do you know? The flies, I mean.''

It took her a moment to get herself together enough to answer lightly, "Yes and no.''

He blinked. "What?''

"Yes, I know how they do it, and no, I won't tell you. I refuse to ruin the mystery of it.''

He laughed again, and she felt a sense of accomplishment that seemed all out of proportion. But she couldn't deny it and didn't try. She just looked at him, smiling her pleasure in the sound.

He went quiet, his smile slowly fading. His eyes looked surprisingly dark in the faint light of the porch. His lips parted, and she thought she could see him take a deep breath. Then, with painful slowness, he raised his hand. So lightly that she could barely feel it, he touched her hair. She held her breath, afraid to move, and not exactly sure what she was afraid of.

He began to pull his hand back, but as he did, he stroked her cheek with the backs of his fingers. She finally took a deep breath of her own at the feel of his touch, at the shiver it sent through her.

"Casey," he breathed, so low it seemed no more than the beating of the fireflies' wings.

She swallowed tightly. She bit her lip, afraid she was going to start trembling at any moment.

And suddenly he jerked away. Sharply, as if burned. He stared at her for a moment. Even in the faint light, she saw shock in his eyes, and more.

What was gone was that dull flatness. His eyes might indeed be full of shock, even fear, but they weren't dead anymore. They were alive. Very alive.

Then he closed his eyes, gave a sharp shake of his head and stood up. He opened his eyes again, but he didn't look at her. He muttered something she couldn't quite hear but that could have been "good night." And then he was gone, out of sight before the door closed neatly behind him.

And Casey sat there, not at all sure what had just happened.

And not at all sure she was happy that it had stopped.

She was going to give it a week of not answering. Maybe two. Because hanging up didn't seem to have slowed him down any, whoever her tormentor was. Nor had leaving her answering machine on; he'd simply made so many hang-up calls that he'd filled up her machine's memory, leaving her without any way to record genuine calls. So if anybody truly needed her for anything, they were going to have to call during daylight. And she would have to hope nothing awful happened, like a fire or an accident where she could have helped but didn't answer the call.

It was either that or go crazy.

And she was already close enough to that, she thought wryly as she reheated the extra beef Stroganoff she'd made when she'd prepared it for the Wilsons' anniversary last night. Between the calls and the disconcerting presence of Clay Yeager, she felt as if she were constantly on a high wire.

It wasn't intentional on his part, she knew that. After that moment the other night, when the fireflies had nearly led to another kind of fire, he'd been scrupulously polite, the wall that had crumbled solidly back in place.

Which was just as she wanted it, of course, she told herself. When she finally decided to risk some kind of relationship with a man, it would be something safe, slow, measured, where nothing happened before she was ready. She knew there was a chance she might never find a man willing to be patient enough, but she also knew she couldn't bear any other kind. She would be better off alone than with a man who would rush her. A man who wouldn't take it at her pace. A man who wouldn't wait—

"Smells great."

Her breath caught as his voice yanked her out of her thoughts, but she had herself composed by the time she answered.

"Thank you. It came out well, I think."

She didn't look at him as he silently went about setting the table, a task he'd taken over without comment. As usual, he was fresh from the shower; he never came to the table without cleaning up from his work first, a fact she appreciated. He had taken to putting on a pair of battered running shoes after his shower; she wondered if it was so he could get out in a hurry when something hit a nerve, as it had the other night.

"Finished stripping the back siding today," he said as they began to eat.

"Already?" she asked. He'd just begun working on the back wall of the house, the wall that got the worst of the heat and weather, yesterday morning.

"It wasn't in as bad shape as it looked at first. I'll get it primed tomorrow, then it'll be ready for paint." He took a big bite of the Stroganoff. "This really is great."

"Thanks. It was a bit of an exotic choice for Mrs. Wilson, but it went over well. Except with her son Matthew, who can't get past the concept of voluntarily eating sour cream."

Clay chuckled. He did that more regularly now, and always seemed to look a bit surprised when it happened. "I remember thinking that myself once. He'll get over it."

"Maybe. Food's not all that important to Matt. He's a teenager, he wants to save the world."

Any trace of the chuckle or its accompanying smile faded. "Didn't we all?" he said softly.

He wasn't looking at her, wasn't even looking at his

plate; she could see that his eyes had gone unfocused, as if looking inward. She wondered what he was remembering.

"Matt hates injustice," she said. "He gets all wound up about it. Passionate. It's good to see."

"I knew somebody like that once," Clay said, his voice still soft, his gaze still turned inward. "Kit was young, earnest, smart and determined. She had that fire, too, the outrage at injustice."

"Had?"

"Maybe she still does. It just might have been strong enough to carry her through."

He came back to himself with a snap that was almost audible. Casey could have sworn he was playing back what he'd said in his mind, as if searching for anything he had said that might...what? Give away too much? Tell her something about himself?

Not likely, she muttered mentally. You never give away an inch.

"Don't worry," she said dryly, "you didn't let out any secrets."

At least, she added silently as she got to her feet and began to gather dishes and silverware, she herself only kept one part of her life buried so deeply. Well, maybe two. She hadn't said anything about the phone calls to him, but then, there was nothing he could do about them, and she felt a little silly being so jumpy over them. It had been nearly four years, and she'd been back in River Bend, far from the scene of the devastation of her life, for three; there was no reason to think this was anything other than some warped little man with a phone book who'd fixated on her for some reason. Maybe he hadn't liked her ad.

"Casey," Clay said.

She stopped, looking at him. Slowly he stood up.

"I didn't...I don't mean to be..."

"Secretive?" she suggested. "Uncommunicative? Tight-lipped?'' He winced. She sighed. ''Sorry. I have no right to criticize. We all have our secrets and should be allowed to keep them.''

He stepped around the corner of the table. ''Do your secrets have to do with why you jump when the phone rings?''

She studied him for a moment as he stood barely two feet away. His expression was unreadable, carefully so, which alone told her something. She just wasn't sure what.

''I'll tell you, if you tell me where you learned that 'the best defense is a good offense' tactic of always turning questions back on people.''

He let out a breath visibly. ''In another life.''

''Hmm. Cryptic, too,'' Casey said. She wasn't sure why this was stinging so, but it was. ''So secrets will remain secrets, then. As they should, between strangers.''

''Casey.'' He said her name again, as a sentence, complete. Then he reached out and grasped her shoulders. ''Believe me, there's nothing about me you want to know or hear.''

She looked up at him, her body tensing at his touch. But it felt different somehow, and it wasn't just that her reaction wasn't based on fear, as it sometimes was.

''Is the story so awful, or simply boring?''

He laughed then, but it wasn't a pleasant sound. ''I only wish it were boring. I wish I'd never had anything in my life to think about but the weather and the fields.''

''Sounds like an empty life. No people.''

Something flickered in his eyes then, something dark and pained that flashed for an instant and was gone. ''Exactly.''

''I've thought that, sometimes,'' she said quietly, very aware of the feel of his hands on her shoulders. ''That life would be less painful if you lived it alone. And there are…people I would have been much better off without ever meeting. But would having been saved from them be worth never meeting the good ones?''

His grip tightened, as if she'd struck some kind of nerve in him. "Wouldn't it?"

"Never to have known my parents at all, instead of having had ten loving years with them? Never to have had my aunt and uncle, who loved me almost enough to make up for losing my folks? No. No, I don't think it would."

He stared at her for a long time, and this time what he was feeling showed clearly in his face. Wonder. Slowly he shook his head. Then, a third time, very softly, he said her name.

"Casey…"

She was in his arms before she realized what was happening and could tense up. She went very still, waiting to feel trapped, to feel panic. But then his mouth was on hers, and she forgot to be scared.

He didn't kiss her fiercely or forcefully. He kissed her like a man who was starving but was still mindful that too much too soon was not a good thing. Gently, like a man tasting something longed-for for the first time. It sent shivers through her, and she was unable to stay rigid. Instead she found herself sagging against him.

And kissing him back. Savoring the feel of warm, firm, but gentle, lips against hers. Wondering what it would be like to taste him more deeply.

And, in some small part of her mind, delighting in the knowledge that she wasn't afraid. Not of this man, stranger though he might be.

But she'd learned well that strangers weren't always the dangerous ones.

And then he pulled away abruptly. She could see him taking rapid breaths through parted lips as he stared down at her.

"God," he murmured, sounding half-reverent and half-fearful.

And then he spun on his heel and left her there, reeling, feeling as if whatever had been holding her up had been ripped away.

Chapter 7

This time Clay didn't stop until he'd run halfway to the river. It was dark, and he was on unfamiliar ground, but getting lost was the last thing he was thinking about. In fact, the idea of wandering forever amid the tall stalks of corn seemed almost appealing at the moment.

He was vaguely aware of movement behind him; the light scrabbling sound told him it was probably Mud. He kept going, running, even knowing he could never outrun this. He'd been trying for five years, and it had always been there, dogging his every step.

He wished he'd never stopped here. Better to have driven the truck until it had fallen to pieces on the road than to be here, now, with Casey Scott stirring up emotions and needs he didn't want to feel, had no right to feel.

But the more time he spent with her, the less he was able to resist the lure of being with her even more. And the temptation to touch her. Then, tonight, he'd committed the ultimate folly of kissing her.

And found it to be more foolish—and more shattering—than he could have imagined.

He'd hoped the chill that had enveloped him would hold forever. He had no desire to ever care about anyone, had no desire to ever feel anything other than the numbness that had carried him this far, had no desire to ever…desire. Anyone or anything.

Yet he seemed helpless to escape the soft, warm, gentle net Casey cast without even realizing she was doing it. She'd never tried any of the traditional feminine lures that had been so meaningless to him for years now, had done nothing more than look at him now and then. And if his peripheral vision hadn't been exceptional, he might not even have seen that; she was not giving him sidelong looks just waiting to be noticed. He doubted she wanted him to know at all.

Yet he'd reacted as if she'd sent him an invitation. Even if she had, he was supposed to be immune to such things. He *had* been, on the few occasions when such an invitation had been issued so blatantly that even he couldn't miss it.

But he wasn't immune to Casey. No, it was worse. For the first time in five years, he not only wasn't immune, but was apparently more than susceptible to her quiet allure. And each time he was unable to resist, he swore to himself that it had to stop, that it couldn't happen again. And when that didn't work, he told himself he had to leave, get away from her, had to break whatever this hold she had on him was and sink back into blessed numbness.

But he'd been as unable to make the break as he'd been to make himself stay away from her. And the strain of it was tearing at him, until he felt caught, trapped, ready to rip himself apart just to get free of it.

Finally winded by the gradual rise of the gravel road he'd been running along, he slowed, then stopped. From here, in the faint wash of moonlight, he could see the thick growth of trees that marked the riverbank. He sank down to his knees in the tall, now-almost-dry grass by the side of the road, his head lolling forward as he tried to breathe.

Was this part of it? Was this part of the hell he'd cast himself into by his own tunnel vision? He'd grown used to, even welcomed the numbness, the lack of feeling, but he'd thought it would last forever. And he had never thought about the agony it would be if it didn't.

Mud nuzzled him, whining. His natural reflex was to pet the worried animal, to reassure him, but he couldn't seem to move. He couldn't even reassure himself, so how could he do it for anyone else? Even a dog?

Mud nudged him again and let out a little yip.

The Border collie was sometimes more human than dog, Clay thought wearily. Hell, sometimes he was more human than most humans.

His breathing slowing at last, Clay realized he was going to regret this run so soon after eating; he was already feeling a bit queasy. His stomach wasn't entirely used to regular meals, even now.

Deciding that keeping moving might distract him from the nausea—he had no hopes of being distracted from his thoughts—he stood up. He swayed slightly, then steadied himself. And looked first up the deserted road, then down. It appeared oddly silver in the moonlight, as if it were some magical path leading to someplace not of this earth.

Quite a choice, he thought wearily. And he wasn't sure he didn't want to just keep on going the way he'd been running; he'd seen the river at the bend that gave the town its name, and he knew it was deep there. Deep, and swift-running enough to make drowning easy.

If you were going to go out that way, you should have done it in the Pacific five years ago, he thought. But you didn't deserve the easy way out then, so what makes you think you deserve it now?

Reluctantly, he started to walk back, wondering if in his mad rush he'd made any turns he didn't remember. "You may have to lead me back, Mud. One cornfield looks just like another to me, even in daylight."

He would finish the painting, he thought as he walked. It was the biggest of the jobs left to do, and the most necessary. Everything else she could either handle herself or have somebody else do. He hadn't promised her that he would finish it all; they hadn't set any time limit on his work. So he was free to leave anytime.

He listened to the steady crunch of the gravel under his feet and wondered that he hadn't heard it at all when he'd been running. It was amazing what you could miss when your emotions were in an uproar. He'd forgotten.

When she paid him for this week, he would have better than five hundred dollars. It wasn't anywhere near enough to do all the repairs the truck required, especially if he bought the work boots he desperately needed, but he could buy parts for the most crucial stuff. He would have to find another place to stop, where he could do the work. He might need more tools than he had to replace the alternator, but maybe he could rent or even borrow them somewhere. Casey kept talking about country people and how generous they were. Maybe—

Mud's sharp bark snapped him out of his ponderings; he wondered half-seriously if the dog had guessed he was planning their escape and didn't care for the idea. The collie had stopped at the edge of the road, where the fields to the south changed from corn to what Casey had told him was the other main crop in the area, soybeans. There was a narrow path between the two fields, and Mud dashed a little way down it, then looked back at him. When he didn't move, the collie barked again.

"You find a shortcut or something, buddy?"

Another bark, then the dog ran another few feet and again stopped.

"Okay, okay, I've watched *Lassie,* I get it."

Figuring he had little to lose, he followed. After a few

yards the road he'd left vanished from view. It felt surreal to him to be able to see nothing but the expanse of tall corn and shorter soybeans. But he found himself back at the farm much sooner than he'd expected.

"Good boy," he said, leaning over to scratch Mud's ears. "Where would I be without you?"

It was a rhetorical question, not simply because it was asked of a dog, but because he knew all too well where he would be. Sometimes he thought the dog, and the need to take care of this tiny remnant of a life that had once been so full, were all that kept him from taking that one-way swim.

Come home, Clay. All the penance in the world won't change what happened.

He didn't know why the words came back to him now; he hadn't thought about that last conversation with his father in a long time.

It wasn't just your fault. You can't punish yourself forever.

He could hear it so clearly, the love, the worry. He hadn't called again after that. It was cowardly of him, but he couldn't bear to hear the pain in his father's voice.

You can't forget all the good you've done, Clay. That has to be worth something.

Maybe, he thought as he crossed the yard to his truck. But it wasn't enough to balance the scales. He didn't think they could ever be balanced.

Casey stretched expansively, luxuriating in several things: she had no jobs pending for two days; she'd managed to clean up everything from the last job yesterday, so there was nothing hanging over her today; and for the first time since the calls had started, she'd been able to relax and had had a decent, peaceful night's sleep. She should have gone ahead and unplugged the darn thing in the first place.

She snuggled back into her pillow, smiling at the thought of actually sleeping in. At least painting was quiet, so Clay's industry wasn't awakening her when he started at his usual early hour.

The urge to sleep vanished.

Casey sighed. If she could just have held off thinking about Clay until she'd drifted off again... But once she had, she knew better than to think she could go back to sleep. She'd tried too often—fruitlessly.

She sat up, yawning. And stretched again, long and hard. She drew her legs up and crossed them in front of her. She rubbed at her eyes. And without realizing what she was doing, she touched her lips.

She was abruptly not only not sleepy but totally, wide-eyed awake. Her fingertips traced her mouth as she remembered. She could almost feel his kiss all over again, and it made her shiver anew.

She hugged herself. She'd gone to the counseling, she'd listened, she'd understood, had tried to believe even when she couldn't picture herself ever feeling secure again. They'd told her it would take time. They'd told her it would be a long while before she trusted enough to let herself feel anything for a man again. And it had been true; she'd held herself aloof for a long time now, at first intentionally, later because she hadn't met anyone who made her want to take the risk.

Clay Yeager made her want to take all the risks at once, and that frightened her as well as thrilled her.

It figured, she thought as she got out of bed and headed for the bathroom for a shower. She couldn't be attracted to someone straightforward and simple, like Mrs. Wilson's nephew, or even Amos Tutweiler's grandson, who was a professor over at the state university, much to his grandfather's pride. She'd even gone out with Aaron; he taught history, made it come alive for his students, and she admired that. But there was no spark, and they both knew it.

She'd been almost relieved that there was never any question of anything beyond friendship between them.

But no, she had to be attracted to someone like Clay, a man who was more mystery than not, who seemed haunted by demons, who was withdrawn and had more sore spots than she could seem to avoid hitting.

He seemed driven by a pain that in an odd way reminded her of her own. For a while she'd wondered if that was it, if it was a simple case of two wounded souls connecting, but as time passed she knew it was more than that. And she didn't know if she dreaded the knowledge or welcomed it.

Not that it mattered, she thought as she pulled on jeans and a sleeveless blouse, glad she didn't have to put her business persona together today. Not when the kiss that had sent her reeling had sent him running.

Her gut had reacted to that hasty, urgent departure instinctively, out of the old pain, wondering if she had disgusted him, if somehow he had guessed, had known and was repulsed. But an instant later all the work of the past four years had kicked in, and she'd fought her way back to rationality. Whatever had sent Clay running, it hadn't been her. It hadn't been disgust or repulsion in his eyes when he'd broken the kiss and looked down at her.

It had been alarm.

And she had wondered in that moment if he had been as shocked as she by the unexpected power of a simple kiss. Had it burned through his defenses as it had hers? Had he run because he was reeling, too?

That question didn't make it any easier for her to contemplate seeing him this morning. Would it be awkward, or would he, as he had before, act as if nothing at all had happened?

"It'll be ready to paint by this afternoon," was what greeted her when she stepped outside, and she guessed she had her answer.

"All right," she said, with what she hoped was unruffled calm. "I'll go into town this morning and get the paint."

He seemed to hesitate, then asked, "Is there an auto parts store in town? Or a repair garage?"

"Alf Taylor runs a garage at his gas station on Third," she said. "He has a lot of parts and can get what he doesn't have fairly quickly."

She hesitated, knowing she was about to open herself up to a storm of gossip. But it hardly seemed fair to expect him to stay isolated here on the farm all the time, seeing no one but her. So she asked, "Do you want to ride in with me? There must be things you need."

He hesitated even longer than she had. Since he could hardly be embarrassed by gossip among people he didn't know, he had to have some other reason. Was he reluctant to spend that much time with her after last night? Or did he have some other reason to not want to go into town?

Right, maybe he's an ax murderer on the run, she chided herself. He had as much right to privacy as she did, and she certainly wasn't pouring out her sorry past to him. He was one of the hardest workers she'd ever seen, and he didn't owe her anything but an answer to her question.

And if he needed time to think about it, she wasn't going to read anything into that.

"I'll leave right after breakfast," she said. "You can decide by then if you want to go."

She left it at that, half-expecting him not to accept her offer. But after they'd finished the fruit, toast and coffee she'd fixed, he washed up and presented himself at her car. Mud eyed them both suspiciously and barked to let them know he wasn't about to be left behind.

Casey looked at Clay.

"He's good at waiting," he said. "He won't hurt the car."

"I wasn't worried about that. You don't think he'll be bored?"

"He'd rather go along and be bored."

Casey's mouth quirked. "Why do I get the feeling that if we didn't take him, he'd follow us?"

For the first time that morning, Clay smiled. "Because he would."

"I thought so. Okay, Mud, in you go."

The little collie scrambled into the back seat of the small station wagon; she'd bought it for the business and had racks built to safely hold her pans and dishes for transport. It had her logo and Casey's Catering painted on each front door; she felt as if she were driving a billboard sometimes, but it had netted her a customer or two, so she guessed it was worth it.

Once inside, Clay lapsed into silence, and they were half-way to River Bend proper before she finally broke it. "Something wrong with your truck?"

"It's just tired," he said.

"It's not that old, is it?"

"Eight years. But a lot of miles."

"Older than Mud, then," she quipped.

She was watching the road, not him, but still she sensed his sudden stillness.

"Yes," he said, his voice calm enough that she wondered if she'd been wrong.

Well, at least he wasn't running this time, she thought. But then, they were in a moving car. In keeping with her resolution not to pry, she turned the conversation slightly.

"I've been thinking about getting a dog myself," she said. "Security and all."

He shifted in his seat to look at her. "You feel like you need that, out here?"

Ouch, she thought.

Now it was her turn to back off. She wasn't really sure why she hadn't told him about the calls, except that it was such a personal thing, and he seemed to shy away from anything like that. Not to mention that he'd absolutely refused to share any information about himself, which didn't exactly encourage her to open up. And besides, she didn't want to admit that a few silly phone calls had her so rattled; it might lead to questions she truly didn't want to answer.

"No, not really," she amended quickly. "But a dog would be company, too."

"They are great listeners."

He said it deadpan, and she risked a quick glance. He wasn't smiling, and something in his face told her he meant exactly what he'd said. She could only imagine what discussions he and Mud had had on the road. The dog no doubt knew all there was to know about this man.

Which was probably more than could be said for any person on the planet, she thought.

She parked in front of the small bookstore, midway between Alf Taylor's station and the Exchange. Clay headed off for the garage after they agreed to meet at the Exchange in an hour, to get the paint.

Casey didn't really have anything specific she needed beyond the paint, but she could always pass an hour in Jean's bookstore. Jean had very eclectic taste, and in addition to a rather varied selection of magazines, you were as likely to find a book on true crime as one on farming, a thriller or the latest romance as a book on local history. It was the only bookstore in River Bend and served other smaller towns farther out, as well, especially for those who didn't want to drive into Ames and wade through all the bookstores and the books they stocked for the Iowa State students.

Which also meant that Jean knew the reading tastes and interests of virtually everyone in town who read anything that didn't come in the mail; she was very observant. If Phyllis Harrington was the town broadcaster, Jean was the source. When Mrs. Tutweiler had purchased a baby name book, the up-until-then secret of her daughter's pregnancy was out. When Mabel Clark ordered a crochet pattern book, the buzz was on about which afghan would be her county fair entry that year. And when Jim Wilson had ordered a book on UFOs, everybody in town wondered if he'd spent one too many hot days out in the fields, until it turned out to be for Matt's school project. Sometimes Casey thought Jean stocked horror novels just to find out who read them.

The bell over the door rang as she went in, which usually got Jean's attention. But as she glanced toward the counter, she saw that Jean was already headed toward her and realized with a qualm that she must have seen Clay and her arrive. Together.

Jean was also not one for niceties when she was on the scent of news.

"Who *was* that scruffy-looking man, Casey? Surely you're not picking up hitchhikers!"

Scruffy? Clay? She thought for a moment and supposed she could understand Jean's observation; she'd thought it herself when she'd first seen him. But she'd grown used to his looks, never thought anymore about the worn condition of his clothes. As for his hair, it was no longer than that of many of the kids of River Bend. And she rather liked it, for all that it could use some trimming and shaping.

But Jean was waiting for an answer. She should have thought this through, Casey realized, or at least discussed with Clay what she should—or should not—say. She didn't really think he was hiding anything criminal, but others in town might not be so generous.

At last she decided on the truth, or at least enough of it to placate Jean.

"His truck broke down near my place."

"But he's not from around here," Jean said positively.

"No. He's from Southern California."

"Oh."

Jean lifted a brow until it disappeared beneath her rather determinedly black bangs. Casey supposed that, in Jean's mind, Clay being from California explained it all.

"I suppose he's some Hollywood type, with all that hair."

"Actually, he's from some place called Marina Heights." Ah, that was something she could do, find an atlas and look that up.

"Marina Heights, Marina Heights," Jean muttered. "I've heard of that somewhere."

"You have?" Casey asked, surprised.

"I can't remember where, though."

Casey left her trying to recall and moments later was looking at a road atlas. California was on two pages; sometimes she forgot just how big the state was, and how long. But she found Marina Heights, a small—by California standards—town just inland from Marina del Mar, which was right on the coast. She wondered what it was like to live that close to the ocean. Did you go to the beach every day you could, or did you fall victim to a sense of complacency, never going because it was always there and you always could?

She reshelved the book before Jean could notice and wonder, took a quick step to the left and began to scan the fiction titles. She hadn't been doing much fiction reading lately. Perhaps she should buy something engrossing; maybe it would help distract her.

By the time she'd selected a couple of westerns—she'd developed a taste for them and their generally clear-cut good and evil—and been lured by a picture book on the seasons of the Mississippi, her hour was almost up. She went to the register and found Jean still worrying about where she'd heard of Marina Heights before. Casey was glad enough that she was preoccupied; it kept her from asking any more questions. Although as she walked toward the Exchange after dropping her package off in the car, she found herself wondering as well why a bookseller in the middle of Iowa had heard of a small place in Southern California.

As long as it isn't famous for ax murders, she thought wryly.

As she crossed the street, she saw Clay waiting outside the front door of the Exchange. He was leaning against the post, out of the way of the few passing pedestrians, who almost universally looked at him curiously as they passed. He appeared not to notice at all, but Casey had the feeling he didn't miss much. That he didn't ever miss much.

She could see why they looked; even if he hadn't been a stranger, Clay Yeager was the kind of man who got noticed. There was just something about his long, rangy body, his stance, that edgy alertness, that made him stand out.

And made her pulse pick up so noticeably that she almost blushed. She slowed her pace until she had herself in hand.

He went still, and then his head came around, his eyes looking for her long before she would have thought he'd been aware of her. His gaze never left her as she closed the distance between them, and she nearly shivered under its intensity.

When she'd been young and foolish, she'd dreamed of a man looking at her like that; she'd never realized that the fantasy had worked because in her mind she'd known what the man was thinking. She had no idea what Clay Yeager was thinking, and that made the look as unnerving as it was electrifying.

"Did Alf have what you needed?" she managed to ask.

He shook his head. "No, but he ordered it. Should be here in two or three days." He paused, then added, "I had to tell him where to reach me. He started to get a little…wary when I tried to tell him I'd just come back to pick it up."

She smiled ruefully. "Alf would. And don't worry about it. Jean in the bookstore saw us arrive, so your cover's blown, anyway."

He gave her a look so sharp it was all she could do not to take a step back.

''What did you buy?'' she asked instead, trying to sound as if she hadn't noticed as she eyed the bag at his feet.

''Boots.''

The short answer, after that look, irked her. She was getting mightily tired of bouncing off his sore spots, and it drove her to say breezily, ''Funny thing, Jean in the bookstore says she's heard of Marina Heights somewhere. She couldn't remember where, though.''

He went even more still. ''You...told her?''

Well, she'd guessed right that time; he'd reacted about as she'd expected. ''She asked. People around here do, you know. I didn't realize it was a secret.''

Something in his face changed then, and suddenly she didn't feel quite so breezy. He went almost pale, and she saw him swallow tightly. His eyes closed for a moment, and his rangy body seemed to slump.

Casey felt a rush of guilt, as if she'd somehow betrayed a trust she hadn't even realized she'd been given.

She was still wrestling with her feelings later that night, when Clay finally called a halt to the painting because it had become too dark to continue. He'd been pushing hard; she sensed he had some goal in mind beyond simply finishing the painting of the house.

She'd helped where she could, since she had the time just now, but he was much quicker than she was. She had urged him to quit when the light first began to fade, but he'd kept on for another hour, until she warned him there were going to be moths permanently imbedded in the fresh paint if he didn't stop. So he'd stopped, with only the bottom few feet of the entire side of the house to go.

As he sealed up the paint cans, she gathered up the brushes and carried them into the laundry-room sink to be cleaned. She'd just gotten them started when she realized she'd forgotten the big roller and went back for it.

She heard him before she rounded the corner of the house.

"I don't know how long I can keep going, buddy."

It was a good thing she'd insisted they stop, then, Casey thought. She'd known he'd been pushing too hard.

She heard Mud whine. She smiled; the little collie sounded almost worried. He had insisted on supervising the job, and now the black parts of his coat were splattered with white paint. She should take him in and clean him along with the brushes, she thought with a grin.

"She likes you, you know. And she's been thinking about a dog, anyway. She'd take good care of you."

Casey stopped midstride, halting just before she would have turned the corner into his field of vision. Mud whined. Still worried.

And suddenly Casey was worried, too.

The allusion in those soft words, the thing he wasn't saying, rang in her mind as if he'd spoken the words. A vivid image shot through her mind of the first day she'd seen Clay. Of the flat deadness of his eyes. Then they'd convinced her she shouldn't be afraid of him.

Now she was afraid *for* him.

Chapter 8

He knew the moment he saw her face that she'd heard him. And Clay's instincts, rusty but still working, told him that she'd read the intent behind his words and there was no use trying to convince her she was misinterpreting.

The bluntness of her words proved him right.

"Whatever it is, it's not worth that."

He tried to ignore her, to simply not answer. But she wasn't having any of that.

"No matter how black it seems, it passes, Clay. Eventually it passes."

He turned on her then, unable to help himself. "That's exactly what I don't want."

She blinked. "You don't want it to pass?"

"No. If it passes, then I'll start to...forget."

"You never forget," she said. "Not completely."

"Forgetting any of it isn't an option."

She drew back slightly. "Remembering every detail won't change anything. And it won't bring you any peace."

He laughed harshly. "I don't *deserve* peace."

"You're a harsh judge, then. Everyone deserves peace."

"I'm sure the murderers on death row everywhere would be grateful for your best wishes."

She flushed. "You know that's not what I meant."

Yes, he knew. He knew that she'd only meant to tell him that *he* deserved peace. And he knew that if he told her the truth about who and what he was, she would have to agree that he deserved nothing of the kind.

But she kept her head up and faced him down. Whatever her own past had been, whatever it was that had put that occasional look of world-weary wisdom in her eyes, it had also given her courage. And if there was anything left in this world he admired, it was that. Perhaps because so many people thought he had it himself, and more than most...but he knew better.

"Yes, I know that's not what you meant," he said softly, sorry now he'd struck back in that way.

"What nerve did I hit that time?" she asked, then immediately added, "No, don't bother, I know you won't answer. But whatever it is that...haunts you, Clay, it's not worth giving up."

For a moment, standing there and looking into her eyes, into those eyes that made the blue of the summer sky seem pallid, he thought she just might really understand, that she, too, had walked this barren ground where the only salvation seemed to be ending the journey. That she had faced her own demons, battled her own nightmares, her own fears, her own memories. That what she said wasn't just platitudes, but hard-won, bitterly learned lessons she was trying to pass on.

In that moment he felt a connection with her unlike anything he'd ever known, something that tugged at a part of him he'd thought had been ripped out and destroyed five years ago. Something he would call his soul if he'd bothered to name it, since *soulless* was the only word that fit the gaping feeling he'd been left with after that day.

And Casey was looking at him as if she'd been where he was, as if she'd fought to keep her soul...and won.

"Clay?" she whispered.

"You know how it feels, don't you?" The words escaped before he could stop them. She would think he was crazy, they didn't make any sense.

"Yes," she answered, with a certainty that made him want to reach for her, made him want to grab her and run until they found a place where they could both hide, where they could both heal, where they wouldn't have to have anything to do with a world that could inflict such wounds.

Then he was reaching for her. And she let him, moving into his arms with only the token resistance of surprise. He cupped her face in his paint-stained hands, tilting her head back. He gave her a chance to protest, to say no, to pull away. It was all he could manage; the heat of his anger at her intrusion onto that desperate moment had suddenly and completely changed to a different kind of heat. For an instant he wondered if the reason he reacted so strongly when she got too close to things he didn't talk about was because he knew, deep down, that she had the power to not just strike but awaken nerves he'd thought long dead. With others, he simply ignored them and didn't answer; with Casey...

And then all rational thought fled, for instead of protesting, Casey held his gaze, her lips parting as if she were finding the air suddenly as thick as he did.

He had to kiss her again. Had to know if her mouth was truly that sweet, or if his imagination had played tricks on him, playing the taste of her back in his mind until he was convinced it was nectar, ambrosia. Or if it was simpler, if it was merely the response of a body long denied the slightest trace of pleasure.

He had to know. Now.

Yet he went slowly, not just for her sake but for his own; in some part of his whirling mind he knew he might not be ready for the answer he was so desperate for. But it didn't seem to matter; the only thing that did was the lure of her lips, the willingness in her eyes.

His imagination had played tricks on him, but only in understatement. She was sweeter than any memory he'd conjured up since that first kiss. She was honeyed fire, and she was flowing over him, warming him when he'd thought he would be frozen forever. And right now, as she kissed him back, willingly, even eagerly, the knowledge that he couldn't do this, that this was wrong, that he was rushing into territory he'd been banished from wasn't nearly enough to overpower what he was feeling. His body, suddenly reawakened, wasn't listening to his mind, no matter how loudly it screamed in warning.

And even if he could have heeded the alarm bells himself, Casey was making it impossible. She was kissing him with every evidence of eagerness, and if his will hadn't already crumbled, she would have finished the job.

His hands slid down her back, slowly, savoring just the feel of her. He tried to tell himself it had been so long that any warm female body would have made him feel this way, but his gut knew that he wouldn't even be here with any other woman. For five years he'd felt not so much as a flicker of heat in the presence of a woman, no matter how attractive. And now he was awash in it, hot waves of sensation rippling through him, over him, sweeping all his apprehension, all his reservations, away like so much dust.

Casey made a soft murmur of pleasure that rocketed through him with a force far out of proportion to the tiny sound. His body responded swiftly, fiercely, and he almost gasped at the sudden rush.

Her arms slid upward, around his neck. He savored the slight weight, welcomed the signal it gave and pressed her more tightly against him. His skin, even through his clothes, seemed electrified; he could feel her every curve, every soft, feminine inch. He slid his hands down her back to her hips, pulling her closer against flesh that was aching.

She whispered something that sounded like his name, and it sent a new burst of fire flicking along his nerves. Her fingers tangled in his hair, stroked, caressed, and just knowing she was touching him like that, that she wanted to, turned the fire into an inferno. His image of himself as a man cold unto death, beyond feeling, beyond reach, vanished; Clay Yeager was alive. Reluctantly but blazingly alive.

And he could no more stop this than he could single-handedly douse a forest fire.

He moved suddenly, almost involuntarily, desperate to have her even closer. He pressed her up against the house, against the wall he hadn't yet painted. Not that it would have stopped him if the paint had been fresh, not with the need raging through him now.

He deepened the kiss, tasting, probing, wanting. And it was still not enough; he needed more. Wanted more. Had to have more. With every sign that she felt the same burning urgency, his own grew, until he was ready to sink to his knees under the force of it.

His hands were shaking as he moved them up her sides. He shifted slightly, just enough so that he could cup the soft curves of her breasts. The warm female flesh filled his palms, and when she didn't resist but actually pressed herself into his hands, he groaned low and deep in his throat.

He broke the kiss, desperate for air, but hating to lose the contact. Now almost mindless with need, he surrounded her with his arms, his legs, wishing he could absorb her somehow. He enveloped her, thinking that if only he could climb inside her warmth, the ice within him would vanish for good...and that he could live without it. That he could go on, that perhaps there was a reason he was still alive.

She squirmed, and he groaned again at the pressure of

her body against his, at the feel of her hands on his chest, pushing....

Agony exploded in his groin.

His legs buckled. He collapsed, a harsh chunk of sound ripping from his throat as his body doubled over, curling in on itself in a desperate and too late attempt to protect itself. His vision faded as pain throbbed through him in waves, the recession between them so slight as to be barely noticeable. All he could hear was an odd, faint buzz. He felt sweat breaking out all over his body, and nausea swamped him, and he thought in some tiny part of his mind that could still function that he didn't have enough air to throw up, and that he would probably strangle if he did.

At last the agony began to recede slightly, enough that he could at least hear. And what he heard were Casey's distressed moans. When his vision cleared, he saw she was crouching beside him, the knee she'd used on him bracing her, her hands pressed to her mouth.

He tried to take in more air, but it was a moment before he had enough to gasp out some words.

"God, Casey..."

Another low moan broke from her. He sucked in another breath and tried again.

"All you...had to do...was say no!"

He heard her take a gulping breath. "The last time I...said no...it didn't work."

She scrambled to her feet, her pale face a study in shock and hideous embarrassment. And then she was gone, running from him as he had run from her last night.

Clay drew his knees up farther, setting his jaw, riding out the gradually easing waves of pain.

And trying not to think about all the things about Casey Scott that had suddenly become clear.

"Oh, God..."

She couldn't believe what she'd done. She'd been willing, more than willing, delighting in the thrill of his kiss, joyous that she could even respond at all.

And then, just when she'd thought them vanquished forever, all the old, ugly memories had crashed in on her. She had felt suddenly trapped. And she had reacted out of pure, terrified instinct, her knee coming up hard and fast, just as they'd taught her in the classes she'd taken in the city. Just as they'd taught her could stop a man instantly.

They'd just never taught her in any detail what it would be like.

Or what to do if she reacted out of her gut-deep fear and attacked an innocent man. A man who'd done nothing to deserve it. A man who'd done nothing but reawaken in her feelings she'd been afraid she would never know again.

She moaned, burying her face in her pillow. She'd retreated to her bedroom in shame at what she'd done and sat on her bed, rocking back and forth, wondering how she would ever face Clay again. If he even stayed around for her to face. She wouldn't blame him if he took off without a word.

Assuming, she thought suddenly, that he could move at all.

Dear God, what if she'd hurt him? Really hurt him?

On the thought, a knock came to the door. Shaking, she dropped the pillow she'd been hanging on to.

"Casey."

It came through the door, sounding steady enough. Relief flooded her; she hadn't damaged him irrevocably if he'd managed to get up and walk inside.

It was the last thing she wanted to do, open the door and face him, but she also knew it was the only thing she could do. She'd hurt him, and she had to face the consequences, including the anger he had every right to.

But when it came right down to it, all she could manage was to unlock the door and retreat behind her pillow again.

She didn't say anything, but he'd obviously heard the lock click, because a moment later the door swung open.

"I'm sorry, Clay." It burst from her before he took a step into the room.

"Believe me, so am I," he said wryly.

She looked at him then, in disbelief. But one look at his face—still a little ashen, she realized guiltily—told her it was true. He wasn't angry.

She saw him glance around quickly, at the brass bed, the matching lamp beside it, the books on her table. He'd never been in her room. He'd never been beyond the living room. And these weren't exactly the circumstances under which she'd pictured him here.

And picture him she had, in the long, sultry hours of the night. She knew she shouldn't, but she couldn't seem to help it. It had been the only thing powerful enough to distract her from the fact that she was lying awake waiting for the phone to ring, for her tormenter to strike again.

He sat down—gingerly, she noticed with another pang of guilt—on the edge of the bed.

"When did it happen, Casey?"

God, he didn't believe in the niceties, did he? She shook her head. "It doesn't matter. Except that I'm really, truly sorry. Are you...hurt?"

"I'll live. Was it when you were in the city?"

"It was unintentional, really."

"Felt pretty intentional," he said. She flushed, almost as embarrassed now as she had been when she'd unmanned him.

"Somebody taught you well," he said.

"I...yes." She'd graduated at the top of the small class. "He was a good teacher, he—"

Her attempt at diversion failed again.

"Where? Why? Talk to me, Casey."

Something about his intensity was beginning to register with her through her own emotional upset.

"Please…"

"You nearly made me a soprano out there. I think you owe me an explanation, don't you?"

Clay clearly wasn't going to drop this. And she supposed he was right; she did owe him at least some kind of explanation. But she couldn't seem to get the words out. She hadn't talked about it in so long, she wasn't sure if she could.

"I…can't," she whispered.

"Let it out, Casey. Otherwise it will eat you alive."

She shivered, tried to stop it, couldn't.

Clay's voice went very low, very soft. "Who was he?"

She crushed the pillow between shaking hands.

"Was it when you were in Chicago?"

She took a deep, shuddering breath. When he reached out to touch her arm, it was all she could do not to pull away. But that he was even willing to get near her after the blow she'd delivered surprised her, and she looked up at his face.

What she saw there took her breath away all over again. Gentle concern, understanding, encouragement and genuine caring—they were all there, along with something else that glowed in the eyes she'd once thought of as dead. How, she didn't know, but he'd suddenly made it easy. Still, she started at the beginning, not the bitter end.

"In Chicago I worked at Creative Profiles, a medium-size public relations firm. Started entry level, gofer work mostly, so I wasn't getting rich, but it was fun and exciting and in the city. Just what I wanted. Or thought I did."

His hand tightened on her arm, encouraging her. She wondered where and how he'd developed this reassuring manner. And why. But she knew she had to get this out or she might lose her nerve.

"I worked with…a man. Jon Nesbit. We became…friends. We both started at about the same time, so we naturally spent some time together. He was charming, polished, not like the boys I'd known. I...liked him.''

"And you thought he liked you?"

She took a tight little breath and nodded. "It was never, ever anything else. We were friends. Good friends, I thought. But one day...we were both up for a promotion. I got it.''

He made the leap faster than she would ever have expected. "And he thought he should have?"

She nodded again, a barely discernible motion, but she knew he would see it. "He went to the boss. Made a scene. Mr. Allen wasn't happy about it and reprimanded him.''

"So he was angry, jealous and humiliated. The worst recipe.''

How did he know? He seemed to understand so well, even before she told him. It made it...not easy, but at least possible for her to go on.

"He caught me one night when I'd been working late, moving to my new office. We were the only ones still there. He...pushed me into a storeroom...''

She couldn't say it, couldn't get it out. She shivered, helpless to stop it.

"And then forced you? Raped you?"

She didn't think she nodded that time, but she doubted she had to; the answer probably showed on her face.

"What was his rationalization?" he asked.

She blinked, diverted. "What?"

"Besides the promotion. Men like that always have an excuse for what they do. They convince themselves the victim had it coming. They're cowards at heart, so they have to work themselves up to it somehow.''

She lowered her gaze to the pillow, which was beginning to look a bit worse for wear. "He said I must have...'' She couldn't say what Jon had really said, so she used the milder euphemism instead. "I must have slept with the boss to get the job over him, so I could...I shouldn't mind doing it with him.''

"Bastard." He said it with a rough, icy anger that startled her. And warmed her. "Just tell me he went to jail."

Her head came up sharply. For a long moment she looked at him, wondering at his intensity. "Yes. Yes, he did."

"Good," he said. "Good for you. It takes a lot of courage for a woman to press charges. To take it all the way." He held her gaze, and she had the oddest feeling he knew exactly what it had taken.

"I fought him," she said. "Clawed him. He...hit me a few times."

The moment the words were out, she wished she hadn't said them; this was an aspect of the whole ordeal she hated to think about. It was so impossible to explain, the humiliation of having to prove you'd fought, the horrible combination of terror and anger when your word wasn't enough.

"Lots of evidence," he said. "They'd need it, going up against a smooth junior-executive type like that."

She stared at him. "That's exactly what they said."

"And I'll bet his lawyers still tried to say it was consensual."

She felt a sudden chill as he hit yet another nerve dead center. "Jon lied and said we'd been...intimate for months. And that I liked it...rough."

"To explain the marks."

She tried to hide the shudder that went through her, but she knew she'd failed. It was just too much, too ugly, too painful, all the memories she'd managed to keep under wraps for so long.

"The prosecutors showed photos, and they were...not pretty. In the end they believed me. But his lawyers, they were..."

"I can imagine. Rape is the only crime where the victim

is put on trial. Where so many people believe she somehow shares in the culpability.''

"They were…decent, the police. And the prosecutors. They tried to explain that too many women used an accusation of rape as a weapon, or because they felt guilty about saying yes. That it makes it harder for the true victims.''

"It does happen. It's not fair, but it does.''

"It was awful. To have to convince them that I hadn't wanted it, hadn't…asked for it, like Jon said. The D.A. said that if I hadn't fought, hadn't had visible injuries or scratched him so badly, it might have gone differently. That's what made me sicker than anything.''

"It shouldn't be that way. None of it should matter. Nothing except that you said no.''

His words were gentle, sincere, and she knew he didn't mean them to remind her of what she'd done to him, but her embarrassment returned in an instant.

"Clay, I really am so sorry. It was… I panicked. I don't know why.''

"You were feeling cornered. I understand.''

She couldn't quite believe he was being so understanding. The sight of him on the ground, curled up in agony, was still too vivid. "But I hurt you. Badly.''

"I can't argue that. But I'll live.'' His mouth quirked. "And by tomorrow I might even be glad about that.''

She blushed, furiously.

"Who taught you?'' he asked.

"A cop.'' He blinked, drawing back a little, suddenly oddly wary. "He ran a self-defense class for women,'' she explained. "Women who'd been…attacked.''

"To teach them how not to be victims.''

It wasn't a question, and she wondered why he seemed to know so much. "He said it had to be our first instinct, that there would be no time to think about it.''

"You learned that part well.''

This time there was a light, teasing note in his voice, but she didn't think she was ready to laugh about it yet.

"I needed something to...think about. During the trial."

He studied her for a moment. "When all you really wanted to do was come home?"

She nodded. "I left the afternoon after the conviction came in."

"Didn't stay for sentencing?"

She shook her head. "I knew that whatever it was, it wouldn't be long enough. Not for me. So there was no point. I came here to try and...heal, I guess. And it worked. At least, I thought it had."

"Casey, what happened out there was...instinct. It doesn't mean you're back in the muck again, it just means you learned well. You can defend yourself."

She looked at him, shaking her head in wonder at his gentle understanding, at the way he seemed to know exactly what to say. And her next words were out before she thought, although she wasn't sure she would have stopped them even if she had.

"I didn't want to defend myself. Not from you."

He went very still. "Casey..."

"You're the first man who's made me want to try again, Clay. The first man I've trusted enough to let get close."

"Casey, don't."

He'd gone oddly pale, almost as ashen as he'd been when he'd been lying on the ground outside. She wasn't sure what was wrong, or what he was saying, thought maybe he didn't understand. "I've never told anyone here, never even talked about it since I left Chicago."

He stood up, and when he looked down at her, his eyes were dark with so many emotions that she couldn't begin to name them.

"Don't, Casey," he said, his voice low and harsh. "Don't trust me. I'll only let you down."

And then he was gone, leaving Casey with the memory

of an expression on his face that was worse than any of the physical pain she had caused.

I've never told anyone here, never even talked about it. The first man I've trusted enough to let get close.

Clay cowered in the darkest corner he could find, in the small toolroom. He was shaking, and he didn't bother to try to stop, knowing he wouldn't be able to.

He'd been sickened by Casey's awful story, just as he'd always been sickened by tales of viciousness and cruelty. And he'd been filled with admiration at the way she'd fought back at the trial—and no one knew better than he what that could be like—and the way she'd gone on with her life afterward. He supposed part of it was envy, too; going on was not something he'd managed very well.

But then, what had happened to Casey hadn't been her fault in any way. What had happened to him had been no one's fault but his own.

But her words had brought back countless memories, memories of a time he'd so distanced himself from that it sometimes didn't seem real. The only memories that were consistently, constantly real were the ones that haunted his dreams.

But even those were overpowered right now by the realization that his fears had come true. Casey trusted him. He'd known it, on some level, from the moment she'd begun to tell him what had happened to her. She never would have talked about it if she hadn't; he'd known that, too, before she'd told him.

He rubbed his hands over his face, pressing his fingers at his temples as hard as he could, even knowing it was hopeless, that nothing would relieve the pounding pressure.

He'd let things go too far. He'd let Casey get too close, let her come to depend on him. It had started out with minor things, but from there it was only a small step to bigger ones. Like trust.

She trusted him.

And he'd already proved resoundingly that he was undeserving of that kind of faith.

There was only one thing he could do. And he should have done it already, the moment he realized he'd been contemplating staying awhile. That should have been his first clue that things were getting out of control.

And now it was too late. There was no way to avoid hurting, or at the least disappointing, Casey, a woman who'd had far too much pain in her life already.

But better now than later. The longer he stayed, the worse it would get. So he would leave.

Soon. Tomorrow. Early.

And if he managed to dodge Casey in the process, all the better. The desire to avoid her didn't surprise him; he'd long ago acknowledged that he'd turned into the worst kind of coward.

And it was past time for this coward to hit the road.

Chapter 9

Casey suspected it when Mud didn't meet her in the kitchen as he usually did, but she knew for sure the minute that she looked out into the empty yard. She hadn't dreamed that noise at dawn, hadn't imagined the sound of an engine starting. Clay was gone.

Still, she stood there staring at the empty spot where the green truck had been parked for so many days. The silence seemed deafening, no sound of work going on, no good-morning bark from Mud...and no racing of her own heart.

In fact, the only thing she felt was a chilly, sinking sensation, followed by a hollowness that was almost an ache somewhere deep inside her.

Don't trust me. I'll only let you down.

But she *had* trusted him. Enough to tell him what she'd never told anyone in River Bend.

Enough to let him kiss her. Enough to kiss him back.

Enough to want that kiss to be only the beginning.

She shivered, despite the fact that it was already warm at this early hour. Had she driven him away with that trust?

Was he so very fearful of being trusted? Or was it *her* trust that had sent him running? Or had she overwhelmed him? Had he not wanted to deal with the wounded soul she'd revealed to him?

Or had he simply been repelled by a woman who'd been raped?

It couldn't be. She would not believe it was what had happened to her that had made him leave. He just was not the kind of man who would look at a woman who had been assaulted that way with distaste. He couldn't be, not when he had talked to her the way he had, comforted her the way he had, held her the way he had. Whatever his reasons were, she was as sure as she could be that that was not one of them. He might not want to deal with it long-term, but at that moment, he'd given her the most peace she'd ever known when the memories were upon her. Surely he couldn't have done that if he'd been genuinely repulsed by her as a result of what had happened?

Maybe it had been a combination of things. Including that knack she seemed to have for treading on forbidden territory. Of course, he also seemed to have more forbidden areas than just about anybody she'd ever known. Which was the only thing that had kept her from prying, despite her sheer curiosity about the man who had so quickly become such a part of her life and thoughts.

Or maybe it was simply that she was a lousy judge of men. She'd thought Jon Nesbit was her friend. And she'd thought Clay Yeager might care, a little.

But instead, Jon had betrayed her trust in the worst way. And now Clay had decamped without a word, in the middle of the night.

Maybe it was just as well, she told herself. Maybe she wasn't ready for…whatever might have happened between them. What had almost happened between them last night. Maybe her reaction had been proof of that.

But all the rationalization, all the maybes, didn't make the empty place inside her go away.

"You've gotten through worse. Much worse. You just made a mistake, that's all. It won't be the last time."

As her voice echoed in the kitchen, she realized that she'd gotten into the habit of speaking her thoughts aloud. Not to hear herself, but because usually Mud was somewhere around. And he was, as Clay had said, a good listener.

God, now she was missing his darn dog.

She made herself turn away from the window. She wouldn't think about it, she told herself. She'd been getting by just fine before Clay had disrupted her life, and she could do it again. Today she would finish the painting he'd started, then get back to her own work tomorrow. She had a birthday party to do, and she had to plan how she was going to coordinate the three possible jobs she had in the works for Labor Day.

She would be fine. She knew that. She knew how the process worked. She would eventually forget he'd even been around. She would stop thinking of him every time she looked at the wind vane, or the fence, or opened her screen door, or came in contact with any of the other things he'd fixed.

And she would even stop expecting to see a flash of black and white and hear a bark of greeting, eventually.

Eventually.

The phone rang. She spun around to look at it, and for the first time her midnight caller was not uppermost in her mind.

Had Clay not really left? Had he just gone somewhere, and was he calling to tell her now? Had something happened?

Her breath caught; what if something *had* happened? Clay had obviously been able to drive, but maybe Mud had gotten ill or hurt. Maybe he'd gone off on one of his hunts and run into something more lethal than a squirrel. She hadn't heard anything like an animal fight, or Mud barking, but maybe—

A second ring came, jolting her out of her racing thoughts and into motion. She grabbed the receiver and answered hastily.

"Hello?"

"That wasn't very nice, Casey, not answering me."

Oh, God, it was him. Again. In the daylight.

"You shouldn't do that. I miss our little chats."

It was too much. On top of everything else, it was just too much, and she was suddenly very angry. She knew she should just hang up, but she couldn't stop herself.

"I didn't think cowards came out in the daylight," she snapped. "Crawl back under your rock."

Then she hung up before he could speak again, before he could say something that would overwhelm her anger with the fear she knew he was trying to instill in her.

"I won't let you win," she said, staring at the telephone as if it were a malevolent beast. "I've dealt with worse than you before."

And now she had to deal with the fact that in the space of two rings of a phone, she'd almost talked herself out of the truth, that Clay Yeager had simply and silently abandoned the work he'd been doing—and her. His reasons didn't matter, not really. What mattered was that he'd done it.

And that now she had to get used to it.

The ominous dropping of the needle on the voltmeter seemed like merely the final blow to an escape that had felt cursed from the beginning. First Mud had been strangely uncooperative this morning, until Clay had had to drag the unhappy dog bodily into the front seat of the truck. Then the truck had chosen to be exceptionally noisy when he'd started it at first light, as if it sensed his desire for quiet and wanted to foil it. Then he'd had a flat barely twenty miles from the farm, which meant he had to practically unload the entire camper to get to his jack to change the tire. Mud had taken advantage of the opportunity to take off running, clearly back toward the farm. He'd spent an hour chasing the suddenly disobedient dog, finally catching him and having to trudge back to the truck and close him up in the cab while he finished with the tire.

After an hour spent on that and reloading the truck, he'd stopped to get the flat repaired, not wanting to risk getting stuck miles from any help without a spare. The only gas station he'd been able to find open had been busy, and he'd had to wait almost three hours until they got to him. Then it was back out onto the narrow country roads, where, eager as he was to put distance behind him, he had to hold it down to a careful speed.

As a result, it was past one before he'd managed to put even fifty miles between him and the woman who'd scared him into flight by the simple act of trusting him.

And now there was that ominous reading on his dash, that needle dropping slowly but steadily, telling him he'd left those repairs too long.

It figures, he thought with a sigh. Apparently fate hadn't liked what he'd been doing. Whether it was his running or that he'd let Casey get too close, he didn't know, and at this point it didn't really matter.

He began to look for a place to pull over. It was another mile before he saw a level spot conveniently shaded by a large oak. He edged off the road, and just in time. The truck died before he could even reach for the ignition to turn it off. He tried the starter and got nothing but a faint click.

"Great," he muttered. "Just great."

It didn't take him long to determine that it was what he suspected, the alternator. He'd probably been running on the battery since he'd left the farm. Not that the diagnosis helped; he certainly didn't have a spare handy. And he had no idea where to get one, even if he could afford it; he hadn't stuck around long enough to get the second week's pay.

And that was assuming he could get out of here at all; this didn't look like a bustling thoroughfare. Besides, who would pick up an obvious transient like him out here in the middle of nowhere? He would probably have to walk, at least until he could find a phone he could use. Not that he expected anybody to let him use their phone, either. Or had anybody to call.

He was pondering which way to start walking when a large black flatbed truck slowed to a halt beside him. An older man, dressed in overalls and a battered straw cowboy hat, leaned over and rolled down his passenger window.

"Gotta problem, do ya?"

"Alternator," he said. "Is there a garage anywhere around?"

"Best one's about fifty miles back, in River Bend."

Now that, Clay thought wryly, really put a capper on his day.

"Unless maybe you don't need a mechanic," the man said, looking Clay up and down as if trying to gauge his ability to repair the truck himself.

"I can do it," Clay said. "I just need the alternator."

"Hmm. Well then, maybe Buck Chapman can help you. He's got a wrecking yard about five miles up the road. Think he's got a coupla trucks like yours, might have what you need."

Well, five was better than fifty. And anything was better than heading back to River Bend.

"Thanks—a lot," Clay added, meaning it.

"I'm heading that way, if you want a ride. Pup, too, if you don't want to leave him in the heat. Can't bring you back, though. I'm already late to pick up the wife."

Clay stared at the man. "I...yes. I'd be very grateful. Thank you."

Casey had been right about the people around here, he thought. He supposed there were people like this everywhere, willing to help even when it wasn't particularly convenient. Maybe they just got lost amid the masses elsewhere.

It took him a moment to locate Mud's long-unused leash, but he didn't think he could trust the collie not to take off and head back to Casey, fifty miles or not.

He thanked the older man profusely when he dropped him at the yard enclosed by a weathered wooden fence. The man just nodded and waved, wishing him good-luck as he drove on.

Buck Chapman was nearly a twin of the man who'd helped him, and Clay almost asked, but decided he'd best just be thankful and shut up. And he was more thankful when it turned out that Buck indeed had what he needed. And when the man offered him a break on the price of the alternator if he would take it out of the wrecked truck himself, he jumped at it; it would take time, but this was already going to eat up most of his small hoard of cash. He shouldn't have bought those new boots, but his old ones had been literally falling apart, and he'd needed them to keep working. Besides, he'd figured he would be back where he'd been financially by the next week.

Too bad he hadn't stuck around to get paid.

He knew by the time he started the walk back to the truck that it was going to be tight, trying to get the job done today. He was going to run out of daylight, and his flashlight, while probably powerful enough, wasn't going to be easy to secure at the right angle.

Not to mention that, after sleeping restlessly at best last night, he was so tired he would probably screw it up, anyway.

And hungry.

He'd gotten spoiled, gotten used to eating regularly and well. And he hadn't done much planning for this, hadn't stopped for food or even water in his rush to get away.

"Coward," he muttered to himself, his self-disgust getting stronger with every step. And for the first time, he let the thought of going back creep into his mind.

He rejected the idea immediately, knowing he didn't dare seriously consider it. The sooner he got the repairs done and got back onto the road, the better. And if he had to finish by flashlight, so be it. He would find some way to do it, some way to tie the light to something.

Some way he could keep running.

He was suddenly more than disgusted with himself. What had he been thinking, to let it go so far? Sure, Casey was the first woman in five years who had roused even a twinge of interest in him. But that alone should have been a warning.

He'd never expected to feel anything like that again in his life, so he'd never really thought about what he would do if it happened.

He obviously hadn't taken into account finding a woman like Casey. A woman who had every right to be bitter, cynical and mistrustful, yet was kind and generous, and trusted a stranger who had trespassed.

Sometimes it's the ones who call themselves your friend that you have to watch out for.

He hadn't understood it when she'd said it. But he understood it now, all too well, after the harrowing story she'd told him. And for a moment an old, once familiar feeling flooded him, a feeling of disgust for being one of a gender that could so brutalize its natural mate. There had been a few times, in that other life, when he'd been amazed women had anything to do with men at all.

You don't have any right to that feeling anymore, he reminded himself fiercely. What you did was just as bad. In some ways worse. You dishonored a sacred vow. You became one of those that Casey meant, the ones you should be able to trust but who betray you.

But Casey *had* trusted him. Enough to hire him when she didn't know the first thing about him. Enough to tell him the ugly story she'd told no one since she'd come home.

Enough to say she hadn't wanted to stop him.

Even, he thought wryly, *when she'd darn near crippled him.*

He knew it had been totally instinctive, and he understood exactly why she'd panicked. In a weird way, after the pain had begun to fade, he'd been proud of her; she would have stopped anybody who hadn't been armed.

What scared him was that she probably would have done the same thing even if it had been an armed attacker. Not that she would ever have to face that, not as long as she stayed in River Bend. But still, she was alone out there, and vulnerable.

"Maybe you should have stayed with her, Mud," he told the collie as they finally neared the broken-down truck, even as he realized that if he'd left the dog behind, he would have little left to convince him to keep going. Especially now.

Mud, who wasn't at all pleased with his reintroduction to the leash, didn't even yip in answer.

"Still sulking?" Clay asked. "Never mind. I can't blame you."

The truck was, thankfully, not overwhelmingly hot; the oak still had its leaves, and the shade was better than tolerable. He found the jug he kept Mud's water in, which he was thankful to see was half-full. He set out the collie's dish and filled it, stole a swallow himself, then capped the jug and put it back as the dog lapped noisily after the long walk.

"Sorry, buddy. I didn't plan this very well. Best I can do for dinner is a couple of cereal bars."

It had been enough for a long time, and it would just have to be enough again, he told himself.

As soon as they were finished the scanty meal, he opened the hood again. He had to get as much as he could done before he lost the daylight. He was lucky it was still light out; if it hadn't been August... It was still August, wasn't it? Or had it slipped into September while he'd been slipping under Casey's spell?

He fought off the memories, trying not to think of her voice, her laugh and the clear blue of her eyes. Trying not to think of the way she had made even him laugh, for the first time in so long that he'd been surprised he still knew how. Trying not to think of how sweet she'd been to kiss, and how hot and swift and fierce his body's reaction had been, the body he'd thought would never respond in that way again.

Trying not to think about what she must be thinking now, about him.

He forced himself to concentrate on his work, even welcoming the distraction of painfully skinned knuckles as he tried to work in the tight quarters. He ended up finishing, as he'd feared, by flashlight, and it took him twice as long as it would have otherwise, but at least it was done. Of course, there was the small problem now of the battery being dead, drained by the malfunction of the charging system.

He should have thought of that before, but he'd been so focused on the immediate repair that he hadn't. Maybe he could talk Buck into coming out and giving him a jump. At least the battery wasn't that old; once he got rolling, it would charge back up.

And he was, he admitted wearily, too tired to go on tonight, anyway. He needed some sleep or he would likely drive right off the road. At the same time, he had doubts about whether he would be able to sleep any better now than he had last night. But he had to try. It wasn't late, but if he slept now, he could get an early start in the morning.

He felt battered as he climbed into the back of the truck. He didn't understand why; he hadn't worked nearly as hard today as he had the whole time at Casey's. But he felt like he'd been caught in a riptide and bounced off every rock on the West Coast.

He stretched out gingerly; at least the rest of him hurt so bad he didn't even notice if he was still sore where Casey had kneed him. He reached out and scratched Mud's ears as the dog settled into his spot. He seemed to have forgiven him, although from the heavy, very human-sounding sigh he let out, Clay wasn't sure it hadn't been grudgingly.

But Clay was suddenly selfishly glad that he hadn't left the dog with Casey; Mud might have been better fed, but Clay knew he himself would be one step closer to the edge. He'd been there once, peering into the abyss, and knew if he ever went back, it would be to jump.

He wasn't even aware he'd gone to sleep until Mud's sharp, warning bark woke him.

He jerked awake. It was still dark. Perhaps some animal had wandered by, rousing Mud's interest. The dog let out a peal of barks, scrambling toward the back of the truck.

Then Clay saw a light. Or rather, lights. Something nudged at his mind, something about the feel of this: car headlights behind the truck, another, single light in motion...

Cop, he thought, coming abruptly and completely awake. And no sooner had the realization struck him than there came a pounding on the tailgate.

Mud subsided into a steady, low growl at Clay's order. Which was followed by an order from outside, in a voice that seemed used to giving them.

"Okay, buddy, come on out! And hold the dog!"

He could see the outline of the figure now and caught a

tiny glint of reflection off the left chest. Badge, he thought, confirming his guess.

"Yes, sir," he said quickly, before the man could get any idea he had somebody uncooperative on his hands. He didn't know how things worked out here in the heartland, but cops were a lot alike anywhere; respect them, and they respected you.

He lowered the tailgate and slid out, cautioning Mud to stay put. He moved carefully, not wanting any quick moves misinterpreted, and made sure his hands were in plain view the whole time.

The cop—a county sheriff's deputy, as he'd expected this far from a town of any size—watched him thoughtfully.

"Done this before, have you?"

Clay nearly laughed; he should have expected that reaction. But he didn't want to get into his history, not if he didn't have to. So he just said, "I've been on the road for a while." Then, figuring some explanation was in order, he added, "I broke down. Alternator. Took me until dark to get it fixed, and now the battery's dead. I was figuring to get a jump tomorrow. And I was tired enough that it wasn't safe to drive, anyway."

The deputy nodded. "Figured it was something like that. But I wish you'd found somewhere else to do it."

Clay drew back a little, not sure what to make of the words, or the regretful note in the man's voice. "I didn't have much to say about it. The truck chose to die here."

"Tough break," the deputy said sympathetically. Then, at the sound of an approaching vehicle, he looked over his shoulder. With a slight grimace, he turned back to Clay. "*Real* tough break," he said. "You picked Harry Snider's place to break down. And he's the worst-tempered, most stiff-necked old buzzard for fifty square miles."

Whatever was going on, Clay knew he wasn't going to like it. The other vehicle, a truck newer than his that looked twice as old, came to a halt behind the deputy's car, and a short, wiry man bolted out of it and hurried toward them. From ten feet away he started yelling.

"That's him, Deputy! Right there, bold as brass, on my property!"

The deputy turned to the wildly gesturing man. Clay opened his mouth to speak, then shut it again, figuring it would be best for him to keep quiet.

"He broke down, Mr. Snider."

The man snorted, running a hand through a rather wild bush of white hair. "Likely story. Do your duty, Deputy."

The deputy sighed. "He's got it fixed now, Mr. Snider." He glanced at Clay. "And I'll give him a jump and he'll be on his way right now, won't you?"

Never let it be said I can't take a hint, Clay thought. "Right now," he confirmed quickly.

"Like hell," the old man said. "He's on my property! Been there all day!"

"I didn't know it was private property. I didn't see a sign or a fence," Clay began, then stopped when the old man took a step closer. Clay saw him glance past the truck for an instant before a crafty look came over his face, a look that was visible even in the stark glare of the headlights.

"'Course you didn't see a fence, you ran right over it! Damn California types, don't care 'bout nothing but yourselves. Trespass, damage a man's property."

Clay turned to look, certain that even in the sunlight he'd never even seen a fence, let alone hit it. He still couldn't see a thing. Apparently the deputy couldn't, either, because he walked around the side of the truck, lifting his flashlight to scan the ground.

After one full arc, he moved the light back to the only thing that even vaguely resembled a fence, an old, broken piece of wood with some wire attached to it. The wood was bleached-looking on the top, and weeds had grown up around it.

"See, right there! Pushed that fence right over."

Clay looked at the old man. "That's your fence? That's been there for months."

The man bridled, turning red in the face. "You calling me a liar, boy?"

Uh-oh, Clay thought.

"Now, he didn't say that, Mr. Snider. Tell you what, why don't we just get this fellow off your property, then you can go back home and I can go back to work."

"Oh, no you don't. He's not going to get off that easy!"

The deputy sighed. Clay felt a pang of sympathy for the man, despite his own untenable position.

"Just what is it you want, Mr. Snider?"

"Do I have to tell you your job?" the man spat out. "I want him arrested!"

"For what, Mr. Snider? There's obviously no intentional violation here."

"He trespassed, and he damaged my property. That oughta be enough, even these days."

"Perhaps we could work out some sort of restitution for the fence," the deputy said, glancing at Clay.

"I'm down to my last twenty, after the breakdown," he said.

"See there, and he's a vagrant, too! Prob'ly have to sell that truck to pay me for my fence, so you make sure it gets towed away and locked up somewhere."

For the first time Clay began to realize that this was not going to end up like some comedy skit, with everyone laughing at the end. The old man meant every word. He'd finally met the exception to Casey's rule; this man would have been right at home in any heartless big city.

"Well?" Snider said expectantly. "Do I have to make a citizen's arrest?"

Clay swore to himself; he knew the position that put the deputy in.

"You sure you want to do that, and have to write a report and appear in court and all?"

"Never shirked my duty as a citizen before. If that's the only way I can get you to do what oughta be done, then I'll do it."

The deputy turned to Clay and said regretfully, "He's got the right, I'm afraid. I'll have to take you in."

And that, Clay thought, was the real capper to this stinking, godforsaken day.

Chapter 10

She nearly didn't answer the phone. Why should she, just because she happened to be sitting in the living room, wide-awake, in the dark, thinking about things she couldn't change?

It rang again, and she set her jaw, determined not to let her mind take off on some wild flight of imagination, thinking it might be Clay, calling to explain, or say he was coming back. If it was anyone, it was probably her phantom caller, back to his nighttime harassment after he'd gotten such a lovely response from her today. She never should have lost control like that. The deputy she'd reported the calls to had told her that reactions like that were exactly what callers like this were after.

At the third ring she turned to stare at the phone, as if she could force it to stop by sheer will.

On the fourth ring, her control broke, and she grabbed the receiver.

"Listen, you slimy worm, find somebody else to bother!"

"Excuse me? Is this…the Scott residence?"

It was a woman. And a stranger. Casey let out a squeak of both relief and embarrassment.

"Yes. Yes, it is. I'm sorry. I've been getting some crank calls."

There was a pleasant laugh on the other end. "I understand. I've been there myself."

"This is Casey Scott, can I help you?" she asked, glancing at her watch. She found only her bare wrist, since she'd taken the watch off before her fruitless effort at sleep. She looked up at the clock on the mantel, whose faintly glowing hands told her it was after midnight. That realization made her sit up straighter in the overstuffed chair.

"I hope so, Ms. Scott. Do you know someone by the name of Clay Yeager?"

Casey's heart leaped. "Yes. Is he hurt?"

"No, he's fine. I'm sorry, I usually tell people that first."

She let out a long breath of relief. "I didn't give you much of a chance. What's wrong?"

"He is in a little jam. He was brought in a couple of hours ago."

"Arrested?" Casey's voice rose slightly.

"It's nothing serious—"

"Sorry, but to me an arrest for anything is pretty darn serious."

She could almost hear the woman smile. "Wish more people felt that way. But really, in this case, the deputy who brought him in said it was mainly to placate a…rather crotchety old man. I'm sure it will all be dismissed eventually."

Casey tried to absorb it all, but one question kept playing back in her mind. "He gave you my number? He wants me to…bail him out?"

"Yes, and no. He gave us the number, but not for himself. He said you wouldn't help him, but you might help his dog. That's all he was worried about."

"Mud?"

"Excuse me?"

"That's the dog's name," Casey explained. "Is he okay?"

"Yes, except that he's locked in the storeroom, making a heck of a racket, and won't let anybody near him. The sergeant isn't happy. He wants to send him to the pound, even if they have to tranq him."

The image of smart, quicksilver Mud in a tiny, cold cage—or, worse, victim to an overdose of tranquilizer—made her stomach knot.

"Mr. Yeager said you were the only one the dog would go with willingly." The woman hesitated, then added, "He said he knew you didn't want anything to do with him, but to tell you that it wasn't Mud's fault."

She was, Casey assured herself later, only doing this for Mud. She just couldn't bear the thought of the live-wire dog, that crazy, squirrel-herding dog, in the pound, all alone and scared. Besides, you heard about accidents all the time, where dogs were put to sleep by mistake.

That his master was in pretty much the same boat was something she tried not to think about as she drove through the darkness toward the sheriff's substation. She didn't care, not after the way he'd vanished in the middle of the night without a word or even a note. She didn't care, even though they'd told her that if the complainant, who was there writing out his citizen's-arrest paperwork, couldn't be reasoned with, Clay would be transferred to the county jail, since they had no facilities beyond one small holding room.

She hadn't been inside a police station since the last day of Jon's trial. The prosecutors and the detectives and even the arresting officers had all gathered there in a show of support for her that she knew she would never forget. They'd all told her there was no way he wouldn't be found guilty, thanks to her steady, unshakable testimony, but that no matter the verdict, she'd done herself proud.

She hadn't felt proud. She'd felt drained, exhausted, battered, and nearly numb. She'd been attacked, her words twisted by lawyers who cared nothing for the truth, their only goal getting their client off. Their lying, vicious, coward of a client.

She shivered, as if shaking off his evil touch, even after all this time. And nearly missed the building she was looking for. The dispatcher had told her it looked like a bunker, and that it did; with low concrete windows narrow enough to be rifle slits.

The lights were low inside, but after the unrelieved blackness of the night, they seemed bright. Behind the sliding window that looked as if it belonged in a doctor's office, there was a rangy older man in uniform who turned as she came in.

"Casey Scott?" he asked before she could speak.

She nodded, heading that way, and he approached the small counter. Before she got there, she heard the barking from down the hall.

"Oops," she said. "I guess he's still wound up."

The man gave her a wry grin. "I will be eternally grateful to you if you can quiet him down."

"I'll try," she said.

She heard a click, and he came around the counter and through the door beside it. He wore a name tag that said D. Vickery, a neatly trimmed, graying mustache, and a small revolver on his right side. He reminded her of the man who had been the bailiff at Jon's trial. The man had been a silent, stoic presence in the courtroom, but he had broken into a smile of satisfaction when the guilty verdict had come in, and had given Casey a short, sharp nod of salute.

It was odd, she thought, as she followed D. Vickery down the hall to a small door, the little memories that stuck with you. It had been a moment of support from an unexpected source during a horrible ordeal, and she'd never forgotten it. It made her feel rather favorably toward Deputy Vickery.

"I was half-convinced I should lock it," Vickery said. "That's one smart dog."

"That he is," Casey said softly.

Then the door swung open and Mud launched himself at her. She barely managed to catch him and hold on. He wriggled in her arms, swiping a tongue across her face wetly. He whined, but quietly. And she was surprised at the strength of her own response as she hugged the black-and-white bundle of fur tightly.

"Bless you," the deputy said fervently. "If he'd still been howling when the sergeant came back, it would have been the pound for him, and I really didn't want to do that. His owner said he wouldn't have gone peacefully."

She was *not* going to ask, Casey said firmly. She was here to pick up Mud, no more. It was bad enough that, whenever he got out, Clay would have to reclaim the dog from her, but she would deal with that when she had to. She took hold of the leash she'd never seen before—and doubted Mud would take to—but she couldn't bring herself to let go of the dog just yet.

"He sure was worried about this pup, more than himself. Practically begged the deputy not to lock the dog up. Said you were the only one who could handle him."

She said nothing, not wanting to encourage him, not wanting to even think, let alone hear, about Clay. But instead the man took her silence as license to continue; perhaps he was just happy to have somebody to talk to, to break up the monotony of his graveyard shift.

"It's a shame, really," Vickery said as they walked back to the lobby. "Old Mr. Snider, he's kind of notorious around here. Always making complaints about ridiculous stuff. But this one was the topper."

Scratching Mud's ears, she bit her lip to keep the natural

inquiry from breaking through. Not that it mattered to the voluble deputy.

"The trespassing was trumped-up enough, but he's blaming the guy for breaking down his fence. The deputy who brought him in said he was sure it was real old damage, though."

"Then why did he arrest him?" It was out before she could stop it.

"He didn't, really. And he hasn't been booked—we're trying to avoid that. But he was on private property, so he had to bring him in, with old man Snider yelling about his right to make a citizen's arrest."

Casey sighed, then asked, "Why was he on his property?"

"Truck broke down. The battery went dead."

Casey stopped in her tracks. "And this Mr. Snider had him arrested for *that?*"

"Told you he was a pain. Yeager even had the truck fixed, could have pulled out right then. Deputy offered to jump him, but Snider wouldn't drop it. My guess is he wants somebody else to pay for rebuilding his fence. Must have figured he had some rich Californian snagged."

"He's not rich," Casey said, adding silently, *The man couldn't even afford food two weeks ago.*

The deputy looked at her curiously. "He doesn't seem much like the typical transient type."

She shifted the now calmer Mud to her hip, not sure what he would do if she put him down, even with the leash on. In a minute, she thought. "No," she answered.

The deputy's mouth quirked. "You're about as talkative as he is. He's got the sarge ready to run a background on him just to find out what he's hiding."

Casey went still. "Nothing…criminal," she said, realizing only when she said it how certain she was of that.

"That's the feeling I got. Whatever's doggin' that boy

is personal. But he sure looked a little desperate when they locked him in that holding room.''

Casey could picture that far too clearly.

And she knew in that moment that she could no more leave Clay here than she could Mud.

''Here's your stuff, Yeager.''

Clay watched as the man who'd locked him in this small room with only a table and two chairs emptied the manila envelope onto the Formica surface. It didn't take long; all there was were his keys, driver's license, what was left of his cash and two small wood screws left over from his work at Casey's.

Then he looked up at Deputy Vickery. ''Sir?'' he asked respectfully; he hadn't forgotten everything he'd ever learned.

''You're out of here.''

Clay's brows furrowed. ''I am?''

Vickery nodded. ''Snider dropped the charges and the property damage claim.''

Clay slowly got to his feet. He didn't reach for his things; he wasn't sure he wasn't going to have to give them back. ''He doesn't seem to be a change-of-heart kind of guy,'' he said warily.

''He's not,'' Vickery agreed. ''But this time he changed his mind.''

There was something in the man's voice, some undertone, that only heightened Clay's wariness. But whatever the reason for Snider's unexpected reversal, he was glad. When Vickery opened the door and gestured him out, Clay grabbed up his scant possessions, stuffed them into his back pocket and stepped outside quickly. He breathed a small sigh of relief to be outside the room; he'd been surprised at how the prospect of jail had affected him.

Only the idea of them probing into his past until they found out who he was made him feel worse. Not just because their probing would open old wounds, but because it would also telegraph his whereabouts to the people and places he'd left behind, intending never to go back.

Not that anybody would still give a damn, he thought as he walked down the narrow hallway beside the uniform. He'd cut his ties too thoroughly, too completely, for anyone to still care. No doubt he wasn't even a passing thought any longer. But he didn't want to take that chance.

It felt both strange and oddly familiar, this trek through the night-quiet building. They paused at a door while Vickery reached for keys on his belt. There was a glass panel about two feet high and a foot wide in the upper part of the door, and through it he could see an identical door a few feet farther on, which he guessed led back to the front lobby; this was a small substation, and he supposed the way he'd come in, through that lobby, was the way everyone in custody came in. It was—

He stopped dead when they moved to where he could see through the window in the second door. Across the lobby stood Casey, with Mud sitting quietly at her feet. They'd told him two hours ago that she'd arrived to pick up the dog, and he'd been relieved that he'd been right in thinking she would not hold his cravenness against the dog. But he'd assumed she was long gone by now, back home, still angry at him, but at least taking care of Mud.

"You're a lucky man, Yeager," Vickery said as he unlocked the first door.

He looked at the deputy, who had apparently been watching him stare at Casey through the two doors.

"Not that I'm surprised Snider withdrew his complaints," the deputy went on. "A lady who looked like that could talk me out of just about anything, too. Of course, being Snider, he wouldn't give up, but when she offered to pay for the damage, he agreed to drop everything."

Clay nearly groaned. "She paid him for that damn fence?"

Vickery nodded as he pulled the door open and gestured Clay through, toward the second door. "Not as much as he wanted, I suspect, but you're free and clear. All you need to do is sign for your truck."

Understanding bit again. "She paid the tow fee, too?"

"Like I said, you're a lucky man."

Right. Now I'm in hock to her for probably ten times the cost of that damned prime rib.

"You know, if I had a rescuer who looked like that, I'd be looking a bit more cheerful," Vickery said with a drawl.

Clay was saved from having to respond by a sudden, joyous chorus of barks from Mud as he leaped as close to the door as the leash would allow, giving Casey's hand a sharp yank.

Vickery winced and hastily unlocked the second door. The moment she saw Clay, Casey let go of the leash, and Mud scrambled across the floor in a crazed run.

Clay stopped, knowing what was coming; from four feet away the dog went airborne, and Clay braced himself for the impact.

"Second time I've seen that trick," Vickery muttered. "That's quite a dog."

So he'd been right about that, too, Clay thought. Mud had been as glad to see Casey as he'd hoped. He'd been desperate when he'd asked them to call her. He certainly hadn't wanted to, but he hadn't been able to stand the thought of the dog being locked up. He knew Mud would go crazy, and who knew what might have happened if somebody lost patience.

Casey didn't speak to him while Vickery quickly filled out a form and handed it to him to sign. Clay wasn't surprised; he hadn't expected her to welcome him. If she was even civil to him, he would figure he'd gotten off lucky.

"You won't be able to get your truck until morning, I'm afraid. Buck doesn't cotton much to waking up in the middle of the night."

Clay glanced at the form again. "Buck Chapman?"

"You know him?" Vickery asked.

"Sort of," Clay said wryly.

"Well, good luck, then," Vickery said. "And watch out for that mutt, huh?"

Then they were alone. Casey's expression revealed little. And Clay had no idea what to say. Finally, rather lamely, he said, "Thanks for coming for Mud."

"I couldn't leave him to be locked up." Her voice was as unemotional as her expression.

You, on the other hand... He was certain that was what she was thinking, that he could have rotted in a cell, were it not for Mud.

"How much did you pay the old man?"

"It doesn't matter. It's done."

"It does. I'll pay you back—"

Her cool demeanor snapped. "I did it for Mud's sake. Just forget about paying me back, and as soon as you get the truck you can be on your way to...wherever the hell you were going."

The uncharacteristic language told him how much his unexplained, unannounced departure had hurt her. But he knew he couldn't do as she pungently suggested. His freedom had cost her hundreds of dollars, no doubt. That was even more impossible for him to walk away from than the cost of Mud's escapade with the roast.

The fact that she probably didn't really need the money only made it worse, in a way he ruefully admitted was probably some perverse trick of his upbringing and personal code of ethics. It made it charity, and he could not accept that. He'd failed at the most important principle, so all that was left to him was to try to keep the smaller ones.

He had to repay her.

Which meant he had to go back.

He couldn't go back.

He had to go back.

For a long moment he just stood there, barely managing to keep from shaking. With a grim burst of honesty, he admitted he was terrified. He was afraid to go back on a very deep, gut-wrenching level.

And he was even more afraid that he knew why. That there was only one explanation for the crazy effect Casey had on him. That there was only one explanation for why he'd run like he had, when he hadn't cared about anything enough to want to escape it for years. And it was something he couldn't let happen.

He couldn't fall in love with her.

Nor could he let her fall in love with him, because he would let her down, he would fail her.

Just as he'd always failed the people he loved. And who had loved him.

A sudden image flashed into his mind, vivid, painful, coming straight out of his nightmare, and he shuddered almost violently.

He would hang on to that image, he thought. He would hang on to it, remember it, replay it until his suddenly unruly emotions—and body—were forced into submission. He would use the brutal memory as a weapon against himself. He would keep a safe distance.

And he would *not* fall in love with Casey Scott.

Chapter 11

Casey knew she was manufacturing work, rearranging her already efficient kitchen, experimenting with recipes she'd perfected long ago. But she had to do something. Otherwise she was quite simply going to go crazy.

Clay was back, yet he wasn't. At least, this was not the Clay she'd known. True, the old Clay had been prickly and touchy on occasion, but he'd also been pleasant enough, had even laughed now and then.

And he'd comforted her like no one had ever been able to the night her guard had collapsed and she'd told him what had happened to her in Chicago. Even after she'd nearly caused him great bodily harm.

But this Clay...this Clay barely spoke. When he did, it was brusque, cool, distant. And he spoke only when he couldn't avoid it; otherwise, he avoided her as if she were lethally contagious. He was as distant as if he'd built a wall between them. He talked only of business, of what chore he would do next, and if she had anything else to be done.

When she'd taken him to pick up the truck, she'd half expected him to turn it in the opposite direction.

Their relationship before, edgy as it was, had been downright affectionate compared to this. He ate dinner in silence, and quickly—no more casual conversation. He wouldn't even come into the house for breakfast, and as always, he ate sandwiches on the run, as if he were desperate to pile up the six hundred dollars—he'd demanded she tell him the amount—as quickly as possible.

Nor did they ever discuss his reasons for leaving. She'd asked him, the first day he'd been back. She'd wanted to hear him say something, anything, to tell her she'd been right, that it hadn't been what he'd learned about her that had sent him running. But she didn't get to hear it. He'd said only that he'd had no choice. And that she should think twice about what he'd done before ever trusting him again.

For three days it had been like this. Clay looked almost as bleak as he had when he'd first arrived, Casey felt as if she'd been walking on eggshells forever, and even Mud was showing the strain. The dog seemed to sense the tension between them, and the collie wore himself ragged going from one to the other, as if trying to send some message of his own.

At this rate, she had at least eleven more days of this to look forward to. And that was assuming—as his glacial disposition seemed to indicate—that he would be taking off again as soon as she was paid back, forgoing the chance to build up his traveling money.

But then, at the rate he was working, top speed and from dawn to dark, there might not be enough chores to last much beyond that. At fifty dollars a day, she was getting one heck of a deal, production-wise.

But there wasn't enough money in the world to pay for the disquiet he was causing.

"I'll need some more galvanized nails to fix those gutters.''

The level, businesslike voice came from behind her. It took all of her already tattered self-control to keep from jumping. She slowly put away the mixing bowls, right back where they'd been before this urge to rearrange had overtaken her, then turned to face him.

"I'll pick them up tomorrow."

He nodded once, short, sharp, then turned as if to go.

"Do you want dinner now?" Casey asked; she'd fixed some pasta salad for herself.

He stopped, but kept his back to her, not even looking at her. "No. Thank you."

"Perhaps you'd like some tea to go with that ice?" she said sweetly.

There was a fractional pause, and she thought she saw the muscles in the back of his neck tighten, but his only response to the gibe was to keep going toward the door without a word.

And suddenly it was too much.

"That's it! I've had enough of this."

He stopped again, but this time he half turned toward her.

"Just go, will you? You can send me the money when you get it, if you're so determined to pay me back, but go." Her voice broke, and to her distress she felt a stinging behind her eyelids. "I can't stand this anymore."

He closed his eyes, and she saw his mouth tighten. He lowered his head slowly.

"Casey," he said, his voice low, sounding as if he were the one in pain, as if he hated this as much as she did, as if he hadn't been the one to put this distance between them.

"I don't know why you left, and I don't know why you've been acting like a Hatfield working for a McCoy since you came back. But—"

"Casey, please. I didn't mean to hurt you."

"I'm past being hurt. Now I'm just confused. And tired of this minefield we're living in."

He let out a compressed breath. He turned the rest of the way to face her but came no closer, choosing instead to lean against the doorjamb.

"I know I've been…" His voice trailed off, and he lifted one shoulder in a half shrug.

"Yes, you have," she said, resisting the urge to tell him exactly what she thought he'd been, although she wasn't sure why she restrained herself. "I told you, I did it for Mud, and you don't need to pay me back. So why don't you just go? You obviously don't want to be here."

"Want," he said tightly, "has nothing to do with it."

A vivid image of that look of anguish on his face when he'd told her not to trust him, that he would only let her down, came back to her. And she wondered just what she wasn't supposed to trust him with. And thought she must have been right.

"Look, I understand. A lot of men don't want to deal with a woman with my…particular brand of baggage."

He came upright in a rush. For a moment he just looked at her; then he swallowed visibly.

"Casey, you don't really believe that, do you? That…what happened to you had anything to do with my leaving?"

He looked so stunned that Casey knew it hadn't had anything to do with it at all. She hadn't been aware how much that had been nagging at her since he'd come back until she felt the rush of relief now. It was so strong that for a moment she couldn't answer him.

"God," he muttered, so low she could barely hear it and wasn't sure she was supposed to, "this is worse than what I was afraid of in the first place." Then he looked at her, almost urgently. "I would never…you've got to believe, the only thing I feel when I think of what you went through is anger at that piece of slime, and…admiration for how you brought him down. I'm not one of those men who wonder what the victim did to bring it on, or who feel she's...somehow less after. I swear, Casey.''

She found her voice at last. "I think I knew that. You wouldn't have been able to...say all those things if you did. All the things I...needed to hear. But when you left like that, without a word..."

He left the support of the doorjamb then and crossed the room to stand in front of her. "I never meant to hurt you, Casey."

"So you said." But she couldn't doubt that he meant it, not when she could see the pain, the remorse, the utter truth of it, in his eyes. She hadn't meant to say it, had sworn she wouldn't ask, wouldn't beg him to explain, but it escaped before she could stop it. "Then why? Why leave like that?"

He sighed audibly, long and weary-sounding. "Partly because I was afraid you'd...start counting on me. Depending on me. And I'd only disappoint you."

"You have a pretty low opinion of yourself, don't you?"

He gave her a look that was so bitterly cold she almost backed up a step. "Some would say it's still too high."

She didn't know what to say to that, so she made the only point she could think of. "If I start to depend on you, isn't that my problem? Besides, I got along on my own before you showed up, and I could do it again."

"I know you could. But I didn't want you to start thinking I might...stay. Because I can't. I won't."

"You made that fairly clear," she said. Then, heedless of the dangerous territory she knew she was heading into, she added, "Partly?"

He looked distinctly uncomfortable.

"What else were you afraid I'd do?"

"Casey..."

"Were you afraid I'd fall in love with you?"

He winced. "I'd never presume that much."

No, she thought, he wouldn't. No matter what signals

she'd sent him. And she had, she knew that. She also knew he hadn't missed those signals. But whatever reaction he'd had, it couldn't have been any more intense than her own shock and surprise at her response to him.

"Besides, you knew you weren't staying," she said softly.

He drew himself up as if she'd delivered a blow. And when he spoke, he sounded as if he were waiting for another one. "Yes. I knew I wasn't staying. Don't ask me for promises I can't keep, Casey."

"I never asked for any promises at all."

For a long moment Casey looked at him, wondering if she had the nerve to take this plunge. Now that she knew why he'd left, that he'd had some idea about protecting her from her own foolishness—and foolish it would indeed be to fall in love with a man who wouldn't stay—she was left with the one fact she couldn't ignore.

"I don't expect any promises, either," she said slowly. And then, taking a deep breath, she made herself say it. "But you're the first man who's made me want to feel like a woman again."

He seemed to shiver. "God, Casey, don't say that."

"Why? I didn't think that would ever happen. I thought I'd be frozen forever after what Jon did to me."

"Sometimes it's better that way, to be frozen," he said, his voice harsh.

It hit her then, what she realized she should have seen long ago. "You, too," she breathed. "That's why else you left, isn't it?"

He turned away from her, sharply, abruptly. He took two steps, and then he stopped. For a long moment he just stood there, and she could almost feel the tension radiating from him. Then he spun back to glare at her.

"Yes, damn it." It came out as a hiss. "You welcomed the thaw, and I...ran from it. I'll always run, Casey. Sooner or later. You'd better remember that."

How had she missed it before? she wondered. How had she not seen that the coldness she'd felt was aimed inward, that it was himself he was furious with, that it was himself who was the target of the aversion in his own voice?

"I'm not asking for forever, Clay," she said.

"What *are* you asking for?" His voice sounded hard, cold, but Casey could see his eyes and knew it was only a sign of the battle going on within him. "Sex? Is that all you want?"

She winced at the coldness of it, even though she knew he'd done it intentionally.

"Because that's all you'd be getting," he continued warningly. He was pacing now, as if he had to have some physical outlet for the turmoil inside him. "You'd just be getting a body, because there's no heart left to give."

She didn't believe him. Oh, she knew he believed it, knew he'd meant every word of his warning. But he didn't seem to realize that the very earnestness with which he warned her proved him wrong.

"You're wrong, Clay," she said softly. "If you didn't have a heart, you wouldn't care about my feelings, wouldn't care if I got hurt. You'd figure it was my own fault if I got in over my head."

He stopped his pacing and looked at her. She could see his breathing quicken and his jaw set, the outward signs of that inner tumult. "Maybe I just don't want any more guilt to carry, all right?"

And again he unwittingly proved she was right. "If anything," she said, meeting his glare levelly, "you have too much heart. No one could hurt so much without it."

He made a low sound deep in his throat, a sound of protest, of pain. "God, Casey, stop trying to defend me. Stop trying to make me something besides what I am."

"Just what is it you think you are?"

He turned on her then, staring at her with an intensity that would have rattled her if she hadn't been so certain that was exactly what he wanted. She made herself go on, guessing, trying to read between the lines of what he was saying.

"Or is it what you think you *aren't* that's dogging you?"

He looked away, dodging her gaze so abruptly that she knew she'd struck deep.

"What is it, Clay?"

He turned again. Started moving again. Quickly, like a man escaping. He was at the rear door to the screen porch in two long strides.

"Whatever you're trying to run from, it won't work," she said, stopping him in the doorway. "You can't outrun a memory, Clay. Believe me. I've tried."

He moved again. Stepped out into the screen porch. Reached for the outer door. And stopped.

Casey watched him, barely aware of holding her breath. Somehow, based on some deep, gut-level instinct she didn't understand but couldn't question, she knew that this moment was crucial. Not just to their relationship, whatever that was, but to something even more important. She knew that what he did now could set the pattern for the rest of his life. That if Clay ran now, he might never stop.

And whatever he was running from, she thought, it couldn't be bad enough for that. Even she had managed to find some semblance of peace; surely there had to be some for him, too.

She hardly dared breathe as, for what seemed like an eternity, he stood there, as if teetering on the edge of a precipice. Which, perhaps, he was, Casey thought. There was a tightness in her chest that she recognized, although it had been a while since she'd felt it. In fact, not since those days of the trial, when she'd spent so many long, dark hours wondering if Jon was going to get away with it, if there truly was no justice in the world.

But Clay looked as if there were not only no justice, but no mercy. He looked like a man who had given up on both long ago. A man who didn't believe in anything. Most especially not in himself.

And finally, as if bending under the pressure, he sank down to the porch bench. Elbows on his knees, he buried his face in his hands. Casey heard him take a gulping breath, and then another.

She took a deep breath of her own to steady herself, then quickly stepped out onto the porch. He didn't look up, even as she sat beside him. Slowly, tentatively, she reached out and touched him, laying her hand gently on his shoulder. She felt a tremor go through him, felt the heat coming off him, as if the conflict within were creating a literal friction.

"Remember what you told me?" she asked softly. When he didn't answer, she went on, pressing harder against his shoulder, wanting to do more, wanting to somehow take away his pain. "You have to let it out, or it will eat you alive."

"Better that than for it to come out. You don't want to hear it, Casey. Believe me, you don't want to hear it."

"I'm sure you didn't want to hear my story, either. But you listened. You listened and comforted me in a way no one's ever been able to. Let me give back that support, Clay."

His head came up then, but he didn't look at her. "That's different."

"Why?"

"You were the victim. And you were still strong enough to do what had to be done."

"So...what? I deserve absolution and you don't?"

He turned to face her then, and she almost wished he hadn't.

"Exactly."

His voice was cold, flat. Unforgiving. She studied him for a long, silent moment, trying to read in the taut planes of his face the reason for his own harsh judgment. She found no clue there, nothing that told her what he was unable to forgive himself for, what made him so implacable in his self-hatred.

"What is it, Clay?" she asked softly. "What did you do that makes you so hard on yourself?"

He looked away again, muttering something barely audible to her. "Didn't do."

"What?"

"What I didn't do."

Didn't do? she wondered. What was it he hadn't done that could leave him so deeply guilty that he couldn't forgive himself? She tried to think of possibilities, but the only ones that came to her were from her own experience: she wished she had stayed here in River Bend; wished she had come home to see Aunt Fay more often, especially after Uncle Ray had died.

But that didn't seem enough, not to cause the kind of guilt Clay was feeling. It didn't seem enough that he might have made some wrong choice, or decided not to do something that he now wished he had. It had to be something worse, something specific, she thought. Had he left the scene of an accident? Had he not tried to stop something he could have? Not stopped to help someone when he could have?

She had no idea and knew she wasn't going to find out this way. Perhaps she should try his favored tactic and hit him with something unexpected; maybe it would come out then. She didn't stop to analyze why she was so determined to get it out of him; she only knew that if he could feel half as relieved as she did, it would be worth it.

His words as he'd left her that night came back to her, and she found her question in them.

"Who did you let down, Clay?" she asked softly, gently.

A sound broke from him then, strained and harsh. It was a painful sound, the sound of a man pushed beyond recovery.

"Why can't you forgive yourself?" she asked. "I'm sure they've forgiven you, whoever it is."

He laughed. He laughed, and it was an awful sound, as cold and desolate as the Iowa plains under six feet of snow. His eyes were wide and unfocused, his expression agonized in the fading light. She didn't know what he was seeing, what memory was playing out before his blank eyes, but she didn't have to to know it was horrible. And she wondered if she could bear to hear the truth, if she could stand to know what had made a strong man look so broken.

"She was so little," he said. "So helpless and so little."

He stopped, and suddenly Casey wanted to run. She didn't want to hear this. She'd been a fool to push; she had no right.

"I loved her so much. More than my life," Clay said, and she felt a tremor go through him.

Instinctively she put her arms around him as if it were cold that made him shiver. And she quashed the urge to run. She'd begun this; she had no right to back out, now that she'd pushed him to the brink, just because she was suddenly afraid she was going to hate what she heard.

"I would have died for her," he whispered. "But I killed her instead." He shuddered then, violently.

"Clay, no..."

Her shocked protest seemed to make him angry. He turned on her, pulling free of her arms. "I did," he insisted. "I closed my eyes to what was happening, pretended not to see all the signs. Me, of all people, who should have known, should have seen, should have recognized how close to the edge she was."

Casey's brow furrowed; something in his tone made her think this was a very different "she." "How close *who* was, Clay?"

She felt the tension flood out of him, saw his normally straight body slump, as if all his resistance had drained away.

"My wife," he said dully.

Casey's eyes widened, but she managed not to let the words that leaped to her lips escape. She held her breath, and after a moment, in that same flat, dull voice, Clay went on.

"I was a cop. In Marina Heights."

A cop? He'd been a cop? She tried to get her mind around it. It fit, she thought, as image after image came to her. The way he'd calmed her. No wonder Clay had known just what to say, what to do that night when she'd told him her horrible story. The scars, especially the one that looked like a bullet wound.

"But then...why did you let them arrest you for that silly thing the other night? The deputy said it was bogus. Surely all you had to do was tell them who you were?"

"I didn't want anyone to know. Didn't want them calling Trinity West, my old station."

"Why?"

"I don't have any right to claim that badge anymore. And they don't want to hear from me."

"What happened, Clay? What made you...cut your ties so completely? Was it when you were shot? Did you stop wanting to be a cop?"

His mouth twisted into a grimace. "I loved it. Too much. I became a cop who got totally wrapped up in the job, who spent all his energy on the scum of the planet, until there was only a little left to give his family."

He had shifted to the third person, she realized, as if that were as close as he could bear to get to what he was saying. As if he'd realized it himself, he went on in the first person in a tone of utter condemnation.

"I knew Linda—my wife—was...troubled. She was up and down all the time. Moody. But I thought it was just the tension of being a cop's wife. It's not an easy thing, the worry, the crazy hours...."

"It must be awful sometimes," Casey said softly, afraid

of breaking the flow of words. "Never knowing, each time they leave, if they'll come back again."

"I thought that was what it was. I didn't understand it was something more. Something worse." He took a deep, shaky breath. "She got…painful to be around. And she didn't seem to want to be with us."

Casey's breath caught. *Us?*

He caught the sudden sharpening of her attention, the holding of her breath.

"My little girl." His voice was an aching, raw thing. "Jennifer. Jenny. The sweetest, smartest, prettiest…"

He broke off. Casey's throat was tight, her eyes stinging; she knew she didn't want to hear the rest, but she could hardly stop him now.

"It hurt. Linda withdrew, and I couldn't reach her. But worse, neither could Jenny." He shivered anew as he said the name, and Casey wondered how long it had been since he'd spoken it. "I kept trying to confront her but she'd insist everything was all right, get angry at me. But it got worse, she got moodier. She never went out, she slept all the time. Eventually it was like she was just sort of there, in the background, in our lives, but not part of them."

"What about Jenny?"

"Linda barely managed to take care of her. I tried to make it up to Jenny, to be mom and dad, but she was only four, and she needed more time than I had. So did Linda. But my job took so much, and I was in the middle of several big cases—" He cut himself off abruptly. "No excuses. There are no damn excuses."

"Clay—"

"I should have known. Damn it, I was a cop, I was trained, I should have known!"

For a long moment he sat there, staring down at his hands, as if their strength had somehow betrayed him. Casey knew the worst was yet to come. Knew she didn't want to hear it, wanted nothing more than to tell him to stop, to keep his demons safely locked up, that she could barely deal with her own.

But he'd dealt with hers. Even carrying this, whatever it was that was bearing down on her like an oncoming jet, he'd helped her deal with hers. She owed it to him to return the favor.

"What happened, Clay?"

"It was a Saturday night. I'd been working late on a stakeout all week. Undercover, plainclothes. Got off it early that night. So I could see Jenny before she went to bed. Stopped to pick up a stuffed toy she'd been wanting. Proceeded home."

He was talking so oddly that it took Casey a moment to realize that he was speaking in the cold, detached phrases of a police report, as if that were the only way he could stand to talk about it.

"It was sunny. Bright. Summer. I was going to take time off. Take Jenny to the beach. Try to get Linda back to normal. Not this...shadow of herself. Thinking about that when I hit the driveway. Hit the garage-door opener. Light should have come on, but don't remember it. It was dark inside."

He was breathing quickly now, not looking at her, not looking at anything. Except perhaps whatever awful images accompanied the memories he was describing. She glanced at his hands; the right was clenched into a fist, the left wrapped around it so tightly his knuckles were white.

"They were there. Garage floor. Linda on the left. Still. Very still. Dead still. Two-foot pool of blood under them. Growing. Spreading." The knuckles got whiter. His face was nearly as pale. "My gun. My service revolver. In her hand."

"Oh, God, no," Casey whispered.

"Both of them. She'd killed both of them. Jenny first.

Then herself. There. In the garage. Where I'd see them first thing. Because I'd failed them. Both of them.''

For the first time, Casey understood the deadness in Clay Yeager's eyes.

Chapter 12

Casey didn't even try to stop the tears. They streamed down her cheeks as the horror of Clay's story formed a too vivid picture in her mind. Even imagining it was too awful; she couldn't comprehend what it must be like to live with a reality like that every day of your life. Her own horror story seemed almost sanitary by comparison.

She wanted to comfort him, but what could she possibly say? There were no words for something like this, nothing that could ease that kind of pain.

Or, she realized slowly, that kind of guilt. Because she couldn't doubt that that was what he was feeling. It was pouring out of him, almost palpable.

"Jenny was the best thing I'd ever done," Clay said, his words more natural now, but his voice still dead and flat. "She was the one bright spot in an ugly world I had to work in every day, the one thing that was still good about my personal life. She was what kept me going, the reason I didn't quit, because I wanted to make the world a little safer for her. But instead I—"

"Clay, stop it. It wasn't your fault."

He shook his head, slowly, like a mortally wounded animal. "It was. I should have known. I *did* know. But I kept hoping it would go away, that it would get better."

"She pulled the trigger, Clay. Not you. She made the choice. Not you."

His head came up sharply. "Did she? Did she make the choice? Or did I make it for her, by being too blind, too busy, too damn obsessed by my job, to give her what she needed?"

"You said you tried to talk to her—"

"I should have done more. Made her get help."

"I don't think it works that way. You can't make someone get help, they have to want it. Or at least not object."

"I could at least have gotten her in a hospital for observation, something."

"Would she have gone?"

He let out a long breath. "Willingly? No. We fought over it. I wanted her to go to a counselor, but she insisted she was fine, and that she didn't want to talk to some stranger."

"Are you saying you think you should have forced her? Handcuffed her and dragged her?"

"If I had," he said flatly, "maybe my daughter would still be alive."

Casey didn't know what to say to that. In fact, she didn't know what to say to him at all. What she'd been through had been awful, but she was alive, able to fight the memories, able to go on, and getting better at it every day. But there was nothing that could change the finality of what had happened to Clay. He couldn't fight death, couldn't run away from it, no matter how he tried.

And he'd apparently tried rather hard.

"What did you do? After, I mean."

"I left. The day of their funeral, I turned in my badge, packed up my truck and hit the road."

"With Mud."

"Yes." His mouth twisted. "He was Jenny's. I almost had him put down, because it hurt so much to just look at him, to remember how she played with him. To remember how she named him when I brought him home and the first thing he did was plop in a mud puddle."

Casey smiled, but her heart wasn't in it; it couldn't be, not when he looked so devastated.

"I told my dad to sell the house and everything in it, do whatever he wanted with the money."

"When...did it happen?"

He took a long breath and expelled it before telling her, "Five years ago."

It seemed like forever. Sounded like a long time. But when dealing with death, especially the death of a child, it was no doubt yesterday.

"You've never been back? To see your friends, or even to see your father?"

He shook his head. "I couldn't stand their sympathy. Not when I knew I...didn't deserve it. I was still alive. It was Jenny they should have been sorry for, not me. She never had a chance."

"So your father has not only lost a grandchild, he's lost his son, as well." Clay winced visibly, and Casey chose her next words carefully. "Maybe some of the blame is yours, Clay. But you can never know completely what's going on in somebody else's mind. You couldn't have known how close Linda was when she kept insisting she was all right."

"I should have known."

"How? Are you omniscient?"

"I should have stopped her. Somehow."

"How? How could you have stopped her? Stayed with her twenty-four hours a day?"

He gave a weary sigh, as if he'd been through this countless times. She was sure he had been.

"I don't know. Somehow. I already kept the guns locked up, always had, since Jenny was born. I had even locked up my service weapon, because I was only carrying the smaller one I used undercover. It never... I didn't even realize Linda knew the combination to the gun safe. She never went near it."

"Then you couldn't have known she would."

"I should have thought about it." He shook his head. "But even if I had, I'd have worried more about pills. I was a cop, I knew women didn't usually shoot. I never would have thought she'd use a gun. She didn't like them."

Casey couldn't help wondering if Linda's choice of method hadn't been another way of striking back at the husband she wanted to hurt. For she didn't doubt that that was what it had all been about. Doing it in the garage, where Clay would be sure to find them the moment he arrived, and with his own weapon, was too calculated for her to think it was coincidental.

"You know," she said quietly, "it probably wouldn't have mattered if you'd taken the guns away, or the car, or every kitchen knife. She'd have found a building to jump off, or a truck to step in front of."

Clay rubbed at his face, his eyes. "Maybe. In her way, Linda was a determined woman."

"You didn't put the gun in her hand, and you didn't pull that trigger, Clay."

"And that makes it all right?" he asked, sarcasm biting deep.

"No," she said. "Maybe some of the blame *is* yours. Maybe you did neglect her for your work, maybe she felt she didn't matter enough to you to change."

"But she never asked!" The words burst from him in a cry of pain and anguish. "She never said a word about feeling that way."

"That's why you don't get to have all the blame to yourself, Clay. She was a grown-up, an adult woman. She should have talked to you, should have been able to express what she needed. Sulking and waiting for someone else to read your mind about what you want is childish.''

He gave her an odd look. ''She…used to say that. That I shouldn't have to ask what was wrong, I should know.''

''Prince Charming Syndrome.''

He blinked. ''What?''

''That's what Aunt Fay used to call it. Women who were convinced there was nothing wrong with their lives that the right man couldn't fix. So rather than get out there and fix it themselves, they wait for the prince to come along and do it for them. The prince who would naturally know just what to do without them having to say a word.''

His eyes went unfocused for a moment, as if he were again looking back over the years to that long-ago time. ''I felt that way, sometimes. Like I was supposed to fix everything, but I didn't know what was broken, or what she wanted it to be like in the first place.''

''It's impossible to make someone like that happy. Either they adjust their expectations, or you continue to fail them, in their eyes. And when you love them, you end up failing in your own eyes, too.''

''I did love her,'' he whispered. ''But God, why Jenny? Why did she have to take Jenny? Could she have hated me that much, and I didn't know?''

''I didn't know Linda, so I can't guess. Maybe it was to hurt you, or maybe she was so confused by then, so caught up in her own despair that she thought she was saving Jenny from what had overtaken her.''

''They told me that. That she probably thought she was saving Jenny. I asked them from what, and they gave me some psychology doublespeak that translated to they had no idea.''

Casey studied him for a long moment. Then, thinking first that perhaps she was risking truly angering him, then realizing that if she was going to, better now than when she got any more involved with him, she said what she'd been wondering since he'd told her the gruesome tale.

"So how long do you pay?"

His head came around suddenly. His gaze was sharp, intent. It was also unsettling. "What do you mean by that?"

She shrugged, trying to make it less of a loaded question. "I just wondered how long you'd sentenced yourself to. Life?"

His jaw tightened, and she knew she'd struck home.

"You're a tough judge, Clay Yeager. No court would sentence you to that. In fact, most people wouldn't sentence you at all. If we went to jail for the things we didn't do that we think we should have, we'd all have done time."

"Most people don't have people die because of what they didn't do."

His voice was as hard as it had ever been. And she couldn't argue with his bottom-line logic. So she tried another tack.

"Were you a good cop?"

His brows furrowed. "That doesn't—"

"Were you?"

He lifted one shoulder in a half shrug. "So they say."

"Save any lives?"

"You think that evens it out?" His gaze narrowed again.

He was angry now, but Casey was glad to see it. Anything was better than that ghastly dead look.

"No. It was just a simple question. Did you?"

There was a pause, and she wondered if he was considering not answering at all. Then, finally, with a grimace, he said, "A few."

"So do you figure you should be rewarded for that?"

"No. I was just doing my job."

"So if you shouldn't be rewarded for what you did, why should you be punished for what you didn't do?"

He looked at her for a long moment. "That's some very convoluted logic, Ms. Scott."

"It makes as much sense as what you're doing to yourself. Even if you'd pulled the trigger yourself, you'd likely get out on parole eventually."

"That," he said sourly, "is the fault of our justice system."

"So no parole for you, ever, is that it?"

"My little girl is dead. That's about as permanent as it gets."

"And you can't bring her back. You can wear this hair shirt for the rest of your natural life, and it won't change. She'll still be gone."

"Do you think I don't know that?" A note of barely restrained desperation had crept into his voice.

"I'm sure you do know it. So the question is…do you really think Jenny would want it this way? Would she want you to torture yourself forever over something you couldn't control?"

"But I should have *done* something! Everybody always talked about how good I was at my job, at reading people, at talking to people, getting people to talk, negotiating hostage situations—but I couldn't see that my own wife was so far gone that she would kill herself." The desperation broke through then. "And that she'd take our baby with her."

"God, Clay," Casey said, abandoning any effort to make him see reason, "I'm so sorry."

Instinctively she reached for him, knowing she couldn't ease the pain but unable not to try. To her surprise, he let her hold him. She thought perhaps he was just too distraught to realize what she was doing, what he was allowing. But then he sagged against her, shuddering, and the why didn't seem to matter any longer. The only thing that mattered was that he wasn't fighting, when she sensed he'd been fighting every day of the last five years.

"You said rape was the only crime where the victim was put on trial. But didn't you do that to yourself? Put yourself on trial and find yourself guilty? And you were as much a victim as I was, Clay. Somebody destroyed your life, too."

As she held him, as she felt the shudders of emotion rack him, heard the gulping gasps for breath, she wondered if he'd ever let himself cry for his loss, or if he'd simply plunged straight into the morass of guilt he was mired in now. And she wondered at the strength of her own desire to relieve him of that pain, to pull him out of that destructive mire and back into living.

And she wondered why she hadn't realized the truth until now, the truth of why his bolting suddenly had hurt so badly. Before, the comings and goings of others in her life had meant little; she'd never let anyone get close enough to matter. No one had ever seemed worth the effort it took to get past the instinctive barriers she put up.

But Clay seemed to have done it without trying at all. Because she cared. She cared a great deal. It had happened, and she hadn't even known it until he'd left and she'd felt the unexpected hurt.

She waited for the fear to strike, the fear she'd come to expect at the very thought of getting close to a man. But it didn't come. It took her a moment to realize why, that her fears were nothing compared to the pain Clay endured every day.

The wonder of it made her a little shaky. Clay had fallen into her life so suddenly, and she knew deep down he was apt to leave just as suddenly. And she knew as well that putting her heart on the line for a man so wounded could wind up leaving her badly hurt yet again.

Yet she didn't seem to have a choice anymore. His pain had lowered her guard, and before she'd realized it, she'd let him in. And now she didn't know what to do about it. Didn't know what he would let her do. Didn't know what she wanted to do.

So she did the only thing she could think of. She held on.

If he'd harbored any hopes that his story would scare her off, Clay soon realized he'd underestimated her.

He'd also, he thought, underestimated his need for her. She probably saw him now as some kind of wounded animal in need of tending. But her tender touch weakened his resolve, made him want to cradle himself in her arms forever. And he didn't even have the strength to be scared at the thought. Even when he realized that he was, for the first time since the door had risen on that horrific scene, crying. It seemed almost natural to be doing it in Casey's arms. She understood, somehow, whether through her own terrible experience, her gentle nature or some combination of both. She understood loss, the kind of loss that was permanent and never fixable. She understood, and it felt so damn good to just let go....

You were as much a victim as I was, Clay. Somebody destroyed your life, too.

He'd never thought of it that way. He'd thought first and foremost of Jenny as a victim, and even Linda, but never himself. In his mind he'd always been the one who failed, the one who'd been blind to what was right before him and had let it all happen.

Survivor's guilt, the shrink had said. It had become his identity, more than the uniform had been, more than the badge had been, more than all the commendations and medals had ever been. It had driven him for years, aimlessly, rootlessly, until he was sure of only one thing: he could never go back. Could never go back to what was left of his family, or to the friends who had once been like family to him.

To all the people who had thought him a hero but who he'd let down.

Casey tightened her arms around him, holding him as if

she wished she could absorb the pain. It was an incredible feeling to Clay, especially knowing the extent of her own nightmarish memories. How could she still give like this, after what she'd been through?

He felt her touch on his hair but didn't realize for a moment that she'd kissed him. He held his breath, waiting, and it came again, this time just above his ear.

God, it felt so good, so warm, so utterly tempting. Did he dare? Could he, just this once, accept her tending, as if he were that wounded animal? He felt wounded, all right. Odd how he'd never felt the lack in his life, the aloneness, never felt much of anything before he'd stumbled onto Casey's farm and into her life. He'd been gliding along, content, if not happy, in his numbness.

But Casey made it impossible to stay numb. Even when he'd tried to run, he hadn't been able to leave her behind. She'd been with him every mile of the way, every hour he'd spent locked in that little room at the sheriff's office. Not even the irony of being on the wrong side of that locked door had managed to put her out of his mind.

He'd fought it with as much determination as he could muster. But some part of him must have known he was going to lose, the part that had made him run at the first sign things were spiraling out of control.

He had that feeling now, much more intensely. But he wasn't going to run. He wasn't sure when he'd made that decision, wasn't even sure he had; he only knew that when he thought of pulling away from her, he felt a pain that made moving simply impossible.

He also wasn't aware of when the moment had changed, only that it had, that soothing comfort had become something hotter, more urgent. Her gentle kisses moved from his hair to his temple, and the feel of her soft lips on his skin sent a burst of heat through him that was startling in its intensity.

Lord, she'd barely touched him and he was on fire, he thought. If she kept going…

She did. Slowly, tentatively, she traced his jaw with a line of tiny, nibbling kisses. He fought down the surging response that was making it hard to breathe. His head lolled back, and when Casey continued that hot, fiery trail of kisses down his neck, he wondered vaguely if he'd hoped she would.

His thoughts were caroming around wildly; he hadn't felt anything like this in years, if he ever had at all. He'd forgotten the power of it, and most of all, he'd forgotten how to deal with it. At first he was afraid she was being motivated by sympathy as much as anything, after hearing his grim tale. But then he remembered her own ugly story and knew it would take much more than sympathy to make Casey risk what she appeared to be risking.

And it was that realization that made him afraid to move, afraid to do anything. He could only begin to imagine what it must be like for her, to make this kind of sexual overture with the memory of what had happened to her lurking.

And it struck him suddenly, as he was thinking that he should—that he *had* to—call a halt to this, what it might do to her if he did. When he'd run, she'd thought that it might have been in response to what she'd told him. He knew there were men like that, had dealt with them, men who could not deal with, who were repulsed by, the thought of a woman who'd been raped. That she'd even for a while thought he might be one of those had hurt. Had hurt when he'd thought nothing could hurt him again, when he'd figured he was beyond pain because he was beyond caring.

If he'd been thinking clearly, that would have been a clue. But it had been so long—forever, it seemed—since he'd had to deal with such feelings.

Just like it had been forever since he'd experienced anything like what Casey's soft, sweet kisses were doing to him now.

"God, Casey," he breathed, "that feels so damn good."

For an instant she stopped, and he wondered if he'd ruined it, if she would withdraw now, if perhaps she hadn't really been thinking about what she'd been doing until he'd spoken. And he knew that if she wanted to stop, he had to give her that chance, no matter how much his body cringed at the idea.

But then she went on, gently brushing her lips over the hollow of his throat, then tasting his skin with the tip of her tongue. Fire blazed anew along nerves long dormant, and he nearly gasped at the shock of it.

He wanted desperately to grab her, hold her, kiss her senseless, give her back some of what she was giving him. But at the same time he knew he had to hold back; he had to let her take the lead. If there was nothing else he'd learned in his years in uniform, it was the fragility of women who had been sexually assaulted when it came to venturing back into intimacy. And suddenly the fact that he wasn't sure he wanted to risk this himself didn't matter.

Not, he thought wryly, that it made a bit of difference; he doubted he could have stopped even if he'd been able to convince himself he really should. Not when her mouth was on him, not when he could feel her warmth, could sense her eagerness despite her hesitancy.

She pressed her lips to the skin in the open collar of his shirt, and an involuntary shiver rippled through him. His hands shot up to her shoulders, and he hung on to her as he slid down to lie on the bench, pulling her with him.

He had a split second to savor the soft weight of her before it registered that Casey had gone very still. He realized abruptly that he was dwelling on the shock of what he was feeling and not concentrating on keeping himself in check. He had to be able to stop if she changed her mind. He only hoped he could; five years was a long stretch of doing without.

He had to, he told himself again. And he thought of the

courage with which she'd faced an ordeal that had defeated many, the courage with which she'd gone on, rebuilding her life, the courage she was showing right now.

He had to let her know that, this time, "no" would be enough.

"You're in charge, Casey," he whispered. "We go as far as you want, no further."

It took a tremendous effort, but he didn't move, despite the fierce ache the feel of her atop him roused. And he bit back the groan that rippled up from his chest when she rose up to look at him, the movement pressing her hips hard against his, capturing flesh already rigid with need between them in a sweet, soft vise.

But when he saw the look in her eyes, when he saw the glow of thanks, of need and of joy, he knew he would stay in control of himself no matter what it cost him.

"I know," she said softly. "Or I wouldn't be here."

"Are you sure…this is what you want?"

"What I'm sure of is that for the first time in so very long, I…want. Like I never thought I would again."

Her quiet, heartfelt words sent a shudder through him. He wondered how long it had really been since he'd felt wanted, for it to hit him so hard. Long before Linda had reached the breaking point, there had been little joy between them. He'd written it off as resentment over the long hours and all-consuming nature of his work; many cops had to deal with spouses who couldn't really understand. He would deal with it, too, as soon as he had time, he'd thought.

But he and Linda…and Jenny…had run out of time.

Casey lowered her head, this time pressing her lips to his in a kiss that was both shy and incendiary.

What I'm sure of is that for the first time in so very long, I…want. Like I never thought I would again.

As her words echoed in his mind, he knew that she had

spoken for him, as well. And that for the first time in that very long time, nothing else mattered except this growing, burgeoning want, this need that was overwhelming even bitter memory.

Chapter 13

Casey knew in the moment when he swept her up in his arms that it was too late to change her mind, even if she'd wanted to. But she didn't want to, and that alone thrilled her beyond measure.

How lucky could she be, she thought, that the first man she'd craved intimacy with since that ugly day was a man who understood so well what she needed, what she had to have to feel safe—the knowledge that she *could* say no and he would listen?

And that he fired her blood as no man ever had didn't hurt, either, she thought with a blush.

"First door," she whispered against his chest as he started down the hall, forgetting for a moment that he'd been there, the night she'd almost permanently damaged him. He didn't point out her error to her.

"Good," was all he said, bluntly, as if going any farther would mean too long to wait.

She felt it, too, that humming need, heating every inch of her body, making her ache somewhere deep and low, filling her with the certainty that this man, only this man, could ease that ache.

She wondered, in some part of her mind that could still think logically, if she would panic at some point, if she would pull back or, worse, react instinctively as she had the last time he'd kissed her. But he moved with such care, kissing her so thoroughly that her head was spinning before he ever touched her anywhere else. And caressing her breasts so gently, so lovingly, that her knees were weak before he tugged her shirt over her head.

By the time he unsnapped her jeans, she wanted nothing more than to be naked with him and to see him naked, and she found herself pulling at his clothes with much more ferocity than he was using. He let her push his shirt off his shoulders but refused to hurry the pace.

"We've got all night," he whispered, cupping and lifting her breasts once more, rubbing his thumbs over nipples already taut and aching for more.

She cried out at the hot pleasure of it and wiggled out of her bra herself. She leaned into him, thinking she'd never felt anything more glorious than the hot, solid wall of his bare chest against her naked breasts. She heard him suck in a swift breath, and his arms came around to her back, pressing her even harder against him.

She put her arms around him in turn. Her fingers touched the round scar on his side, and she felt him go still. She kept her hands moving, brushing over the thin lines on his back as she spread her fingers over his skin. She felt the unnaturally smooth hardness of the burn scar beneath the tips of her middle fingers, and he seemed to be holding his breath.

"Your scars are beautiful," she said, turning her head and pressing her lips to the center of his chest.

He let out the held breath in a long sigh that seemed to catch in the middle. She trailed her mouth sideways over heated skin and kissed him again, then again, and at last, feeling a bit reckless, she shifted slightly and pressed a kiss to one flat male nipple.

Clay let out a broken groan, so thick with pleasure that she couldn't stop herself from flicking the tiny nub with her tongue. He groaned again, whispering her name with a needy sound that made her own pulse leap.

As if by some tacitly agreed-upon signal, they shed their remaining clothes in a hurry. Any thought of panic vanished; all Casey could think of was that he was beautiful. His lean, rangy and thoroughly aroused body seemed the perfect male form to her, and the scars only made him more precious. Someday she would learn the story behind those marks, would learn what ugly part of his life as a cop had caused them, but now all she could do was look at him and be glad he was here and, for the moment, hers.

"You're sure?" he rasped out, giving her yet another chance to change her mind.

In answer, and more than a little surprised at her own boldness, she slipped her hand down between them and curled her fingers around hot, erect flesh. He jerked sharply and let out a harsh sound, his eyes closing as he clenched his jaw.

"Casey…" It came out as a hiss, between gritted teeth. "What about—" She moved her hand lower, and his words were choked off. She could sense him fighting to go on coherently. "You…I can't promise…to stop in time."

It took her a moment, as she dreamily caressed him, to realize what he was getting at. "It's all right," she said. "Wrong time of the month."

"Not…safest method," he panted.

"But better than none," she said, leaning forward to flick her tongue over his other nipple. "And certainly better than stopping."

He growled something low and unintelligible, and the next thing she knew she was down flat on the bed, Clay on top of her, enfolding her. For an instant the old fear flickered, tried to catch. As if sensing it, he rolled quickly to one side, pulling her with him, then over him. His hands slid down to her hips, but gently, as if he were only doing it to balance her, not hold her there.

"Whatever you want," he said roughly, "however you want, at the pace you want. No more. No faster. And *no* is still the magic word."

He was, she realized, giving her control. Utter and complete control. And in that moment she had no doubt at all that if she said no at the last possible second, he would stop. Despite the rigid hardness she could feel pressed between them, he would stop.

And the silent cry of her body at the mere idea of him stopping told her worlds about how far she'd come, how much healing had happened while she'd only thought of getting through each day. And told her how much she wanted this man. She felt a rising urge to straddle him swiftly, to take him inside her to fill this hollow ache as fast as she could. A tiny moan escaped her at the thought of him filling her.

He shifted beneath her, as if the sound had made it impossible for him to stay still. Her legs parted, slipping down on either side of his narrow hips. The movement brought that most intimate part of her tight against him, and with a little shock she felt her own heat, her own wetness; there was no doubt her body was ready.

And she'd never once thought of Jon herself. If it hadn't been for Clay being so careful, making it so clear that she was in control, she doubted it would have occurred to her at all. They'd told her it would take time, but that eventually she would be able to disassociate the act done in love from the act done in violence, but she'd had her doubts. So it was with pure joy that she let herself savor her own response and the wonder of it. That response was fired to an even higher pitch by the look of intensity, of urgency, on Clay's face. It was in direct contrast to the taut stillness of his body.

She realized then that his hands had left her hips and were knotted in the coverlet beneath him. She felt a little thrill of feminine power that he was having to fight so hard...and a flash of pure gratitude that he was able to.

She reached out and touched him, running her hand from the sprinkling of dark hair at the center of his chest down to the narrow path over his belly. She stopped below his navel, just before the band of hair broadened again, and felt another thrill at the ripple of clenching muscles she felt beneath her fingers and the low sound he made.

"Casey," he groaned, "it's been too long. Don't put so much faith in my willpower."

"All right," she said, her voice so husky it surprised her. "If you stop being so careful."

He went very still, his eyes searching her face.

"It's all right," she promised. "*I'm* all right."

It was, it seemed, all he needed to hear. And he took her at her word. He sat up, lifting his knees at the same time to cradle her in the curve of his body. His hands went to her waist, then slid up over her ribs to cup her breasts. Casey leaned forward, pressing herself into his hands, wanting, needing, more. And then Clay lowered his head, capturing one nipple and drawing it into his mouth.

She cried out at the burst of hot, fiery sensation. He repeated the action with her other breast, at the same time slipping a finger between them, probing, until he found the small knot of nerves that made her gasp. He began a slow circular caress. Her back arched involuntarily, and this time she cried out his name.

"Please, Clay," she moaned. "Now."

"I thought you'd never ask."

His voice was tight, harsh. And as he reached for her waist, his hands trembled slightly. He lifted her, and she helped him, drawing her knees up under her. She felt the touch of blunt male flesh, probing, and instinctively reached down to guide him.

He groaned at the first moment of entry, and Casey held her breath at the slow, sweet invasion. He stretched her exquisitely, reawakening flesh that had not forgotten its true function, to be joined in pleasure, not pain; in gentleness, not violence; in desire, not hatred.

At first she settled down on him inch by inch with languid pleasure. But after a moment it wasn't enough. She needed more; she wanted all of him, and she enveloped him in one sharp, breath-stealing movement that made them both gasp.

Clay fell back on the bed, his hips lifting slightly, driving himself in to the hilt. Casey opened to him even more, wanting to feel him so deep inside her that she would never be the same. She wanted every trace of the ugliness erased, and she knew Clay could do it.

And suddenly she didn't want to be in control. Didn't *need* to be in control. She knew this was different, that this was what it was supposed to be, and most of all that Clay wouldn't hurt her.

She was beyond words, but she stretched out on top of him, then slipped to one side and tried as best she could to show him what she wanted even as she lamented the loss of the intimate contact.

Clay lifted his head to look at her, his eyes betraying uncertainty over what signal she was sending. "Casey?"

"Please."

It was begging, pleading, and she didn't care. She only knew she needed him to take the lead now, that it was the only way to vanquish the last of her nightmare memories.

He moved then, rolling onto his side, sliding one leg over her. Then he stopped, as if waiting for some sign of panic from her. Instead, she slid her hands down his back, grasping his hips and urging him over her, parting her legs for him. He responded to her silent request quickly, slipping between her thighs and thrusting back into her swift and hard, as if he'd felt the same loss she had.

"Yes," she whispered fervently, complete again.

Her hands moved again, downward, until she could cup the taut curves of his buttocks, urging him even deeper. With a low growl he began to move then, fast, driving, pumping, until Casey amazed herself once more by arching up to meet him, wanting it harder, faster, and feeling as if her body would turn itself inside out if she didn't get it.

She heard him groan, saw him bite his lip until she was surprised it didn't bleed. He probed between them with one hand again, found that hotly aroused spot and caressed it anew as he continued to stroke her clasping flesh with his body.

Casey heard a low, continuous moan and barely recognized it as her own. Clay uttered a panting guttural sound at the depth of each stroke. She looked up at him, saw his face drawn tight with need and urgency, and no sign of his own haunting memories. She had a moment to realize that their coming together might be exorcising some ghosts for him, as well, but then sensation began to build unbearably, billowing out in hot, swelling waves.

She felt it seize her, inexorably, powerfully. Her body tightened, as if it wanted to hold him forever. She cried out at the strength of it, arching her hips upward one more time as the feeling swept over her.

Through the haze of pleasure she felt him grab her shoulders as if to brace her, and then he drove into her hard and deep once, twice more. Then he shuddered, uttering her name in a harsh cry, grinding his hips against hers, burying himself deep, as if he wanted to climb inside her and stay.

Little echoes of sensation rippled through her, and she felt small tremors going through Clay as he collapsed, panting, atop her. For a long moment they lay there in silence, heartbeats gradually slowing, breathing deepening.

When Clay finally spoke, it was an oath delivered in low,

awed tones that warmed Casey to the core. She held him tight. And suddenly she didn't want to hear any more, didn't want to discuss what had happened between them, didn't want it to be changed somehow by words. She knew all that would come, knew that they would pay for the incredible pleasure they'd had with an unavoidable complicating of their lives, but she didn't want to face it now.

Now she wanted nothing more than to let this lovely, languorous feeling steal over her until sliding into peaceful, dreamless sleep was not only possible but inevitable.

Almost as soon as the thought formed, it was reality, and that coveted, sweet sleep was upon her.

The shrill ring of the phone startled him awake. For a moment Clay thought he'd dreamed it, both the phone and the night spent in Casey's loving arms, exploring sensations he'd never known were possible so often that he couldn't help thinking he'd made a sizable dent in those years of abstinence. But he could feel the soft warmth of her snuggled against him. He fought off the knowledge that he had to face the aftermath of what he'd done last night, clinging for a few precious moments more to the fierce sweetness they'd found in the dark.

That such fierce sweetness and the gentle, healing power he'd found in her arms could come from only one source was something he didn't dare think about, and that source was something he didn't dare name.

The ring came again, and he wished uselessly, he who had long ago given up on wishes, that it would simply go away and let them stay in this warm cocoon, with reality held at bay for at least a little while longer.

Casey said nothing, although he knew she was awake; he'd felt the change. The phone rang again, but she made no move to answer it.

Sleepily, he shifted against her, wondering if, now that they were awake anyway, she was too sore to take him again. He wanted a replay of that, of her taking charge, controlling her movements and his, taking him deep with a fearlessness that thrilled him more than he would ever have expected, even knowing what it meant, what memories she'd had to fight to become so eager with him.

His body was quickly rousing at the thought when she finally reached for the phone. Odd hour for a phone call, he thought. Did she get emergency catering calls? Maybe that nervous bride she'd told him about, who'd changed her mind three times about the wedding cake, was changing it again?

And then he came abruptly, sharply awake as he realized Casey had gone stiff. He lifted his head to look at her.

"No," she whispered. "No, it can't be you."

The vicious laugh was so loud that even he could hear it. But Casey wasn't laughing. In fact, she was terrified. He could feel it in the rigidness of her body, hear it in the shakiness of her breathing.

He moved instinctively, without thinking. He took the receiver from her and held it to his ear. He heard the voice, low, raspy and ominous-sounding.

"You think I'd let you get away with stealing my life from me? I'm coming after you, bitch, and you'll find out what I did to you that night was nothing. I'll show you what you are. I'll beat you to a pulp before I screw you this time."

"Thanks," Clay said into the phone. "You just gave me enough to throw your sorry, cowardly ass back in the slammer."

He heard the quick intake of breath on the other end. Then the phone was slammed down sharply, as if the man had panicked at the sound of Clay's voice.

Clay waited to be sure he was gone. Then he leaned over and hung up the receiver and took the shaken Casey in his arms. He held her, willing his body to forget the idea it had roused to moments before.

He waited, silently, for her to explain.

Chapter 14

Casey buried her face against Clay's chest, avoiding looking at him. She'd been too shaken to protest him taking the phone from her. Realizing it really was Jon who'd been calling her all along made her queasy, in part because she realized how desperately she'd been trying to convince herself that it wasn't him.

Clay waited, and she knew he expected her to say something, to explain. But she couldn't seem to speak, couldn't find words. All she wanted to do was cry because such ugliness had shattered the sweetness of the night. She'd found a joy with Clay that she'd never expected to feel again in her life; to have it tainted by Jon Nesbit filled her with both anger and despair, and it was not a pleasant combination.

"It was him, wasn't it?" Clay said softly. It wasn't really a question, but Casey nodded mutely. "I assume he's why you've been jumping every time the phone rings. How long has this been going on?"

"A...awhile," she managed to say.

"Did he just get out?"

"I...don't know. I didn't want to believe it was him, so I didn't check."

"You said he got four years. Means he'd be up for parole about now."

"I...don't know. I didn't want to know. I wanted to believe he'd never get out, that I'd never have to deal with him again. I told myself it couldn't be him."

"Who else did you think it could be?"

"I...anybody. He didn't say anything to make me think it was Jon, and his voice was...raspy, unrecognizable, not like Jon's at all, so I thought it was a stranger, just some guy who got my number from my ads, or the sign on my car." It sounded so silly when she said it out loud, now that she knew the truth. "But it's Jon. I know it is now. He...said something that only Jon would know."

She cringed inwardly as she waited for him to ask what Jon had said; she didn't think she could repeat the crude words, the words that reminded her so bitterly of her humiliation and degradation that day years ago. Especially after the long, tender night she'd just spent with Clay, who had changed sex back into something beautiful, instead of the ugly weapon it had been turned into for her.

But he didn't ask. He simply took her word for it.

"Great legal system we've got, isn't it?" His tone was cynical, biting, but it cheered her slightly. "How much did he know about you?"

"Do you mean how could he have found me here?" she asked. Clay nodded. "I told him about my aunt, and how she raised me, even though it was Uncle Ray who was my dad's brother. Back when I thought..."

Her voice trailed off, but Clay finished the sentence for her, softly. "When you thought he was your friend?"

She nodded, wondering if she looked as pitiful as she felt. "I may have even mentioned River Bend to him, and my aunt was the only Scott in town."

"You said he didn't say anything to make you think it was him before."

She nodded. "Nothing...until now. This is the first time. Up until now, it could have been...anyone."

"What changed? Why do you think he let you know now?"

She frowned, thinking. She'd begun to hang up, then she hadn't answered at all, and then... "I yelled at him," she said at last.

Clay blinked and drew back, looking at her. Slowly one corner of his mouth curved in a crooked grin. "You did what?"

"Well, I started just not answering the phone, but then he called in the daytime. Before it had only been at night," she explained. "But he called the afternoon of the day you...left," she finished, unable to meet his eyes.

There was a pause, but then he said simply, "And?"

"I got really angry. I called him a coward and told him to crawl back under his rock."

She heard him chuckle. "Good for you," he said, the approval in his voice warming her. "So he called at night first, giving you no clue who it was, then got peeved and called in the daytime when you quit answering. Then you told him what you thought of him, and he decided it was time to let you know who it was. That about it?"

She nodded slowly; it made sense, that he'd gotten angry when she'd stopped answering his nightly calls, and that he'd been prodded by her refusal to be cowed into revealing himself.

"Did he threaten you, Casey? During the trial? Or after?"

"He called once, to try to get me to drop the charges. He even tried to convince me I was wrong, that it had been...consensual. He told me then that I'd regret it if I went ahead. He was furious that I'd already ruined his life."

"What about *your* life?" Clay snapped, holding her so closely that she couldn't help but be comforted. He rubbed a hand up and down her back; she found the rhythmic, warm touch oddly soothing. "What did you tell him?" he asked finally.

"That the only thing I regretted was thinking he was human."

Clay startled her with his laugh. "That's my girl," he said, and a little thrill shot through her. "This bozo didn't have any idea who he was picking on, did he? He probably thought you'd never have the guts to take him down."

"He told me I didn't. It just made me madder. Aunt Fay always taught me that you have to stand up for yourself, and not to expect anybody else to do it for you."

"She was a very wise woman," he said. "And she raised a wise niece."

"If I was so wise, why did I fall for his act and believe he was a friend?" It was the question she'd asked herself countless times, wondering how a person who was supposedly relatively intelligent had been so blindly stupid.

"He's probably had a lot of practice putting on a smooth front, making people think he's a class act."

"That's how he comes across. He's smart, witty and charming."

"And," he added, "he probably knew a threat to his future plans when he saw one."

She looked at him curiously. "What do you mean?"

"If he's as smart as you say, he probably knew you were his competition. And he wanted to keep an eye on you."

Her breath caught. "You think that's why he...was so friendly? Pretended to be friends?"

He shrugged. "People like him are generally always on the lookout for those they think can threaten them. They like to keep an eye on them, so they can try to sabotage them."

It made a certain warped sense. It had seemed only natural at the time that they talk about work, what projects they had been assigned, how their employee evaluations had gone, what supervisors they got on with, which ones they didn't. But now it seemed entirely possible that there had been an ulterior motive, that instead of carrying on a conversation, he had been subtly pumping her for information.

Several silent moments passed before Clay said gently, "You need to report this, you know."

She shivered, and he tightened his arms around her. It was so strange to have someone there, to not be alone to deal with the shaky aftermath of the caller.

"I don't even know where he is. What can they do?" she said, only realizing when she heard the forlorn sound of her own voice just how much she was reeling. That the caller was now confirmed as Jon made it so much worse. She wasn't sure if she could have dealt with it at all, except that Clay was there, holding her, even as he began to give practical advice.

"To a convicted rapist who harasses or stalks his victim after his release? A lot," he said grimly. "We'll call the locals. Get a report on file. Call the prosecuting attorney. Make sure he's really out. They'll know where he was paroled to, and who his parole officer is. Call the cops there. He'll have to have been registered as a sex offender."

Casey took more comfort out of that single "we" than she did out of all his brisk and professional suggestions. She also knew that it meant little more than a caring man trying to comfort an upset woman, and that reading more into it was worse than foolish, it was stupid.

It was a knowledge she found hard to hang on to as the sun rose and the entire world seemed different to her. The passionate night had brought her back to a sense of herself as whole, no longer among the walking wounded. She wasn't silly enough to think one tender night had healed her; she knew she would forever carry scars from the attack. But she'd been more afraid than she realized that she would never be able to respond normally to a man, and Clay had vanquished that fear.

Not, she thought wryly, that she thought the way she had responded had been normal. She hadn't known it was possible to need so much, want so much, be so mindless with arousal that nothing else mattered. She hadn't believed it, even before Jon had shattered her very being with his vicious betrayal.

Now she believed it.

The morning would have been awkward if it hadn't been for the distraction of doing all the things Clay had suggested. The world had indeed changed, Casey thought ruefully, if dealing with Jon's apparent lingering zeal for revenge was almost welcome, giving her something else to think about other than what would happen now with Clay.

She thought he might have welcomed the distraction, as well. He'd said nothing about the night that had passed between them, had only hovered until he was sure she had begun the phone calls he'd outlined; then he'd gone out to work. As if it were just another day, like all the days before. But she was unsettled enough herself not to take offense at it; she needed some time to think, and he made her too restless, too edgy, to do that.

She didn't like having to call the local sheriff's office and amend her original report; they were, as she'd expected, not happy that she'd kept the fact of the rape from them. And now her reasoning, that she'd just wanted it to go away, and that it had been so long and the voice so unfamiliar that she genuinely had thought it had no connection, seemed a bit lame even to her.

However, she was gratified by the reaction of Michelle Carter, the attorney who had prosecuted Jon. The woman let out a string of obscene names that almost made Casey giggle, so incongruous was the image of the elegant, polished woman using such language. Michelle promised she would find out everything she could, and that before the week was out, Jon Nesbit would know that he had stepped in it in a big way, and she would see his parole violated if he so much as sneezed in Casey's direction again.

Casey didn't doubt it; Michelle had been a rock, a fiery, righteous presence in the court, and Casey knew she had contributed greatly to the conviction. She would take care of it all, Michelle said, her anger fairly vibrating in her voice, calling the parole board, the agency where Nesbit had been paroled, all of it.

"It shouldn't be, but sometimes an official voice has a bit more weight than the victim's. Let me handle it."

"I will," Casey said gratefully. "And thank you."

She sat there for a long time after she'd hung up, the memories flitting through her mind in short clips: the awful, painful reporting process; the long, agonizing court process; the nastiness of Jon's attorney's constant attempts to trip her up, to get her to say something, anything, that would lend credence to Jon's claim that it had been consensual. But Michelle had warned her that acquaintance rape was the toughest kind of case to prosecute, had grilled her end-lessly in practice sessions, until she'd been primed for every nasty insinuation the shark had tossed at her.

And she'd done it. She'd gotten through it, and well enough that Michelle had hugged her fiercely after, telling her she'd just won the case for them.

And none of it had the power to make her shake any-more. None of it made her heart pound or her palms sweat. Not like it once had. Jon's call had rattled her, but she'd recovered fairly quickly. Thanks to Clay. He'd changed it from emotionally charged to a practical thing, given her a course to follow, made her feel there was a way to fight back.

"You're smiling."

She turned quickly, barely aware of the smile spreading across her face merely at the thought of him. He was in the doorway, leaning against the jamb, and for a moment she forgot to breathe. She'd always thought him good-looking in that lean, rangy way she liked, but now, knowing the body beneath the worn jeans and shirt intimately, she thought he was beautiful. She even liked the way his shaggy mane of hair fell forward over his forehead, thick and shiny.

"Yes," she said, trying not to blush as the memory of that silken hair brushing over the skin of her thighs last night came to her in a vivid rush. "I'd forgotten how much I liked Michelle. The prosecuting attorney," she added in explanation. "She's going to handle everything. She was...very angry."

"Good," Clay said succinctly. "Nothing liked a pissed ADA to get things going. Did you make the call to the locals?"

A qualm struck her as she suddenly realized he was keeping his distance, not moving from the doorway.

"Yes," she said. "They weren't happy that I hadn't told them about the assault before, but they took the information. Are you coming in?"

She hadn't meant to ask it, hadn't meant to comment on it at all, but it had slipped out before she could stop it.

"No."

That was blunt enough, Casey thought, wincing inwardly. Then Clay nodded downward, and she realized his new work boots were coated with mud.

"The outside pump works again now," he said.

"Oh." Feeling more than a little foolish, she added, "Thanks."

He shrugged. "Couldn't start the gutters without those nails."

"Oh! I forgot. I'll go get them right now." She gave him a sideways glance. "Do you want to go into town?"

He shook his head. "I'll get things ready so I can start as soon as you get back."

"Okay." She didn't know if she was disappointed or relieved.

He turned to go, then halted. He seemed to hesitate for a long moment before looking back at her. He started to speak, then stopped. Nervousness skittered through Casey as wild ideas about what he could be trying to say shot through her mind. Was he regretting last night? Was he looking for a way to tell her not to assume anything? To remind her that he would be leaving again, and soon?

"If we're going to...replay last night," he finally said, "you might want to think about something a little more reliable for birth control."

"I'll do that," she said softly, blushing a bit herself at the happiness that bubbled up inside her; he wasn't going to run. It seemed her trust hadn't been completely repaired yet, she thought. He'd only been embarrassed, or maybe uncertain how to bring it up.

She was so relieved at the implications of his words that it was only later, after she'd picked up the nails at the Exchange, that she thought about the actual sense of what he'd said.

"Birth control," she muttered under her breath as she stood on the sidewalk. She could call her doctor, she supposed, and get a prescription. But if she got it filled at Clark's Drugs, word would be out before the day was over that Casey Scott had a sudden need for the pill. Besides, she wasn't sure it was immediately effective.

Condoms? she wondered. Same problem—if she bought a box at Clark's, that would get around even faster than the pill news.

She sighed; there was a price for the intimacy of a small town where everybody knew who you were and the grape-vine hummed light-years faster than the corn grew. It wasn't that she was ashamed, or trying to keep Clay a se-cret, but she wasn't quite ready to run an ad yet, either. He *was* going to leave, she told herself, and she didn't want to have to explain that. Or why she'd let the relationship go so far even so.

But she would have a lot more to explain if she got pregnant.

She quashed the image of a miniature version of Clay, a little boy with a shock of dark hair and vivid hazel eyes, and determinedly headed down the street. She would stop at Harvey's Books to see if that vegetable cookbook had arrived; then she would figure out what to do about...the other.

Jean Harvey was on the phone when she went in, and she waved at Casey rather urgently, which Casey knew meant she had something to tell her. The cookbook must have gotten there, she thought. She wandered around, idly looking. She wondered if she would ever again be able to read the suspense novels that had once been her favorites. She used to curl up in bed, reading by the warm light of Aunt Fay's big brass lamp. But after what had happened to her, the fear the characters felt had become too close, too real, and she could no longer enjoy the scary tales with the comforting knowledge that it would never happen to her.

Maybe someday. Or maybe not. But at least she had hope now. And even Jon's threats couldn't crush them. Not now, not—

"Casey, I've been hoping you'd drop in."

Jean was hustling toward her as fast as her considerable bulk would allow.

"Hello, Jean. My cookbook came in?"

For a moment the older woman looked blank. Then, "Oh! Yes, it did, a couple of days ago. I have it set aside for you. But what I wanted to show you was this."

She handed Casey a hardcover book with a dramatic black-and-red dust jacket. *Pack of Jackals,* it read, with a subtitle of *The Destruction of a Street Gang.* Casey looked at Jean curiously.

"I knew I'd heard of Marina Heights before," the woman said. "I saw it in a publisher's catalog."

Marina Heights? Casey looked at the book again. She flipped it over to see a portrait of a handsome, muscular black man wearing a black beret at a jaunty angle.

"That Lang fellow," Jean said, "he went undercover, joined a street gang out there in California. Spent over a year with them. The book's all about that, and how the police out there also had somebody undercover, and how he broke up the gang."

"The Marina Heights police?" Casey asked, her breath catching slightly.

"Yes. It's really quite fascinating. But awful. I don't know how those folks live like that out there. Might have better weather, but what good does it do if you can't step outside your house?"

Casey murmured something as Jean ran on with one of her favorite topics. She opened the book in what she hoped was a casually interested manner, flipping through some pages, quickly scanning a section of photos in the middle, searching the captions. She realized it was silly to expect anything, that Clay had been long gone before any of this had happened, but still she couldn't help it. She even checked the index. And nearly gasped when she found the entry. *Yeager, Clay, 350-351.*

It was all she could do not to flip to the page immediately. With an effort, she closed the book and gave Jean a smile. "Interesting. Maybe I'll buy it, to remind me how glad I am to live here and not in earthquake country."

It was shameless, the way she played to Jean's pet subject, but it worked. Jean kept chattering, apparently not having noticed anything unusual in Casey's reaction to the book. Or in her decision to buy it.

She was back out in her car, a few doors down, before she took the book out of the bag and opened it, turning large sections of pages until she got close, then leafing to page 350.

She read a description of Marina Heights detective Ryan Buckhart, the undercover officer who had himself run with the vicious adult street gang known as the Pack for months, risking his life to gather the evidence necessary to take them down. Curious, she flipped back to the photo section and blinked when she saw the picture of a tall, broad-shouldered, exotically—impossibly—handsome man of Native American heritage.

All that and guts, too, she murmured to herself.

Quickly she went back to the text and read on. She gathered from the context that it had been quite an adventure, that neither the writer nor the cop had really known who the other was, yet they had both sensed there was more to the other than met the eye.

And then she hit Clay's name and forgot the rest. It had been Ryan who had mentioned him, who had told Carny Lang, the writer, that he'd simply learned from the best. And the best, according to Ryan, was Clay Yeager.

"I was a wild kid, but he pulled me off the street," Ryan was quoted as saying. "He saved me. I would have been a real member of something like the Pack until I got myself killed. But he never gave up on me, and when I became a cop, he was still there for me, taught me what it took to be a good one. Wherever he is, I owe him more than I can ever say."

Lang had added a footnote to that on the next page: Clay Yeager, it said, was a legend at the department known as Trinity West, and beyond. The three-time Medal of Valor winner had resigned and disappeared after a personal tragedy, but his reputation hadn't faded in the intervening years.

Casey closed the book and sat holding it for several moments.

Three-time Medal of Valor winner.

It didn't surprise her. It didn't matter what he thought of himself after his "personal tragedy;" it was obvious that others saw things more clearly. Others like Ryan Buckhart and Carny Lang.

She wondered if Clay would even want to look at the book. Or if it would only upset him, bring back unpleasant memories he'd managed to put behind him. She tucked it back in the bag and started the engine.

She was out on the highway before she remembered the crucial thing she'd forgotten. She hit the brakes and then looked in the mirror, hoping this wasn't the one day when there was traffic on this road. Thankfully the empty strip of asphalt rolled out behind her until it vanished in shimmering heat waves.

In a way, she realized, she'd sort of solved her problem. By going only an extra fifteen miles—well, thirty, round-trip—she could go to nicely anonymous Ames, among all the college students there for the start of the new term, where a purchase such as she had to make wouldn't even be blinked at.

She hesitated another moment, then made the turn. It would take her another hour and delay Clay's work, but she didn't know what else to do.

As it turned out, when she got back he was only worried at how long she'd been gone. Stammering in the face of his concern, she tried to explain. He noticed the name of the drugstore on the bag and lifted a brow at her.

"It's not that I'm trying to hide it, really, it's just that they gossip so, and this would set them off like wildfire, and Ames wasn't that far, so I—"

"Casey," he said with a crooked grin, "I'm not about to complain, considering."

She blushed, but the joy of last night blossomed again, warming her until she felt a bit giddy with it.

She completely forgot about the book sitting on the front seat of her car.

Chapter 15

Clay lay back, restless tonight. Casey was sleeping peacefully beside him, and as glad as he was to see it, it also made him nervous. She'd been so cheerful for the past few days, and while he rather sheepishly admitted to himself that he'd been feeling pretty good himself, he knew it was more than simply the pleasure they'd found with each other in the night.

He guessed the something more was the fact that the phone calls had ceased. She'd told him she thought that perhaps his taking the phone that night had been the key, that realizing she wasn't alone had frightened Nesbit into stopping.

He hadn't had the heart to dissuade her. And it could be true, he thought.

But deep down in his gut, long-buried instincts were screaming. The long-buried instincts of a cop. A well-trained and experienced cop.

That voice he'd heard on the phone, reeking with venom, wasn't the voice of a man who was going to just give up and go away. He knew it just like he'd once known when a suspect was lying, or when he'd entered a darkened warehouse and known the burglar was still there.

As he lay there in the dark, his mind kept trying to wander, and he kept yanking it back to Nesbit. He knew too well where it wanted to go, straight to the woman beside him. Every moment since the first night he'd spent in her bed he'd felt like he was stealing time, stealing pleasure and, above all, stealing a happiness he had no right to.

And telling himself that it was for Casey's sake, that she deserved what they'd found together even if he didn't, was a cop-out and he knew it. Not that it wasn't true that she deserved it, but he couldn't imagine why she'd picked him, why she wanted him when, with very little effort, she could have any man she set her heart on.

What scared him was the thought that she might have done just that, set her heart on him. He'd thought nothing could scare him more than being trusted by a woman, but the idea that Casey, sweet, gentle and incredibly courageous Casey, might fall in love with him was terrifying. Because he would hurt her. There was no way he could avoid that.

And when that happened, he knew he would find out if there was any small piece of his own heart left, because it would die.

Casey stirred beside him, and he realized he'd once again lost his focus, that he'd let his mind tread on that ground he was trying so hard to avoid.

And then she reached out for him, murmuring his name sleepily, and none of it mattered.

He'd never known anything like this. At first he'd credited at least some of the intensity of their passion to his long years of celibacy, but they'd been together every night since, and it hadn't abated in the slightest. And once he'd been sure she was truly all right, that she wasn't frightened—after she'd told him, blushing, that she never even thought of what had happened to her when they came together—once he hadn't been worried about holding back when every part of him was screaming, it had gone from fire to inferno. She had only to touch him, as she did now, and he responded so swiftly it made him groan.

"You're awake," she murmured.

"If I hadn't been," he said gruffly as her hand came to rest on his belly, "I would be now."

She rose up on one elbow to look at him. Her hair was tousled, falling in a red-gold mass almost down to her breasts. Even in the darkness of the night, he could see it gleam, and he remembered tangling his fingers in the heavy silk of it as she lay beneath him, remembered watching it frame her face as she rode him.

The memory hardened him in a rush. She'd been so tentative, yet at the same time eager, and the wonder of what she was feeling had been reflected so clearly in her face that she'd humbled him completely. He didn't know if it was the shock of being wanted so much, or the pride of being able to bring her such pleasure; he only knew it was something new and undreamed-of.

And he knew it proved what he'd suspected for a long time now: Casey Scott was a hell of a lot braver than he was. She had overcome her tragedy, had had the courage to try again, to not let it break her, to not let Jon Nesbit win by destroying her. She'd fought the ugliest memories a woman can have, and she'd triumphed.

He wished he had half her nerve.

She planted a warm little kiss where her hand had rested on his belly. Then a little lower. Then lower still. Clay held his breath as she hesitated.

"Clay?" she whispered.

"You...don't have to. Not just because I did."

He'd been unable to stop himself last night, had been overcome with the need to taste every inch of her. She'd been as hot and honeyed as he'd imagined. And when it had become clear to him that that kind of intimate kiss was something she'd never experienced, he'd been determined to show her just how spectacular it could be.

Her lips brushed his distended flesh, and he nearly jumped. "I don't…know much about it, but…would you like it?" she asked.

Just the thought had him fighting down the boiling tide that threatened to break free.

"If I survive," he replied through gritted teeth, "I'd adore it."

"I'll take that as a yes," Casey said, almost teasingly.

And then her mouth was on him, soft and uncertain at first, but then more confidently, as he showed her by fervent reaction just how good it felt. Her lips, her tongue, stroked him until he thought he wouldn't be able to hold back another instant; then she moved slightly, experimenting, and it began all over again as she found more sensitive, charged spots that he hadn't realized existed.

Her learning curve was going to kill him, he thought as she took him deeply into her mouth, as if she loved the taste and texture of him.

Finally, gasping her name on a groan, with trembling hands, he reached for her.

"Casey, stop." His hands went to her arms to tug her up his clamoring, wire-drawn body.

"But—"

"In another minute this lesson is going to go further than a first one should," he growled.

For a moment he thought she was going to protest, and he doubted if he would have the strength to dissuade her; he'd just used up every ounce of his willpower. But she looked down at him, at the flesh she'd roused so thoroughly he thought he was going to die, and the most erotic smile he'd ever seen slowly curved her soft, full mouth, the mouth that had just driven him nearly mad with need. He nearly erupted at the sight of it. His hands shook as he fumbled with protection.

And then she moved, straddling him, and he knew what had caused that expression; she'd been remembering those moments he'd thought of himself just minutes ago. She had the knack of it now, and she took him in a slow, luxurious slide that made him close his eyes and gulp for air as he gasped out her name in the tone of a fervent oath.

When he was sheathed in her, hard and deep, she stopped. His body screaming, he waited, but she didn't move. He opened his eyes, thinking he would beg her if he had to, but the moment he saw her face, the moment he saw her awed, joyous expression, he knew he would die before he would hurry her, before he would do anything to disrupt what she was feeling. What he wanted, what his body had been demanding mere seconds ago, was nothing compared to the feeling that look on her face gave him.

And for the first time since that appalling night, he had the brief, flitting thought that maybe he shouldn't wish so hard that he'd died when his family had.

All the old emotions rose to swamp that flicker of brightness, all the guilt he'd so carefully nurtured all these years. But then Casey began to move, rocking in a motion that drove him deep and hard inside her, until he swore there wasn't a fraction of an inch of him that her hot, slick flesh wasn't clasping, stroking, urging. And in those fiery moments there was room for nothing else in his mind, not even the vicious memories, only the woman who was driving him over the edge.

He tried to wait, wanted her with him, but it was too late. He felt the hot tide rise in pulsing beats and arched beneath her, wanting every ounce of her weight bearing down on him, wanting to be as near to climbing inside her as he could get. His hands went to her hips, and he held her tight against him as the incredible sensations swamped him, and he cried out, heedless of what he said, if it was even words or simply a scream as he poured himself into her.

And then he heard her call his name, that cry he'd come to know and treasure, felt the sudden clenching of her body around him, grasping flesh that was already throbbing. He couldn't breathe, he felt his toes curl, and his head felt on the verge of spinning as the moment went on and on, until he thought he was going to get his wish, that he was simply going to pour himself into her until there was nothing left of him.

When she fell forward on his chest with a heartfelt moan, her breath coming in quick little pants, he didn't have the strength to do anything except lift one hand to rest it on the small of her back.

He fell into a deep, dreamless, satiated sleep with Casey sprawled atop him like a living, silken cover.

Casey had never felt like this. It was as if she'd somehow recaptured the joy of childhood, before the crash that had ended it. Each day seemed filled with infinite possibilities, each night filled with wonder and a pleasure she'd never even fantasized was possible.

But her happiness was not absolute. Clay seemed to be getting more tense, more on edge, with every day that passed. More than once she'd awakened to find him staring into the darkness, his expression troubled.

But he was never less than responsive to her touch. He seemed always hungry for her, in a way that fed that new, wondrous sense of feminine power she was reveling in.

It would have been puzzling if she hadn't had a fairly good idea what was wrong. She was almost certain he was reacting to their relationship, resisting any happiness of his own. She knew he hadn't let go of the guilt he still felt.

What she didn't know was what to do about it. Her mind was telling her nothing had really changed with him, that he would still leave when he felt he'd paid her back, though her heart wanted to believe he wouldn't. And no matter how foolish the one called the other, she couldn't quite let go of that hope.

"Hello, Mud," she said as the Border collie nudged the door open and trotted into the kitchen. "Come for a snack before dinner?"

She had never been able to resist the dog's gentlemanly approach. He never begged, merely came in and sat down, watching her intently, his ears alert, his head cocked. When she offered him a piece of whatever she was preparing that he might like, he accepted it gravely and thanked her with a quick swipe of his tongue over her fingers.

"Here," she said, tossing him a bit of the shredded beef she was filling tortillas with for burritos. After he'd gobbled it down, she told him, "These are about ready. Why don't you go get Clay?"

She knew it was likely that all he understood was "get Clay," but she couldn't seem to stop talking to the dog as if he understood much more. And so far Mud had responded as if he'd comprehended every word. Now was no exception; without hesitation, the dog headed back to the screen door he'd learned to nudge open and scampered down the steps. Casey knew he would return shortly, his master in tow. For now, at least, the routine they'd developed was intact.

She wondered how long it would remain that way.

It wasn't just for her sake that she wanted him to stay, she told herself, although she was honest enough to admit she was no altruist when it came to her emotions. But she sensed that if Clay did leave without facing down the memories that haunted him, if he ran again, he would be running forever. And that made her sad in a way she'd never known. It was different from the wrenching grief of death, but she wasn't sure it was any less powerful; the thought of Clay wandering endlessly, forever carrying the burden of his self-imposed guilt, never finding peace, never realizing he'd tortured himself far too much and too long, brought stinging tears to her eyes and a painful tightness to her throat.

But she wasn't fool enough to believe she could make him stay. In the end, he would do what he had to do, and if she tried to force him, tie him, she would only add to his misery. She knew—because he'd made it clear—that he hated the idea of hurting her. It hadn't been a great jump from that to the realization that he knew he would.

They didn't discuss it. He never brought it up, and she was afraid to broach the subject herself. She selfishly wanted things to continue as they were for a while, and she was superstitiously afraid of planting an idea that might not be in his mind at the moment.

And in some deep part of her mind, she was aware that she was also collecting. Collecting images, memories, as a hedge against the time when he left, things to draw on to fill the emptiness she already knew she would feel when he was gone. When he would, as he'd said, let her down.

Don't trust me. I'll only let you down.

As his words echoed once more in her mind, she stopped in the middle of tearing lettuce for a salad.

She hadn't thought of those words since he'd told her his awful story. And now that he had, she understood how completely he'd meant them. How completely he believed them.

"Smells great."

His voice came from close behind her, and she barely managed not to jump.

"Thank you. It's almost ready."

"I'll wash up."

Her thoughts seemed to have her mind in a jumble, and she was almost afraid to speak, afraid she would blurt out what she'd been thinking. He gave her a curious look that told her he noticed, but he didn't push for conversation.

The silence wore on her, though, as if all the things they weren't talking about had taken up residence at the table.

Finally, as she served up the chilled caramel mousse from the new recipe she'd found, she couldn't bear it any longer; she had to do something. So as she passed it on the counter, she grabbed the book she'd found lying forgotten on the seat of her delivery wagon.

"Jean found this for me," she said, setting it down beside his plate. "After I mentioned Marina Heights, she thought I might be interested."

She suddenly remembered his reaction to her mentioning Marina Heights to Jean. She supposed that made sense now. If he'd left cops behind, trained investigators, and he didn't want to be found, the less mention of where he was from, the better, from his point of view.

He was staring down at the book, looking puzzled. He turned it over, glancing at the photo on the back; no sign of recognition. So he didn't know the writer, she thought.

"It's about a street gang the Marina Heights police broke up last year."

"*Pack of Jackals,*" he read slowly. Then his eyes widened. "They took down the Pack?"

He flipped open the cover and began to read the inside blurb.

"Son of a bitch," he breathed earnestly, closing the cover again and staring at the front. "They did it. They finally did it."

"You know about that gang?"

He didn't look up from the book. "They ran for years. Robbery, burglary, car theft, they did it all. And murder, if they had to, or wanted to make a point or send a message. They used the youth gangs as their minor leagues—if a kid survived that, they figured he might be useful to them."

"They sound...ruthless."

"And vicious. Unfortunately, they were also clever, or at least their leader was. We tried for years to get enough on them to break them, but we could only get pieces, make single arrests here and there."

"I didn't read it all, but according to what I did read, a protégé of yours practically did it single-handedly."

His head came up then, sharply. "Of mine?"

She nodded. "Named Ryan Buckhart."

A series of expressions flashed over his face, first shock, then contemplation, and finally what she could only describe as pride.

"Ryan? Ryan did it?"

"It says he was undercover as part of the gang for months. Worked his way to the top."

"And brought them down from the inside," Clay said, almost reverently. "Damn. Ryan. How about that."

"He says in the book that you saved him."

Clay looked startled. Then he shrugged off the praise. "I just gave him a hand when he needed one. He was a smart kid, too smart to end up bleeding to death in a gutter. He just needed somebody to believe in him."

Casey had the feeling there was a lot more to it than that, but it was clear from his tone that Clay wasn't about to accept any accolades for pulling a wild kid off the streets and probably saving his life.

"Kid?" was all she said.

"I was seven years older," Clay said, "but sometimes I got the feeling he was a hundred years older than I was, in grim experience."

Until your life fell apart, Casey thought. Then, before his thoughts could go to that same place, she said quickly, "He's rather...spectacular looking."

Clay smiled crookedly. "Women always said that about him." And then, as if the implication of her statement had just registered, he asked, "There's a picture of him?"

She nodded. "Page two of the photos."

He moved with a haste she was sure he hadn't meant to betray to find the page. "He looks good," he said softly.

"It says in the afterword that he remarried his ex-wife after this was over."

His head came up again, and she saw a flash of pure pleasure in his eyes. "Lacey? He and Lacey got back together?"

"They have a little girl now. Amanda."

He stared for a moment, then looked away, but not before Casey caught the sudden glint of moisture in his eyes.

"They had a baby," he said, his voice nearly a whisper. "They lost their first one. It's what split them up. But there were never two people crazier about each other."

Casey watched him, her heart beginning to pound in her chest. This was somehow important, she knew, this clear demonstration of emotion about someone he'd left behind.

You're not dead inside, Clay Yeager, no matter how hard you try to convince yourself you are, she thought.

She wasn't sure what that realization meant, or if it was really an indication of any change in his state of mind.

What she *was* sure of was that it gave her hope.

Clay hung up the phone. He was glad Casey hadn't come home before he'd finished. He would have to explain about the two calls when she got the phone bill—if he was still here by then—but he didn't want to tell her just now what he'd done.

And he didn't want her to know what he'd found out.

It was selfish, he admitted, but he didn't want to destroy her mood. She'd been so unfailingly happy, certain now after several days of peaceful, uninterrupted nights, that Nesbit had given up and gone away.

But Clay's instincts had refused to be convinced, and his uneasiness had grown until he'd done something he hadn't done since he'd left Trinity West—acted like a cop.

It had taken him a while to get through to Charlie Nantz, an old academy mate and Trinity West cop who had transferred to Chicago a couple of years before Clay had left.

Charlie had been more than startled to hear from him. And what he'd told Clay that morning had made him feel more than a little strange.

"Yeager? Damn, man, I half thought you were dead!"

"Not yet," he'd said dryly. Funny, the idea wasn't nearly as appealing as it had once seemed.

"Damn," Charlie had said again; his vocabulary had always been a bit limited. "You finally surfaced. Guess Trinity West can call off the dogs, huh?"

"The dogs?"

"Hell, yeah. Every couple months, like clockwork, we get the information request on you."

"But...it's been years," he'd said, a little stunned.

"Well, they finally called off the personal search, but we still get those flyers."

"Personal search?"

"You didn't know? We had one of them here, even."

"One of...who?"

"A bunch of your old buddies. They pooled money and vacation time, and each one took a turn looking for you."

He stared at the phone for a long, silent moment, unable to believe what he was hearing.

"That Sergeant Walker who was here," Charlie went on, "guess she organized the whole thing. Quite a looker, that one—"

Kit? Kit Walker had organized a search for him, had gotten people to donate time and money just to look for him? He sat down heavily in the kitchen chair beside the phone. An image formed in his mind of a young, trim, tousled-haired blonde with eyes like his own in color but much more innocent, looking at him with a serious intensity as he explained to her what she could expect trying to be a cop, a woman in what was still very much a man's world.

"—made you call out of the blue?"

Yanked out of his stunned reflections, Clay struggled to regain his bearings. He'd made his request, and Charlie had promised to check right away. Charlie had been true to his word, and when Clay had called back that afternoon, while Casey was out on her second job of the day, he'd had the info.

It wasn't what Clay wanted to hear, but it was about what he'd expected.

After mentioning that they'd already been alerted by the D.A.'s office that Nesbit was being a bad boy—Casey's friend Michelle had kept her word—and that he was due to meet with his P.O. in two days, Charlie told him Jon Nesbit had left his home the morning after Clay had spoken to him on the phone.

Now Clay stood there for a long time, staring out the kitchen window at the peaceful surroundings. It seemed nothing evil could invade this homespun setting. It seemed a good place to do what Casey had come here to do, heal.

But Clay was very much afraid that the sound of his voice hadn't scared away the evil but instead might have been the trigger that brought it down on this serene place.

Chapter 16

Clay was acting very oddly. For the past two days he'd seemed edgy and almost nervous. Yet he didn't, as she constantly feared he would, pull away from her. In fact, he seemed to be watching her closely, so closely that she was starting to feel strained. Even Mud seemed to be hovering, although the slender little dog was much too quick and agile to really be underfoot.

Maybe it was the book, she thought. It seemed to have happened about then, the change.

She sliced another carrot into neat, thin strips and added them to the pile she'd already done for the salad. She'd read the book over the last two days, when it seemed Clay wasn't going to. She supposed she couldn't blame him. It couldn't help but bring back memories, memories he perhaps wasn't ready for.

She'd found it grimly fascinating. The author had a flair for keeping the reader engrossed despite knowing the outcome, that the vicious gang known as the Pack had been vanquished. He wrote modestly, as well, playing down his own courage in daring to join the gang, in managing to survive in that world while he gathered information. The real hero of the piece was Ryan Buckhart.

Lang had written in his preface that, as a journalist, his intent had been only to do a piece on life in a gang, an exposé of their workings and the appeal that drove people to join. But when he inadvertently became witness to the downfall of the Pack, orchestrated by Trinity West detective Ryan Buckhart, his vision changed.

He also said he'd always been a skeptic about that nebulous thing known as a cop's instinct. He wasn't skeptical now, not after watching Ryan Buckhart. The man had sensed from the start that Carny Lang had been more than he seemed.

The rest of the story had been as exciting as any movie, and more frightening, because it was all true. The reality of long-term undercover work, not the glamorous fictions of movies and television, came through, the hours of routine, the moments of terror and, most compelling, the danger of losing yourself in the lies, of seeing the cash flowing on the other side while you took home a paycheck that was barely a drop in that ocean, of working so hard to appear one of the slime that you started to become one.

Had Clay ever done the kind of work Ryan Buckhart had? Casey wondered. Had Buckhart's statement that Clay had been his teacher meant he'd taught him this, too, the kind of steely mentality it took to go up against a gang of cutthroats like the Pack on their own turf, and win?

She didn't doubt it for a moment. Not with three Medals of Valor to his credit. She wondered what they had been awarded for. Not that it mattered. Not when it was clear that all the people he'd ever helped or saved couldn't make up for the two he hadn't.

I'd failed them. Both of them.

Don't trust me. I'll only let you down.

How long? she wondered. How long would he make himself pay for someone else's decision?

She thought of the hero in the book again and wondered how he'd felt—for that matter, how all the cops of Trinity West had felt—when Clay's life had shattered around him. And when he'd left, cutting all ties, even with those he'd been closest to, like Buckhart. She'd always heard about the bond between cops and that it was unlike anything in the world. Something between friends and brothers, and often beyond both.

He'd had friends like that. And a father who loved him. Who was wondering where he was. Perhaps wondering if he was even alive.

And now he was alone, his only companions a clever, loyal dog and a punishing conscience that had never heard of the concept of mercy.

It was too painful to think about, and Casey tried to stop. She wiped back an errant strand of hair from her forehead. After a day of baking for the upcoming Labor Day town picnic, one of her prime advertising tools, Casey was hot and sweaty. She cleaned up the kitchen, stuck the lasagna in the oven for dinner and escaped for a long, cooling shower. When at last she returned to the kitchen, Clay was already there, sitting in the chair by the telephone, Mud beside him. When she came in, Mud looked over his shoulder at her as Clay stood up quickly, his boots in his hands, as if he'd just been taking them off.

"Dinner will be ready in about fifteen minutes," she said.

He nodded. "I'll get cleaned up."

He moved quickly, almost as if he were nervous about being in the room with her. With a sigh, she went to the refrigerator and got the salad. She couldn't keep up with this, she thought.

"I thought women were supposed to be the ones with mood swings," she said to Mud as she set the table.

It was a silent meal; she lost both interest and her appetite about halfway through. And she was just testy enough to bring up what she'd been thinking about, not even bothering to ease into it.

"When was the last time you spoke to your father?"

He blinked, a forkful of lasagna midway to his mouth. "What?"

She wasn't sure if he was angry that she'd dared to ask, or just shocked.

"I asked when was—"

"I heard you."

"I thought so."

He set down his food untouched. "Look, just because we—"

He broke off suddenly, but Casey sensed what he'd been about to say. If she hadn't known his story, hadn't known what he'd gone through, she might have taken offense. But she did know, and so she couldn't.

"I'm not expecting you to share your life with me just because we're sharing a bed," she said. He flushed, telling her she'd been right, he had been about to use that defense. "It was a simple question."

His expression almost amused her; he seemed embarrassed that she'd read him so easily, ashamed at what he'd almost said, but he was still clearly reluctant to answer her.

"A couple of years ago," he said finally. Then, after a pause, "No, probably three."

"You don't know?"

He shrugged. "It was when my driver's license expired. I had to ask him to do the mail renewal. He was already doing the truck license."

The mundaneness of it startled her. And then the rest sank in. "And if you hadn't had to do that, would you have called at all?"

He hesitated, looking at her. She watched him steadily.

And finally, in a tone that told her he was being utterly honest, he said, "Probably not."

"Did he condemn you, as you did yourself?" she asked bluntly.

After another second, he lowered his gaze, breaking the contact. "My father," he said softly, "never condemned anyone in his life. Said that was God's job."

"Too bad you didn't learn from him."

His head came up.

"Too bad you didn't learn that it's not your job to take the blame for someone else's decision. That some things are truly out of your control."

"I should have known—"

"And I should have known Jon Nesbit couldn't be trusted. So we're both blind."

"That was different."

"Why? Because I was naive and you weren't?"

"Something like that," he said, but he didn't sound convinced.

"Did you know anything about clinical depression? Isn't that what they call it?"

"No."

"Ever known anyone else with it?"

"No, but—"

"Sorry, Yeager, but you don't get to be omnipotent. You don't get to judge. Or to condemn. That's somebody else's job. Something at least your father knew."

He stared at her, and for a moment she thought she saw hope flicker in the depths of his eyes. But it was quickly hidden behind that practiced mask she'd come to hate. She got to her feet, staring down at him. She tried to put it in terms that would get through.

"You've tried, convicted and sentenced yourself as if you had the right. And your judgment is based on the assumption that you could control Linda's actions. A bit arrogant, isn't it?"

"I never tried to control her. Just the opposite," he protested.

Her point made, Casey changed tack. "Maybe you should have seen she was in trouble, just like I should have seen Jon *was* trouble."

"Casey—"

"But neither of us did. So if you're going to condemn yourself, you have to condemn me, too. But you don't. Or was all that just talk? Was it really my fault I was raped?"

"No!"

His tone was horror-filled enough to make her feel a touch of comfort. But she knew she couldn't dwell on it. There was something more important at stake; Clay needed to think about this, and hard.

"I rest my case, Officer," she said.

And then she turned and left him, unable to bear witnessing his torture any longer.

Clay sat staring into his half-empty plate. He vaguely realized there were chaotic emotions churning within him, more emotions than he'd felt at once in a long time. But above them all, glowing amid all the confusion, was Casey. She'd been victimized in the worst way, but she hadn't let it defeat her. She'd come out whole and strong and so gallant it made him ache inside.

She'd methodically hacked away at his defenses, at all the things he'd lived with for so long, all the assumptions his life had been based on since the death of his family, until he was beginning to question them himself. She'd been strong enough to fight them for him, strong enough to use her own pain against his in a way he couldn't possibly refute.

But as strong as she was, she was no match for the madness that was about to descend on her.

He crossed his silverware neatly on the plate and stood up. Slowly, methodically, he cleared the table. He put the dishes in the dishwasher, covered the last of the lasagna and put it in the refrigerator. When he was done, he stood looking out the kitchen window into the shadowy yard.

Charlie's words echoed in his mind. He'd sneaked in the call while she'd been in the shower tonight; she didn't have any jobs until next weekend, so she'd been home, and he hadn't been able to get to the phone before.

But when he had, he'd caught Charlie just before he was leaving.

"I was hoping you'd call back," he said. "Wish you'd left a number."

"Let me guess," Clay had said, already knowing in his gut. "Nesbit didn't check in with his P.O. today."

"Nope. No call, no show up, nothing. P.O.'s already put the parole violation through, after the word from the prosecutor."

"Good," Clay said, although he doubted it was going to do him—or Casey—any good. If Nesbit was the kind to follow the rules, none of this would be happening in the first place.

"I thought you might want to know, so I checked—he hasn't been back to his place, either."

"Thanks, Charlie," Clay said, meaning it.

"No prob," his old friend said. "I'm just damn glad to hear from you."

Clay had hung up just as he heard the shower turn off. He'd quickly sat and tugged off his boots; he needed to think about this, decide just what he was going to tell Casey. She had the right to know the possibilities, but he didn't want to scare her, didn't want to destroy the peace she'd found.

But he knew a confrontation was coming. He could feel it in that bone-deep way he'd long ago learned not to discount. Nesbit was on the move—if not already here, then on his way.

One part of him fiercely wanted it, wanted to crush the animal who had savaged Casey.

But another part of him knew that wasn't the only battle approaching, knew that he had to confront more than just an external enemy. And that deeply buried part of him where the nightmares lived knew that Nesbit might be the smaller of the two. Because that part of him knew too well the demon in his own soul, the demon who mocked him, laughingly assuring him that he would yet again fail someone he loved.

Someone he loved.

He braced his hands on the sink as he stared unseeingly out into the darkness. He was sure that if he didn't, they'd be shaking. It couldn't be true. He couldn't let it be true.

He couldn't love Casey.

And then he remembered again the way she'd just stood up to that inner demon, the way she'd fought so hard for him. He remembered the nights in her arms, the zest, the fire, the pure joy and pleasure he'd found when he'd thought himself incapable of such feelings. He remembered the hours he'd spent simply watching her sleep and taking a quiet enjoyment from it. He remembered the way she teased Mud, the way the aloof Border collie responded to her like he did to no one else.

He remembered how he'd felt when he'd heard that vicious, threatening voice on the phone, and how his gut had heaved when he'd realized Nesbit was on his way here, that Casey was in danger of much more than a few sleepless nights.

Then, finally, an image formed in his mind, of Casey, cold and lifeless, like Linda had been, like Jenny had been. And he knew that if that happened, this time he would not survive it himself.

And he knew that he'd committed the most unbelievable folly of his entire life.

He *had* fallen in love with Casey Scott.

He saw it all before him in the darkness of the yard, the choices that were no choices. He could run, leaving Casey to face the deadly threat alone, or protected only by someone who had no personal stake in her safety. Or he could stay, and perhaps fail her as he'd failed before.

But this time, he thought, shifting his gaze down to his hands, to the whiteness of his knuckles as he squeezed the unyielding porcelain of the sink as if he could crush it with his fingers, this time he would die in the effort. Because if he did fail, he was as good as dead anyway.

He stood there for a long time before he dared to move. Though he'd spent years putting his life on the line, the thought of putting his heart on the line again terrified him.

But he could no more abandon Casey now than he could bring his family back to life. And that he even thought of them in the same context scared him even more.

At last he turned away from the sink. Casey had gone to her room, but he wasn't sure he would be welcome if he followed. Nor was he anywhere near being ready—or able—to sleep. Restless now, he left the kitchen, wandering through the living room he'd once found warm and welcoming. Now he simply felt out of place, as if the atmosphere had closed up, deciding it had been a mistake to let him in in the first place.

He tried to laugh at his ridiculousness at giving a mere house thoughts and feelings, but it came out as more of a groan.

He turned to leave, but the sight of the book Casey had brought home, sitting on the table next to her favorite overstuffed chair, stopped him. He stood there looking at it, thinking about things and people long forgotten.

And despite believing he'd completely cut his ties to Trinity West years ago, he couldn't stop the sudden burst of pride that surged in him.

"Ryan," he said softly, "you done good."

He crossed the room and stared down at the book for a

while. And then, reluctantly, yet feeling driven, he picked it up. He looked at the cover. He looked at the back. He looked at the blurb on the inside flap. And finally he turned to the center section and looked at the photo of Ryan Buckhart. Slowly, reluctantly, he sat down.

Three and a half hours later he was closing the book. It had been an incredibly odd sensation, reading the text, seeing familiar places and familiar names, both friend and adversary. Odder still to see his own name there, and bittersweet to read Ryan's quiet praise and transfer of credit.

And he was surprised at the amount of pleasure he took in reading about the destruction of the gang that had been the bane of the existence of everybody at Trinity West for years. The pride he'd felt in Ryan, the wild, almost crazy kid he'd once arrested, only grew. He'd known the boy was just scared, afraid there was no place for him, with his size, ethnic looks and unknown heritage, in this world. Clay had seen a sharp, quick mind that was suffocating, and known it was only a short trip from that to destroying it with alcohol or worse.

Surprisingly, the fact that he'd been so thoroughly proven right mattered to him. He'd seen Ryan become a good cop, but what he'd pulled off with the Pack went beyond that. And for an instant he wished Ryan was there, wished he could congratulate him personally, wished even harder that it would mean something to the man if he did.

That idea rattled him so much he slapped the book shut.

He'd never had any desire to go back, either to his onetime home or to Trinity West. Or at least, if he had, it had been stillborn. He couldn't have allowed it to flourish, to grow into need, not when he knew there was no way he *could* go back, no way he could face the people who knew what had happened, the people who felt sorry for him or, worse, those like Linda's parents, who had publicly and loudly blamed him for neglecting what they said were their daughter's obvious cries for help. The fact that he believed just that himself made it almost impossible to bear.

Yet here he was, thinking about just that, going back. Thinking that he would like to see how Ryan had turned out. That he would like to see Lacey, see the baby they'd finally created after the tragic loss of their first. And Cruz, and his little girl, who probably wasn't at all little anymore. And how was Gage? Was he still driven to the edge of obsession by his work?

And Kit... God, had she really done what Charlie had said, organized all of Trinity West into a relay search team, looking for him? Had the chief really sanctioned that?

His mouth curved slightly at the thought of Miguel as the chief. Miguel de los Reyes was a fine cop, and Clay had always known he had the brains and the savvy to go far. That he was a good, decent, honest man would make it perhaps a little harder, but Clay had the feeling that if anybody could do it, Miguel could.

Besides, having him as a boss must be driving Robards crazy.

Clay couldn't help but grin at the thought. The snarly, bigoted, cigar-chewing dinosaur had been the curse of Trinity West for years before Clay had gone to work there. He hadn't changed in the years Clay had worn the Trinity West badge, and he doubted the man had changed much since he'd left.

You want to remember, think about Robards, he told himself. Remember how he came up to you at Linda's funeral with that charming statement that was apparently supposed to make you feel better.

Sorry, pal, but women are unstable anyway, so what do you expect? You'll be better off without her.

Clay had wondered briefly how anybody who had Kit Walker working for him could possibly believe women were unstable or inferior, but he'd been too shell-shocked to take the man on. Too crushed by his guilt to flatten him as he should have when he'd added that kids were a nuisance, anyway, and he was lucky to be a free man now.

Robards, and the few others like him who were still around, were more than enough reason to stay away from Trinity West, the place that had once been home.

But until now, he hadn't thought of all the reasons to go back, all the people who had meant so much to him. He hadn't dared. He'd locked those memories away in a place where they couldn't torment him, where they couldn't remind him constantly of all he'd lost.

And now they were back, brought vividly to life by the story of one young street kid who had matured into a tough, brilliant cop and triumphantly brought down one of the most vicious adult street gangs in the country.

Clay found himself fighting off a wave of nostalgic longing unlike anything he'd felt before.

He let his head loll back on the chair, his eyes closing wearily. He'd thought that part of his life was buried too deep to resurface. And he didn't understand why it was hitting him now, and so hard. Had staying here done it, giving him time to become used to his surroundings and thus free to think about other things? Or was it more complex than that? Had coming to care for Casey opened the door for other things?

He should have followed his urge to run. When she'd yelled at him to just leave, to send her the money when he could if he was so set on paying her back, he should have gone. He'd known it the minute he'd seen the sheen of moisture in her eyes and known that he'd brought her to the verge of tears. Tough, brave Casey, about to cry, and over him.

It should have driven him out of here like a shot. But instead he'd stayed.

And now the idea of leaving hurt more than he'd thought himself capable of feeling.

A sudden, prickly sensation at the back of his neck pen-

etrated his sleepy fog. He shot upright, half-expecting to
see a dark, threatening figure in the shadows, half-expecting
that Nesbit had been here and he'd missed him, that he'd
failed Casey while lost in his silly memories and wishes
for things that couldn't be.

But instead it was Casey herself, standing before him in
the simple cotton robe he'd peeled off her countless times
in the past days, looking down at him with an expression
he couldn't fathom.

Her eyes flicked to the book still in his lap, then back to
his face.

"You...read it?" she asked, her voice husky with sleep
in a way that made the glowing embers that seemed to have
taken up residence within him flicker to flaming life.

He nodded, slowly, his gaze fastened on her with an
intensity he couldn't fight, couldn't hide.

"I hope you're as proud as you should be," she said,
her voice soft with that hope.

"Ryan...did a great job."

"Just like you taught him."

He blinked, then lowered his eyes, but after a moment
he couldn't stop the slight smile that curved his lips. "He
was the best student I ever had."

"If he were here, what would you say to him?"

His gaze shot back to her face. "I...what you said. That
I'm proud of him." He lowered his eyes once more and let
out a long breath. "I'm just not sure it would mean anything to him anymore."

"Then you didn't read very carefully," Casey said.
"What he feels for you came through rather clearly, I
thought."

"Maybe," Clay admitted grudgingly.

She just looked at him for a moment, as if pondering
something she wanted to say but wasn't sure she should.
At last it came out, in that unerring way she had of voicing
thoughts he didn't dare acknowledge.

"He still thinks of you, Clay. Worries. It comes through, even you can't deny that."

He couldn't deny it, so didn't try. *Wherever he is, I owe him more than I can ever say.* Ryan's words held a certain poignancy, even in print, and caused a tightness in Clay's chest that he couldn't make go away.

"And I'm sure your other friends there feel the same," Casey added. "They haven't forgotten you, haven't given up."

Your old buddies. They pooled money and vacation time, and each one took a turn looking for you.

No, they hadn't forgotten, hadn't given up.

"And it's quite clear they don't blame you," Casey went on, gently relentless. "Only you do that."

"Casey," he whispered pleadingly, not sure what he was asking her for, except perhaps mercy. But Casey, the kindest, most giving woman he'd ever known, suddenly didn't have an ounce of mercy in her.

"Did they deserve that, Clay? Did they deserve you vanishing, leaving them wondering, worrying, afraid for you?"

"What do you want me to do?" he asked, horrified at the broken sound of his own voice.

"What I want has nothing to do with this. It's what you know you should do. What you have to do. This will be hanging over you forever until you face it."

Hearing her say it, hearing her put words to the knowledge he'd secretly carried for so long sliced through him like a hot blade. He tried desperately to bury it again.

"I can't...go back. It's been too long, they won't..."

"Won't what? Care? Welcome you? Even remember you?" She gestured at the book in his lap. "Even I know that's not true. And even if it were true, it wouldn't matter. You need to do it for yourself, Clay."

"I..." He stopped, staring at his own white-knuckled hands, grasping the book as if it were a lifeline, knowing that without it to hang on to he would be shaking. Casey dropped to her knees before him, put her hands over his, hanging on as if she could absorb his anguish. The action nearly shattered his already precarious composure.

"It's killing you by inches," she said, her voice now as shaky as he felt. "I know you feel like that's no more than you deserve, but it's not true. Damn it, Clay, it's not."

He shuddered helplessly. And suddenly Casey seemed to rediscover her sense of mercy. She stood up, pulling his hands with her. He looked up at her, knowing he must be staring at her like some wounded animal, eyes wide with a pain he'd never really faced, the pain of having lost his family in a larger sense than his wife and child.

"That's enough, it's late," Casey said softly. "Come to bed."

He was powerless to resist her gentle urging. And when he crawled into bed beside her, when she took him in her arms and simply held him, stroking his hair, his cheek, his back, when she did nothing more than offer a pure, sweet comfort he'd never known before, Clay felt himself letting go, felt himself clinging to her with something that wasn't quite desperation, something that was need but not needy, desire but not sexual. And after a while, something quietly broke inside him, flooding him with a warmth that was unlike anything he could remember. A warmth so powerful that the pain ebbed at last, leaving him feeling emptied. Not hollow, but scoured somehow, and waiting, not painfully but expectantly, as if for the first time he thought that perhaps he could be filled again, could be alive again.

And the warmth was so strong that the thought didn't scare him, merely held him tenderly until he drifted into the most peaceful sleep he'd known in years.

He was so deeply asleep that it took a moment for him to realize what had awakened him. But Mud let out another round of raucous, angry barks, and he snapped into alertness. The dog was outside, he thought. Had he found something on his nightly rounds? Or had he heard something and gone to investigate?

Clay sat up. Casey was stirring beside him, rubbing at her eyes. He looked at her. And then it hit him, every instinct coming awake with a clamor, every nerve suddenly drawn and taut.

The showdown had come.

He wasn't sure how he knew, only that he did. It had taken him years, as a young cop, to learn to trust that instinct. But now it only took seconds for him to rediscover that trust.

"What's wrong with Mud?" Casey asked sleepily.

He kept his voice level and as detached as he could. He'd waited too long to tell her, and now it was too late. He had to move fast. "I don't know. I'll go look."

With an effort, he managed not to hurry. He swung out of her warm bed and pulled on his jeans as if he thought Mud had done nothing more than corner a rampaging raccoon. But he skipped his boots, hoping Casey would assume it was because he expected to be right back rather than from urgency.

"Be right back," he said, stopping short of ordering her to stay put, knowing too well that nothing would be more likely to send her after him. He only hoped she was sleepy enough to slow her reactions, giving him enough time to get this done before he had to worry about her.

Mud was still outside, and still barking furiously, so Clay went through the house hastily, giving only a cursory check to rooms as he passed. He paused on the screen porch, listening to pinpoint the dog's location. The barn, he thought. And inside. After a moment spent scanning the yard and seeing nothing, he headed that way in a running crouch.

He pressed himself against the wall, listening. With a last yelp Mud went quiet except for a muffled whine, as if he'd sensed Clay's presence. For a long moment that seemed to last forever, Clay strained to hear any movement inside, but he could hear only the small rustling, scratching movements of the collie. Maybe Mud really had just cornered some night creature; maybe it wasn't Nesbit at all.

He edged around the corner, intending to slip through the sliding doorway. And then he stopped in his tracks.

The door was closed. The scratching was Mud trying to claw open the heavy door. The door they always left open for him. The door he never could have closed behind him. The door that could not have slid closed on its own. Which meant somebody had closed it, trapping the dog in the barn.

Somebody who wanted the dog out of the way.

Somebody who wanted Clay outside.

His heart began to hammer in his chest. He reached out with a foot and nudged the door open. Mud bolted through, barely sparing his master a glance. Head down, ears flat to his head, teeth bared, the dog raced for the house. And as his heart sank and his stomach knotted violently, Clay knew he'd made a very bad mistake. His instincts were rustier than he'd thought.

Nesbit was here.

And now he had Casey.

Chapter 17

Casey knew, the minute she heard the footsteps in the hall, that it wasn't Clay coming back. He never made noise like that; he moved quietly, gracefully. She scrambled out of bed, searching for something, anything, she could use as a weapon. The only thing she could see was the heavy brass lamp she'd just turned on, and the moment of hesitation while she decided which was more important, light or a weapon, cost her; he was in the room by the time she grabbed it.

She knew it was Jon. In some primitive level of her brain, she would swear she could smell him. Her lip curled, and she felt herself baring her teeth like some cornered animal as the gut-level fear swept her. The sensation sickened her; she'd sworn she would never be that afraid again. Anger, both at him and at herself, flooded through her, carrying the fear away like the river carried the leaves in the fall.

She spun around, ripping the shade off the lamp and

reversing the base in her hold, freeing the heavy end for a blow as she moved.

"You're mine now, Casey," Jon said, his voice still oddly raspy, as it had been on the phone. "Now you'll pay."

"Like hell," Casey said, heartened by the sound of her own voice so low and steady. And working on an impulse she didn't quite understand, she didn't wait for him to come after her. She went for him instead, jabbing fiercely with the heavy lamp. Startled, Jon jumped back. She jabbed again. He fell back again.

"You bitch!" he yelled. His hand went to his waist, and Casey guessed instantly that he was armed; he wasn't brave enough to come after even a woman without help. Acting instinctively, she swung the lamp this time, bringing the heavy base down on his arm before he could reach the gun butt she could now see above his belt.

He howled and grabbed his arm with his other hand. The sound was oddly echoed by a canine howl, and Mud burst into the room. He went for Jon without hesitation, snapping, growling with clear and deadly intent. Jon yelled again and backed up against the wall as the Border collie latched onto his right leg. Mud withstood the rain of blows, never loosening his grip, never letting go as Jon wailed and swung at him.

Then Jon had the gun out and was turning it on the dog.

"No!" Casey yelled. She lifted the lamp again, ready to swing, even knowing it could get her shot. But a movement at the bedroom window distracted her.

An instant later a dark figure exploded through the window into the room. Jon's head jerked around, but he had no time to react. Clay was on him, low and hard. Jon's arms flew up as Clay took him down to the floor. Casey saw something go flying. Heard the clatter of the gun hitting the floor. Sliding.

She had never seen anything like this, this brutal, vicious,

hand-to-hand fighting. The sounds were hideously fascinating. The impact of fists on flesh. The grunts of both pain
and grim satisfaction. The thud of bodies rolling on the
wooden floor. The crash as something else was knocked
over in the fray. Mud's angry barks as he snapped and bit
whenever he could.

Don't be an idiot, do *something,* she ordered herself. And
in an instant she was on her knees on the floor, searching
in the darkness for the weapon Jon had dropped.

She heard a heavy blow, then a guttural sound she knew
had come from Clay. Jon might be a coward, but he spent
long hours in a gym perfecting the physique he was so
proud of, and he was no weakling. Suddenly afraid for
Clay, she moved faster, feeling her way across the floor.

At last, under the bed, her fingers encountered cool
metal. She grabbed the weapon, thankful it was nothing
more complicated than a revolver. The solid butt of the
weapon felt oddly comforting in her hand.

She got to her feet. Turned toward the two men, the end
to the bloody fight in her grasp. They were entangled, Jon
on top of Clay, pressing his forearm across Clay's throat
as he had pressed it against hers that long-ago day. She
aimed the weapon carefully. Moved so that she could be
certain to hit only Jon. And as Clay flailed, trying to break
Jon's grip, she had no doubt in her mind that she could and
would fire.

I should have done something!

I'd failed them. Both of them.

Clay's words, the words that had haunted him for years,
played back in her head like some crazy counterpoint to
the fierce battle that was playing out before her.

She didn't shoot.

With a sense of clarity and certainty she'd rarely felt in
life, she knew she couldn't. Clay needed to—*had* to—win
this fight. He had to succeed this time. If he lost again, if

he felt he had failed her as he'd failed Linda and his little girl, he would be dead even if Jon didn't kill him.

She realized she couldn't let that happen. And with a sudden shock she realized why.

She loved him. Irrevocably and completely, she had fallen in love with this complex, haunted man with the merciless conscience and the gentle strength. The man who might never heal if he didn't exorcise his demons.

With a much greater effort than it had taken her to find it and aim it at another human being, Casey set the gun back down on the floor, out of her hands but still within reach.

As if her decision were some kind of signal, Clay suddenly found some extra bit of strength. He wrenched Jon sideways, and she heard a howl of pain from the man she'd once wanted to hurt as he'd hurt her. But now all she wanted was for Clay to win this battle—and the battle within himself.

Jon's howl became a scream as Clay reversed their positions. Casey heard the blows. Saw Jon's head snap back and forth. The scream became a whimpering that filled her with distaste that she'd ever let this coward frighten her. Even Mud backed off, either sensing that the enemy was beaten or that his master didn't need his help now.

And then it was over. Jon was facedown on the floor, groaning. Clay was standing over him, panting, but steady on his feet. Quickly Casey nudged the pistol out of sight under the bed, then crossed the room and flipped the main switch, flooding the scene with light. Clay kept a foot over Jon's kidneys but looked at her.

"Are you all right?" he asked, his eyes searching her for signs of damage.

"I'm fine," she answered quickly. "He barely touched me, and then...you were here."

She didn't know if she could have fought Jon off.

It made her shiver just to think about it. But she hadn't had to. Clay—and Mud—had been here.

She smiled at him, although her smile was a bit wobbly with reaction now. But the sight of him filled her with a joy she couldn't deny. His face and his knuckles were bloody, his lip was split, but his eyes were alive. Vividly, vibrantly alive.

Unable to restrain herself, Casey ran to him. He opened his arms for her without hesitation and hugged her to him fiercely. Casey looked into his eyes once more and saw her own joy echoed there. And she knew this demon had retreated at last.

Casey was still amazed at the way River Bend had taken the shocking revelations. There had been no keeping what had happened a secret, not after the sheriff had had to come out and drag Jon away in handcuffs. It was then that she'd seen the odd scar across his neck; he'd been attacked in prison, it seemed, by another inmate with a sharpened spoon who didn't care for yuppies. His voice had been permanently damaged, which made Casey feel a little less foolish for not having been sure it was him on the phone from the start.

There had been, of course, the first flurry of gossip after that night. Rumors had been flying about what had happened to her in Chicago, and who Clay really was and why he was here. But now, weeks later, River Bend had settled on its own version of events, a version that cast her as heroine for putting away a twisted, city-bred psycho and Clay as an ex-cop good guy who had done the really dirty work.

But most of all they had closed ranks protectively around both of them, until Casey could do nothing but shake her head and smile at the oddities of small towns. They were welcomed wherever they went, stopped on the street to chat more often than not, until even Clay got used to it and quit blushing and looking like he wanted to run.

Which was, she thought now, amazing, considering that there was one thing that stayed the same no matter who they encountered—they were treated by everyone in River Bend as a couple. Casey had already heard the rumblings—Mrs. Clark muttering about what weekends the church hall was available, Sally at the bakery suggesting Casey look at her album of wedding cakes, and even Phyllis Harrington lamenting that her aunt wasn't here to see her little niece with a man at last.

So far she didn't think it had gotten as far as Clay himself, and she prayed it would stay that way for a while; while he seemed to have settled into a pleasant routine here, she didn't know if or how long it would last. But he'd found the peace she'd prayed he would that night. It wasn't, she thought, so much that he'd saved her from Jon—he never said it, even told her she could have done it without him. But it was that he hadn't failed again. It was a fine line, but Casey understood it.

And she never told him about the gun. Clay was whole again, although still and forever scarred, and she would never, ever risk that by revealing something that, in the long run, made no difference.

They'd had long, quiet days of reveling in each other and exploring their relationship, now untainted by the hovering shadow of her tormenter. And Casey had been relieved that he'd said nothing about leaving, while at the same time she knew she was about to encourage him to do just that.

Carrying a pitcher of icy lemonade, she stepped onto the screen porch, where Clay sat on the lounge she'd bought when she'd insisted he take Sundays off as the heat of September at last began to ebb toward the promise of the cooler days of October. They'd spent some lovely hours here in the past weeks, Casey telling him stories of her beloved aunt and even of her parents, what she could remember.

And finally, perhaps because she didn't prod or pry, Clay began to talk, as well, began to tell her stories of the wild street kid Ryan Buckhart had been, about Cruz Gregerson and his too wise little girl, about Gage Butler and his devotion to the job, which bordered on obsession.

And now he told her, after several false starts, about Kit Walker and how she'd started the search for him.

Casey felt a slight pang when he described the gutsy, attractive blonde, especially when she had her own little secret to deal with. But when he told her what Kit had done, how she'd recruited those Clay had been important to, organized the intensive search, she couldn't feel anything but gratitude for the woman she'd never met.

"I'd like to thank her someday," she said.

"So would I," he agreed softly, almost wistfully.

Casey held her breath. Then, almost shakily, she said, "Then do it."

His head came around, and he met her eyes. She'd been afraid to see rejection of the idea there, or anger at her suggesting it. But instead she saw an uncertainty tinged with longing that gave her hope.

"Go, Clay."

She hunted for the words that would convince him, trying not to sound as desperate as she felt. They'd been happy here together, they'd found laughter and joy and unbelievable pleasure, but she knew deep inside that there was no real future for them until he faced his past. And she desperately, more than ever, wanted a future for them.

"Go," she said again. Then, guessing at what would reach him, she added, "Never mind that you deserve it, *they* do. They deserve to know that you're all right. Gage, Cruz, Miguel, all of them, but especially Ryan. And Kit. They've worried about you for five years. That's enough."

She saw the wavering in his gaze, knew he was on the

edge. "I..." He stopped, swallowing tightly. "I don't know...."

"I'll drive you to Des Moines, and you can get a direct flight from there. Just say when."

He looked startled. "I thought... I was hoping..."

"Hoping what?" she prompted when he didn't go on.

He lowered his eyes, and she barely heard him say, "That you'd go with me."

Casey's heart leaped. Not only had he decided to go, he wanted her with him? She didn't know what to say, wasn't sure if it would be the right thing for him.

"It's not because...I need you there, or because I won't do it without you," he said, as if he'd read her hesitation. "I *want* you there. I want you to...meet Ryan, and Kit, and the rest."

And Casey knew then that there was no other answer she could give but yes.

All things considered, she thought ruefully as she sipped at her lemonade and wondered if her stomach would accept it, perhaps there never had been.

He wished he hadn't let Casey talk him into this. It was going to ruin everything. He had no right to be here; it was all wrong.

But she'd been so certain. From the moment they'd arrived in California and found out about this event, she'd insisted it was perfect. And his father, darn it, had agreed.

Clay tugged at the unaccustomed tie as he thought of his father. He'd felt like the original prodigal son when his father had opened the front door two days ago. For a moment, while shock had frozen a face so familiar yet changed by time and worry, Clay had wanted to run; he'd done this to him, to the strong, vital man he remembered. He'd put those new lines in his face, the new gray in his hair.

But then Robert Yeager's face had changed. An expression of unmistakable, pure joy came over him, and moisture pooled in his eyes. He'd drawn his son into a hug with arms that were shaking, and welcomed him home so fervently that Clay had found himself crying, as well.

Casey had, after a brief introduction, announced that she had some errands to run now that they were here, tactfully leaving Clay alone with his father. He'd tried to protest, but she'd insisted, and in the end he supposed it was for the best; they had hashed out a lot of things. And Clay knew now that his father had not forgiven him, had never had to, because he had never blamed him for what had happened. Just as Casey had told him.

Casey, who had gotten him into this. Casey who, when she'd found out about this event, had seized upon it with all the zeal he'd once had for his job.

Casey, who took his hand now, squeezing it tightly. He looked down at her, into those reassuring eyes, and tried to convince himself that she was right about this, as she had been about so much else. No matter that here he felt more like a wayward son.

"There's your father," she whispered.

He looked up and spotted him amid a group of people wearing suits and dresses. Bob Yeager looked like a kid with a secret he was busting to tell. He nodded his head in the direction of the front of the large, crowded room, toward the couple who were the center of all the commotion.

Clay looked, and felt his eyes tearing up again, as they had so many times since he'd come back. He didn't know where all the emotion was coming from, but suspected that when Casey had broken through that wall of ice that had surrounded him, she'd set loose the denied feelings of years.

"Now," she said suddenly. "They're done with all the formal stuff, the cake, the toasts...."

He gulped in a deep breath. So far they'd stayed on the edge of the crowd and no one had noticed them. Once he stepped out among them, he would be committed to this, and he wasn't sure he could do it.

But Casey was sure. And he would die rather than let her down. So when she plowed through the crowd, he followed her. He kept his head down and prayed nobody would recognize him, but he followed. And came to a halt when she did.

She'd planned this all with a glee he hadn't been able to deny her; he would do it just as she said, despite feeling that she was overestimating the impact his return would have. She had told him bluntly he was wrong, and that this would be the best possible way to do it. He didn't argue, couldn't argue, not with the woman who had made life worth living again.

He watched as she stepped up to the formally dressed couple. Clay caught himself sniffing as he looked. And holding his breath as he listened.

"Mr. and Mrs. de los Reyes?"

The tall blond woman in the lovely pale green dress that made her eyes look nearly the same shade turned, as did the taller, aristocratic man in the black formal suit with a bright red tie. They both looked absurdly pleased at her use of the brand-new appellation.

"I know you don't know me," Casey said with a smile so wide that they couldn't seem to help but smile back, "but I've brought you a wedding gift."

The newlyweds looked puzzled. Until Casey stepped sideways and Clay stepped forward.

Kit was the first to react. Her mouth curved into an *O* of shock, but almost instantly changed to that joyous look Clay had seen on his father's face. And then she moved, throwing her arms around him, enveloping him in a cloud of satin and flowers and the sweet scent of gardenia that she'd always worn.

"Clay! Oh, God, I was so afraid you were dead! Where have you been? Are you all right?"

She backed off at last, but she didn't let go. Tears were streaming down her face, but he couldn't doubt that their source was joy, not when she was cupping his face with hands that were trembling.

He felt a strong hand grasping his shoulder and found himself looking into the steady gray eyes of Miguel de los Reyes, eyes that betrayed all the emotion Kit had shown in her voice and reaction.

Mayor de los Reyes, Clay corrected himself. Or soon to be. His father had told him the June primary had been a runaway, and it was predicted the November election next month would be, as well.

But the man who was looking at him now wasn't the mayor, or even the chief, it was the cop he'd worked with— his friend.

"Congratulations," was all Clay could manage to say.

"This is the best present anybody could ever have given us," Kit said fervently.

"The very, very best," Miguel agreed, equally fervent.

Then, as if remembering, Kit looked at Casey, who had been watching silently, jubilantly. Clay saw that her cheeks were damp, as well, and felt that tug of sweet feeling that had at last become familiar because she was so moved.

He held out his hand to her. A little shyly, she took it and stepped forward.

"This is Casey Scott," he said. "And without her I...wouldn't be here." He meant it in more ways than one, and when he looked at the newly married couple, he saw that they knew it.

"Then we owe you a very great deal, Casey Scott," Miguel said with soft emphasis. "Because this man means more than we can say—to all of us."

Clay shifted uncomfortably, but before he could say something deprecating, Kit forestalled him.

"All of us," she repeated. Then, with a gesture behind him, she added, "But some more than others."

Slowly Clay turned.

He realized when he did that he'd known who it was. Who it had to be. And he hadn't really changed much. If anything, he seemed taller, more broad-shouldered and solidly strong. With his long dark hair, bronze skin and high cheekbones, Ryan Buckhart was still exotically striking. A far cry from the skinny, scared kid he'd once been.

The look in his eyes now made Clay wish he'd come home sooner. There was pain, haunted memories, years of worry reflected in the dark gaze. But overlaying them all was the same sense of joy and relief he'd seen in Kit's eyes, in Miguel's.

And then he was in a bear hug that took the breath out of him. Ryan swore colorfully in his ear, telling him just what he thought of him for leaving his friends to worry about him for so long. Yet beneath every word was an undertone that warmed Clay to his once battered soul. He might be the wayward son, but he was still welcome. Still loved.

Casey had been right.

Casey was always right.

This was home—not this place, but these people he loved—and he'd been away far too long.

Chapter 18

It all became a near blur after that. People crowded around, and Clay tried to introduce them to Casey. They all welcomed her warmly and thanked her for returning him to them, but so much had changed that he was having trouble keeping up. Finally, laughing, Miguel spoke up.

"As chief," he began, ignoring with a grin the "Not for long!" exclamations that came from various quarters, "I guess I should straighten this out. For Casey's sake, if nothing else."

He turned to his left, gesturing to the couple at his right, a man with a thick shock of nearly platinum blond hair, standing beside a tall, obviously pregnant woman with long, gleaming dark hair.

"Gage you remember—he's finally abandoned that obsession of his and is happily fishing his life away in Seattle—and this is his wife, Laurey. And of course their soon-to-be son or daughter."

As Casey and Laurey exchanged greetings, Clay looked

at the man he'd always known had carried his devotion to the job to the extreme. Funny how he'd been able to see it in Gage but not in himself.

"We both had it to learn, didn't we?" Gage said softly.

Clay heard everything the man intended and nodded. "Congratulations," he said, meaning it.

"I'm glad you've come home," Laurey said, surprising him; had he been a topic even with those he'd never known?

Moving on, Miguel gestured at the trio beside the Butlers. "Casey, this is Cruz and Kelsey and Samantha Gregerson."

Casey smiled and shook hands first with Cruz, whose dark hair, bronze-tinted skin and bright blue eyes were still a striking declaration of his mixed heritage, then with Kelsey, a woman with deep red hair and eyes that looked at both Cruz and Sam as if they were her own and always had been.

"My husband once told me that any good in the cops of Trinity West started with you," Kelsey said to Clay.

His eyes shot to Cruz, who met his gaze levelly, as he always had. "If that's true," he said tightly, "he's the walking proof."

Cruz smiled, a salute without words, and Clay had to look away. This was almost too much, all of this. But then Casey bent slightly to greet Samantha, who had grown so big Clay barely recognized her as the six-year-old he'd known.

"The raccoon got well," the girl said solemnly to Clay after she'd politely acknowledged Casey.

It took him a moment to remember the creature he'd found by the road that long-ago night, scratched up by a nasty feral cat. The wounds hadn't been that serious, but he'd known if he left the animal it would be easy prey for some other predator. So he'd taken it to a vet for treatment, and then to Sam. Even at six she'd had a knack, and a sense of responsibility much larger than she was.

That she remembered it moved him immensely.

"I'm glad," he said softly, reaching out to touch her hair. "How big is the menagerie now?"

"Big," she admitted. Then, with a glance at Cruz and Kelsey, she said in a mischievous voice, "I have to do *something* until I get a sister or brother."

Laughter rolled around the group, Cruz and Kelsey included, although there was something in the way they looked at each other that made Clay think it might not be long until Sam's wish came true.

"There's somebody else you need to meet." The voice came from his left, and Clay recognized it immediately.

"Lacey," he whispered as he turned.

She looked as she always had, long, sandy brown hair, clear blue eyes, and where she'd always thought herself too curvy, Clay had called her, teasingly, luscious. She and Ryan were meant for each other, always had been, and it had broken his heart when they'd lost sight of that after the tragic miscarriage.

She hugged Clay fiercely, not even trying to hide her tears. He soon gave up that attempt himself. But after a moment she pulled back and looked at her husband, who had come up beside Clay once more.

Clay looked, and his chest tightened. Big, powerful Ryan Buckhart was tenderly cradling a child in his arms, a sleepy little girl who looked about a year old. She had Ryan's dark, straight hair but Lacey's big blue eyes, and Clay knew she would be a beauty at all stages. He nearly backed off when Ryan held her out to him. But Ryan just looked at him, steadily, encouragingly, and after a moment he took her, with shaking arms, nearly overwhelmed by the feel of a baby in his arms again. And he didn't even try to hide the warm, salty drop that suddenly appeared on the child's cheek.

"She's beautiful," he whispered, looking up to see a teary-eyed Lacey and a suspiciously blinking Ryan watching him with expressions that took away what little breath he had left.

"Amanda," Casey whispered beside him. Lacey looked at her curiously, and Casey explained. "We read about her in the book, about the Pack."

To Clay's amusement, Ryan blushed. It looked odd against the darkness of his skin. "Darn that Lang, anyway," he muttered.

"Don't," Clay said quietly. "That book is what...got me thinking about coming back. To tell you...how proud I am of you."

Ryan's color deepened, and, characteristically, he shrugged off the praise. "In that case, if it got you back here, I'll forgive Carny. He's here somewhere, I think."

Lacey gave a little laugh. "Find Roxy and you'll find him. I think he's smitten."

"Roxy?" Clay said, the name immediately triggering a memory. "Dr. Roxy?"

"The same," Ryan confirmed. "Roxanne Cutler, doctor extraordinaire and general savior of Trinity West."

"Amen," Miguel and Kit chimed in with a fervency Clay made a note to ask about later.

"Did you hear about Robards?" Gage asked as Clay handed the baby back to her mother. Clay turned to look at the blonde, remembering that his problems with the old-school tyrant had been different but no less serious than those of the targets of the man's sexual and racial bigotry.

"No," he said.

"Miguel took him down," Kit said proudly, and gave him a quick version of the murder and subsequent belated investigation that had ended the twisted and ugly reign of the autocratic lieutenant.

"If anybody took him down, you did," Miguel told his bride. "I just handled the formalities."

"So he's in jail?" Clay asked.

"Was," Ryan said with some satisfaction.

Clay lifted a brow and looked at Cruz when the man let out a compressed sound that was half chuckle, half snort. "Sorry," Cruz said. "It's not PC to enjoy such things, but I can't help it."

"He murdered an innocent boy in cold blood just to make a point," a woman said harshly.

"And he'd been shaking down scared street kids for money for years," Kelsey added.

"He was corrupt, evil, vicious, a traitor to the badge, and he had it coming," Kit said.

The women of Trinity West had most definite opinions about the man, it seemed. Clay looked at Miguel, who seemed as if he were struggling to look solemn. He cleared his throat. "We recently got word that Robards met with an...unfortunate fatal accident in prison. Another inmate with a shiv took offense at his...racial attitudes."

Memories of those racial attitudes, especially when the brutal Robards had turned his venom on a young, uncertain Ryan, came back to him. Memories of the man belittling and demeaning every woman he came across. Of the man ruling by fear and intimidation, getting away with it until his ego had apparently grown to the point that he thought he could get away with murder.

And he'd paid, it seemed, the appropriate price. Clay couldn't find it in him to feel very badly about it.

After that, the greetings came thick and fast, from people he remembered and some he didn't. And from some he'd only heard of.

One he remembered was Caitlin Murphy, the strawberry

blonde who'd opened her club for kids, the Neutral Zone, in the midst of the worst part of Marina Heights just before he'd left. They'd all tried to convince her to move it to a better neighborhood, but she'd stubbornly refused. And had, by all accounts, including a mention in Carny Lang's book, made a rousing success of it. As Kelsey Gregerson had made of her youth shelter right next door.

The Trinity West cops had picked spouses to match their nerve and grit and dedication, he thought. And he felt a pride that had an odd, almost paternal feel to it in all of them.

Caitlin introduced him to her husband, Quisto Romero, a former Marina del Mar cop, now of Trinity West. And to their little girl, Celeste, a beautiful child who caused no end of teasing for her father, who apparently had been quite the ladies' man before he'd run into Caitlin.

"She's going to run you ragged, and rightfully so," came the amused observation from a tall blond man beside them. "Not," the man amended with a glance over his shoulder to where a lively little boy of about three was playing with a toy truck complete with sound effects, "that my boy, Sean, isn't doing the same to me. Chance Buckner," he added, extending a hand to Clay. "I had the misfortune of being this reprobate's partner at Marina del Mar."

Clay blinked. Chance Buckner? *The* Chance Buckner? "I've heard of you," he said, shaking the man's hand. "A lot."

"Ditto," Buckner observed with a grin.

"Ah. The two legends meet at last."

Clay shifted his gaze to the woman who'd come up beside Buckner. Her dark, smoky gray eyes and mass of dark shiny hair looked vaguely familiar. She was smiling widely, one hand resting on her swollen belly. Pregnancy seemed to be in the wind around here, Clay thought.

"I'm Shea," she said. "And it's wonderful to meet the legend of Trinity West at last."

Clay mumbled something as he realized why she looked familiar; she was Shea Austin, a famous songwriter he'd seen on some television special in a bar one night when he'd been using alcohol to drown memories that wouldn't die. He remembered it despite the haze, because her words had seemed to cut so deep, as if she'd been where he was, knew his pain. It had finally driven him out of the bar, unable to face what her sweet voice said.

"Welcome home," Buckner said. Then he added, with a glance at Casey, "In more ways than one."

He had the look, Clay thought, of a man who knew all about hell. And it came to him then, the memory that Chance Buckner had lost his first wife and unborn child in a bomb explosion that had been meant for him.

Buckner nodded, as if he knew just what Clay had been thinking. "We'll talk," he promised Clay. Then he reached out and gently laid his hand on his wife's belly, heavy with his child. "I think I've learned some things you need to know."

Almost numbly, Clay nodded. And only then realized he was hanging on to Casey's hand as if it were his sole life-line.

Maybe it was, he thought. Maybe she was.

A tapping on a glass from the front of the hall drew the crowd's attention. Miguel de los Reyes stood before them, looking almost regal in his formal wear.

"I know it's not tradition that the groom speak at his own wedding, but I've never been much for tradition for its own sake."

A small cheer arose from those who knew exactly what tradition he meant, the tradition of ruling by coercion that had been his predecessor's approach.

"So I'd like to propose a toast," Miguel continued, holding up his glass of champagne. "To the cops of Trinity West, the best there are. To those who have found the love and the courage to go on even when it becomes a job you hate. To those who have found the courage to quit when they had to. To those who have come home at last," he said, lifting his glass in Clay's direction. And then, in a quiet but powerful voice, he added, "And most of all, to those who never will."

"Here, here," echoed through the crowd in hushed tones.

It was the same feeling he'd known before, Clay realized, that feeling of kinship beyond anything outsiders could understand. And yet it was different; the people of Trinity West were different. It was a sense he got from all the people he'd known as they took this joyous occasion to renew their own commitment to one another and marvel at the changes love had brought to them all.

They'd had the nerve, Clay thought later as they followed his father back to the house. The nerve to reach out and take what they'd found, despite the odds. Despite the memories. Despite everything.

He wondered if he could find the nerve to do the same.

Casey stood quietly, feeling more than a bit nervous as she watched Clay's still figure, even though it had been her suggestion that they come here. He'd looked surprised at the idea—or the fact it had come from her—and then thoughtful. Then he had nodded, and they had driven to the hillside cemetery in silence.

But now she was wondering if it had been such a good idea. He'd been there so long, between the two graves marked Yeager. She could only imagine what he was thinking, what memories were running through his mind.

She'd seen photographs of his daughter; Bob had shown them to her. She'd been a lively, bright-eyed child, and if, as Casey guessed, her father had been holding the camera in the large picture Bob Yeager had framed, she had adored Clay. The look in the little girl's eyes made Casey ache inside. How could anyone get over the loss of such a child? Even a man as strong as Clay?

For he was that. She'd always known it, but she'd learned just what kind of man he was at the wedding reception. She'd heard the tales of Clay Yeager, had heard what he'd meant to all those he'd helped. She'd heard the tales of his heroism, including the acts that had won him three Medals of Valor: the accident where he'd dragged a baby out of a flaming car, giving him the burn scars on his shoulder and the deep gash on his arm; the bank robbery where he'd taken a bullet protecting an elderly woman who had wandered into the line of fire; and the most incredible, the hostage situation where he'd given himself in exchange for four children being held by a crazed, barricaded suspect, and had nearly died from the resultant torture.

And she had also seen the guilt in those who had been his friends and colleagues, guilt that they hadn't done more when he'd needed their help.

"He was the rock that held us all together," Kit had told her. "He helped us all, was our mentor, our coach and our chaplain, all in one. He always listened, always helped. But there was no one to listen to him."

Ryan had echoed her sentiment in short, blunt, pained words that told Casey exactly how it had eaten at the big man. "He saved my ass. I would have died for him. But when it came to the crunch, when his life fell apart around him, I didn't do a damn thing to help."

"No one could have helped him then," Casey had told him gently. "He was already gone."

Ryan had looked at her intently, then smiled, and what it did to his stern, bronzed face was startling. "But you brought him back. And for that, we all owe you. If you ever need anything, you just call Trinity West. Any of us will be there for you, anytime.''

Can you help him let go? she asked silently now, not sure who the question was directed to.

At last Clay stood up, and her pulse accelerated. She knew a great deal depended on the next few moments. Perhaps everything. As he approached her, she was almost afraid to look at him, afraid to see that she'd been wrong to suggest this, that she'd only opened up old wounds.

But she made herself look up. Made herself meet his eyes. The quiet peace she saw there gave her hope. And when he came to a halt before her and smiled, a soft, gentle smile, she felt a flood of relief.

''Thank you for suggesting this,'' he said solemnly. ''I feel like I've...really let go, for the first time. Like I've finally said goodbye.''

Casey blinked rapidly.

''And thank you for coming with me,'' he added. ''You were right. About going to the wedding, about everything.''

She floundered for words, wishing he hadn't sounded so...final. ''I...I'm glad it's all working out. Very glad. For you.''

He looked puzzled. ''For me?''

''Well, yes,'' she said, feeling miserably awkward. ''That was the point, wasn't it? I just want you to be...if not happy, at least at peace.''

He was staring at her with a sudden intensity that was nearly unnerving. ''Why, Casey? Why do you want that so much?''

She thought of a dozen things to say, ways to dissemble, things close to the truth but not the truth, things that hinted at it but didn't say it, things that were safe and comfortable to say.

She said none of them. In the end, she gave him that simple truth, because she could do nothing else.

"Because I love you."

He let out a long breath, closing his eyes for a moment. "Thank God," he murmured. Then he opened his eyes and searched her face. "It's not just...pity? Sympathy?"

"Is that what you feel for me?" she countered.

"No!" It was swift, emphatic and satisfyingly urgent.

"I rest my case," she said.

He gave her a small, rueful smile. "You're really something, Casey Scott."

She remained silent, waiting. She knew, had known the minute he'd breathed that heartfelt "Thank God," but she needed to hear him say it, needed to hear the words. No matter how odd the place. And when he finally said them, they were sweeter than she'd ever hoped for.

"You know I love you, don't you?"

"Knowing and hearing aren't the same thing," she said.

He reached out and grasped her shoulders, looking down at her with that intensity that made the deadness she'd once seen in his eyes seem a dim memory.

"I love you," he repeated. "I never thought I'd say that again. Never thought I'd be able to say it. And I've never meant it in quite this way."

As a declaration, it was eminently sufficient.

"Do you...understand?" He looked concerned, almost worried. "Why I couldn't say it before, I mean?"

She lifted a hand and put it over his, savoring the warmth of him, the life force that had once ebbed so low.

"I understand," she said softly. "You had to face your goodbyes."

"You gave me back my life," Clay said, and before she could protest, he added, "But that's not what this is about. This is about the future, Casey. And feeling like I have one again. If you'll marry me, and share it."

Casey had to fight down the tears welling up to get out her answer. "Yes, Clay. Yes."

He pulled her into his arms, holding her tightly, murmuring her name over and over. "We'll work it all out later," he promised. "I want as much of forever as we can get, Casey."

She let him hold her, wanting this. Needing this. Knowing it might not last. It was a long time before she finally worked up her nerve to ask the crucial question.

She waited until they were away from the reminders of tragedy, until they were, at Clay's suggestion, walking arm in arm along the beach in Marina del Mar.

Only then, when they were nearly alone on the fall-weekday-empty sand, did she come to a halt. She pulled back a little, looking up at him, knowing this could change everything, but knowing she had to do it.

"Now that you've said your goodbyes," she whispered, "do you think you could manage a hello?"

His forehead creased in puzzlement. "Hello?"

Casey took a deep breath. And plunged on. "To a new little Yeager."

For a moment the puzzled look remained. Then his eyes widened. "You're...pregnant?" he asked, his voice hoarse, tight.

This breath Casey held on to as she nodded.

"Pregnant," Clay repeated. "A baby."

"That's usually how it works," she said, hating the panic that was building in her. She had to look away, and lowered her eyes. "It must have been that...first time," she said, also hating the need she felt to explain, when she knew he knew perfectly well they'd been careful about protection.

"A baby," Clay said again. "We're going to have a baby?"

We.

Casey could suddenly breathe again. And when at last she looked up, she saw everything she could have wished for in his face. Surprise, awe, wonder, a touch of fear, even a faint trace of regretful memory…but most of all, love. It was there, shining in his eyes, and now she could feel it in his touch.

"I know no one can ever replace Jenny," she began, but stopped when he shook his head.

"No. No one can. But…*our* baby!"

His emphasis said it all, Casey thought, feeling a bit delirious with joy. Clay had indeed found his way back. And somehow he'd found the courage to try again. For her. With her. And their child. The child that could never replace the one he'd lost, but could perhaps do the final healing of his lacerated heart.

And she knew then that, however much of forever they got, it would be enough.

*   *   *   *   *

COMING NEXT MONTH

#931 THE LADY'S MAN—Linda Turner
Those Marrying McBrides!

When special agent Zeke McBride was sent to protect wolf biologist Elizabeth Davis from death threats, his usual flirtatious ways came to a complete halt. The lady's man was suddenly tongue-tied around the gorgeous scientist. And when Zeke's duty came to an end, he knew the job might be over, but a lifetime with Elizabeth was just beginning.

#932 A HERO FOR ALL SEASONS—Marie Ferrarella
ChildFinders, Inc.

Savannah King was desperate when she entered Sam Walters' detective agency. An expert in finding missing children, Sam was an amateur when it came to love. He knew Savannah had come to him for help, but suddenly he found himself wanting more than just to get her daughter back—he wanted to give her a lifetime of love.

#933 ONCE MORE A FAMILY—Paula Detmer Riggs

Social worker Ria Hardin was dedicated to helping everyone—except herself. Then she received a call from ex-husband Captain Grady Hardin and relived the day their son was kidnapped. She was determined to help Grady solve his most important case—finding their lost little boy—and reunite the family she missed…and recover the love she'd *never* forgotten.

#934 RODEO DAD—Carla Cassidy
Mustang, Montana

Marissa Sawyer and Johnny Crockett had spent one passionate month together—before he was arrested for a crime he claimed he hadn't committed. But now Johnny was free, and Marissa knew she had to help him clear his name, uncover the truth about *their* nine-year-old son—*and* admit that they belonged together.

#935 HIS TENDER TOUCH—Sharon Mignerey

As soon as Audrey Sussman got to the Puma's Lair Ranch, she had the feeling she wasn't exactly welcome—except to ex-cop Grayson Murdoch. While they tried hard to deny their attraction, both were caught up in a long-buried mystery that threatened to destroy any chances at survival—and the future they were desperate to share.

#936 FOR HIS EYES ONLY—Candace Irvin

Duty demanded that undercover agent Reese Garrick keep the truth of his identity hidden from his sexy new "partner," U.S. Navy lieutenant Jade Parker. But how long could the lone lawman conceal the dangerous truth of his mission—and his secret, burning desire to make Jade his partner...for life?